Praise for T.A. Ridgell's When Opportunity Knocks

"TA Ridgell is a bright new voice in contemporary fiction." –Hope Tarr, *Tempting*, Reviewers Choice Award Nominee

"Don't miss this fast and funny romp from talented new author TA Ridgell." –Judi McCoy, Waldenbooks Best Selling Author of *Heaven in Your Eyes*

"This book serves up sizzling chemistry in a superb love story, laced with a whole lot of humor." –Round Table Reviews

"...this was one of the most entertaining romances I have read in a long time. The plot was wonderful and the suspense kept me engrossed throughout the entire novel...I would highly recommend this book to those readers who like terrific suspense united with a charming love story. –A Romance Review

"The conversation is lively and works from two points of view seamlessly. The reader can simply sit back and enjoy the double meanings to the fullest..." –Scribblers

"A masterpiece of reading pleasure! This one has it all–suspense, sizzling romance, wicked wit, fabulous characters! A jubilant two thumbs up !! You don't want to miss–"When Opportunity Knocks!" –Pamela Johnson, *Tides of Autumn*, 2003 Reviewers Choice

Diamond Club Best Selling Novel

OPERATION: *Stiletto*

T.A. RIDGELL

This is a work of fiction. Names, characters, places, and incidents are products of the author's imagination or are used fictitiously and are not to be construed as real. Any resemblance to actual events, locales, organizations, or persons, living or dead, is entirely coincidental.

Echelon Press
56 Sawyer Circle #354
Memphis, TN 38103

www.echelonpress.com

First Echelon Press paperback printing: January 2005

ISBN: 1-59080-392-2

10 9 8 7 6 5 4 3 2

Cover Artist: Nathalie Moore
Editor: Emily Carmain

Printed in United States of America

Dedication

In loving memory of my sister-in-law, Beth Reynolds. I will always treasure your enthusiastic support, even as your young life slipped away. May we all have your courage and spirit to live life to its fullest no matter the hand we are dealt.

Acknowledgements

Tara Greenbaum and Shannon Greenland, two fantastic critique partners and authors. This book would not have been possible without your excellent insight.

Lori Pepio and Sandra Tibbetts who recognized Python for the hero he is even in WHEN OPPORTUNITY KNOCKS.

Emily Carmain and Karen Syed, my wonderful editor and publisher, who tolerated my author eccentricities while getting this story ready for publication.

Chapter One

"Baby, I'll play with you any day, any time. You just name it." Stubb had the audacity to lean back in his chair and leer at Special Agent Kendal Smart with an insolent stare. His thick tongue licked dried, cracked lips. "I'll even provide the balls."

The sharp retort Kendal wanted to lash back with died unsaid. The Special Agent in Charge, her supervisor, sat behind the two-way mirror. If she ever had a prayer of going undercover, the last thing she needed was for him to see her lose her composure.

She planted her hands on the surface of the cool metal desk, then bent toward Stubb, breathing through her mouth in an effort to avoid his foul stench. "Tell us what you know about Sloan Rusen."

"He's the booker."

"We're aware of that fact." As if she didn't know Rusen arranged which pro wrestlers competed against each other and who would win. Her jaw started to ache from grinding her teeth. "We want to know about his extracurricular activities."

"Hookers?" Still leaning back, he propped his feet on the table. "He's got a bunch of 'em. You want to join 'em or bust 'em?"

She reined in her automatic reflex to grab him by his grubby shirt and heave him across the room. Male special agents could get away with sweating a suspect. She knew the supervisor wanted to see more finesse from her. "Neither. That's not where our interests lie. What do you know about his businesses?"

"I don' know nothin'. Why don' you let me go? You ain't got nothin' on me."

How she wanted to slam his head into the wall. That would be much more satisfying than making a deal with this sleazebag. "Have you forgotten why you're here? You're one short step from being locked up."

"Aw, I didn' do nothin'. Just a little crack and coke. Why don't you go ahead and bring in the big boys? Then you can go rest that pretty little head of yours."

That's it! One handed, she shoved his feet off the table. "Hey! Don't confuse the fact that I have breasts with the idea that I don't have brains or power." She put her face only inches from his. "I can put you so far away no one would ever know where you are. So if you want to keep your scrawny butt from being best friends with an inmate named Bruiser, I suggest you get a grip and start selling me on how you can help the FBI."

His eyes grew the size of saucers and his gaze bounced at everything in the room but her. Kendal straightened. Tugging her suit jacket by the bottom hem, she slipped back into the seat across the table. "Now that I have your attention, tell me what I want to know."

An hour later, she sat at her desk in the small cubicle, wishing she'd stayed in control during the interview. The other special agents' murmured voices drifted over the five-foot wall divider in the spacious room, and she wondered if they were already discussing her outburst.

Stubb hadn't been much help, and to top it all off, her supervisor had witnessed her momentary loss of control. The last thing she needed was for him to think she couldn't keep it together. Getting an undercover assignment meant proving over and over again she could handle the pressure. Hadn't her parents always said there was nothing more important than controlling all outward signs of emotion? *Never let them see you sweat* had been the family motto. She needed to remember that more than ever now.

Stubb didn't know any details. What good was he going to be? Her fingers started to drum on the top of her desk. She jerked them into her lap.

Could they trust him enough to send him back and expect

him to report in? They couldn't disclose any details. Their only hope would be that he learned something without realizing it.

He'd probably run. Wanting to beat her head on the desk at her thoughts, Kendal rubbed her temples instead. How could they use him?

Shuffling from one foot to the other, Python conquered the urge to tug at the constrictive collar of his tuxedo. After twenty minutes of standing around, he was ready to walk away.

"I want one with Tiny and Python," Mega said from across the room. Maybe he should call her Megan now that she was married. Nah, he mentally shook his head. She would always be Mega to him.

"Of course," said Joe Franconi, her new husband.

A fleeting thought to try and hide occurred to Python. He knew it'd be useless, considering his size. Joe turned and grinned at him and Tiny, Mega's cousin, hulking in the corner.

"Tiny, Python. We need you."

As they ambled over, Python knew, since they were both built like tanks, that they looked like a couple of overblown king penguins. Tiny owned a tattoo shop, so naturally he was covered in vivid body art. Fortunately for Tiny, his tuxedo covered them, which made Python wonder about his own choices.

Why he ever decided to tattoo his entire bald head, he didn't have a clue. In his ordinary life the fact didn't bother him. But out of respect for Mega and her wedding, he was wearing a black kerchief.

Always ready to give Joe a hard time, Python asked, "You need something lifted, Law?"

The FBI agent chuckled. "No. Megan wants you for a picture."

In one step Python sidled up next to him and leaned in close. "You remember what I said, Law. You hurt, cheat, or abuse Mega in any way and you're gonna wish you were never born."

Clearly undaunted, the agent held Python's stare. "You know I love her."

"Yeah, I know." Even though it was begrudgingly, Python admitted the truth. Joe had shown beyond even the most cynical of doubts that he would do anything to be with Mega. And if Python was completely honest, he had known from the beginning that they were going to be together.

"There you are!" Mega grabbed their arms.

The photographer placed her in the middle between Python and Tiny. They must make a comical picture, Python thought, like a couple of bulldozers squashing a butterfly.

"All right. Now I want all the bridesmaids and groomsmen," the photographer said.

Python stepped aside as the other members of the wedding party took their places. When he caught the eye of the bridesmaid he'd escorted and she immediately glanced away, he tried not to interpret her look as one of revulsion.

When he'd been introduced to Alyssa, he'd had a fleeting moment of hope that she might be interested in him. Then her eyes had widened before narrowing to take in his painted head. That's when Python had known it wasn't going to happen.

It wasn't that she hadn't been polite. At the rehearsal dinner, they'd been seated next to each other. She'd chatted easily with him, yet neither of them had pried into the other's background.

Not once had she commented on his choice of clothing or his tattoos. Deep down Python knew she was only being cordial. He was fully aware, since he towered over most men and was built like a steamroller, that petite women found him nothing but an oddity. Hadn't he learned anything since grammar school? Even back then the girls had thought he was too big, too awkward.

"This is the last picture. Then the eating and dancing can begin." Megan twirled and her sparkling beauty lit up the entire reception.

Python wondered, not for the first time, what it must feel like to have a wedding like this. If only Mega could've seen past his size and the body art to the man inside.

She'd been the first classy, real woman he'd ever had the opportunity to be around. Probably the only one he'd even stood a chance with, and now she was someone else's. He felt foolish even dreaming he'd had a chance.

Bulbs flashed and seconds later, Python blinked at the dots swimming before his eyes. As he started for the buffet, a slight hand touched his sleeve.

"Are you planning your escape?" Alyssa asked.

Confused, Python wondered if she thought he was out on parole. "Escape?"

Thumbing over her shoulder, she pointed at the other guests. "I thought you might be scared you were next, with all these women ogling you."

"What women?" Python turned three hundred and sixty degrees.

Grabbing his arm, she laughed again, a musical sound. "As if you wouldn't notice."

When she tugged, he bent to hear her next words.

"Actually, I don't blame you. Something about people and weddings, all of a sudden all the singles in attendance stand out like fresh meat to the marriage-minded or matchmakers." She patted his arm.

Dazed, Python followed the dark-haired vixen to the buffet. Who were these women? Did they really see him as potential dating material? Of course, even if they did, the moment they learned about his past, he'd be dropped like a hot potato. No woman wanted a murderer for a husband.

He picked up a plate and mindlessly piled on food just as Joe and Mega passed by, their heads tilted toward each other. Mega said something, making Joe smile and kiss her lightly.

What would it feel like to have that kind of relationship? To have a wife make some kind of comment that could make a man feel like a million bucks. Python seriously doubted he'd ever find out.

After choosing a small yellow pie, he popped it in his mouth. He chewed and frowned when the sweet taste he was expecting didn't happen.

"What's wrong? The food bad?" Tiny approached, two full plates in his hands.

Python shook his head and swallowed. "Nope, but I wouldn't eat the little pies if I were you. They're not sweet."

Laughing, Tiny shifted a plate to his arm. "That's because they're quiche." He clamped Python on the shoulder with his free hand.

"That's quiche?" Python picked up another one, eyeing the flaky concoction. "Eggs, right?"

"Yeah, and I think cheese, too."

In one bite, Python ate the whole thing, chewing with new interest. "Not bad," he said when he finished. "Now that I know it's not supposed to be dessert."

With a sudden thought, he shoved his friend's shoulder, bobbling the plates on his arm. "How do you know what it is? I woulda thought you'd be a card-carrying member of the real-men-don't-eat-quiche club."

After grabbing one of the plates, Tiny shoved back with his elbow. "Yeah? Well, when you get married a lot of things change. I gotta get this food back to the ball and chain." He winked.

"You better not let Linda hear you call her that."

"Good point." Tiny grinned. "At least you know that much for when it's your turn. I can't wait."

When it's your turn. The words reverberated through Python's head. *My turn*?

He chose another flaky concoction from his plate just as Joe and Mega made their way around the room laughing and talking with the guests. Was there a wife in his future? Somehow, he didn't think so.

"Python! You're Python!"

The young, eager male voice made him turn to see who it was. The blond man rushing toward him didn't look familiar.

"I can't believe it. I mean, man, I can't believe you're here. The tux." He waved at Python's clothes. "That threw me. I kept racking my brain, and then I knew."

Confused, Python only stared.

"Man, you were the best. The best. I never missed a match."

Python's stomach bottomed. *No–not a fan. Not here, not now.* "Listen. I don't want everyone–" he was talking to the back of the blond head.

"Joe! Did you know what a celeb–"

Python jerked the guy around, stepping forward into his personal space. "Hey, pipsqueak." He shoved his fist in the man's face. "Unless you want that perky nose in the back of your head, I'd keep my freaking mouth shut if I were you."

The young man seemed to pale a bit, then looked at him with a peculiar frown. Python stepped back. There, he'd gotten his point across.

"What're you yelling about, Tommy?" Joe joined the two of them, looking from one to the other.

Not taking his eyes off Python, Tommy shook his head. "Uh, nothing, Joe. Nothing. I made a mistake."

Joe glanced between the two of them. Python knew his Fed suspicions had been raised.

"Have you two been introduced?" Joe asked.

"Not really." And Python could care less about meeting Tommy.

Joe knocked Tommy in the shoulder. "Boden and I work together."

Damn, Tommy Boden's a Fed. That's all Python needed–more Law around. Of course, most people had only recently learned that Joe worked with the FBI. A fact Python knew only too well.

The blond agent's peculiar look transformed into a more determined expression. "You're the one that helped at the warehouse."

His fists curled at his sides, Python took a menacing step toward him. "I don't–"

"How about a bite? You look hungry." With a hand on Tommy's shoulder, Joe pushed.

"Yeah, sure." After another quick glance at Python,

Tommy left.

"I wasn't going to hurt him."

Joe nodded, gazing out at the crowd. "Yeah, I know. I'd just rather not rehash anything about that day. I've got better things to think about."

Python leaned back against the wall as Joe walked away without looking back. There'd be no talk about Mega being kidnapped, and he was just as glad. His rehabilitation had been grueling. He still felt a twinge now and then when he thought back to being shot. That Mega had come out of the ordeal unscathed was all that mattered.

Now, if only he could get out of this reception with the same fate.

"Hey, Get Smart."

Already impatient and irritated at her lack of results with the dead-end case, having Tommy call her that blasted nickname was enough to put Kendal over the edge. Not only was he younger, since she was the newest addition to the Baltimore office, even her seniority couldn't keep the wet-nose boy from enjoying her annoyance. She'd love to know who from her last assignment had let him in on the overused joke.

"You know, Boden. One day you're going to regret calling me names."

After rounding the divider, the lean agent plopped onto the edge of her desk. "Yeah? When?"

"The day your butt needs saving and I may decide to let you hang out to dry."

"Aw, you'd never do that, Smart. You're too nice."

"Don't bet your last dollar," she muttered.

"Okay, I'll lay off."

Suspicious of his easy capitulation, Kendal tented her fingers. "Why?"

"Because I should."

"I don't think so. But truth is, I really don't care." Dismissing him, Kendal pulled out a desk drawer.

"I think I have a way we can use Stubb," said Tommy.

About to rummage around for a notepad, she halted. "How?"

"There's a wrestler I know. I think he could get us inside."

The notepad forgotten, she slammed the drawer shut. "Are you telling me you've had a wrestler in your back pocket all this time, and you just now felt like bringing it up?"

He jumped up. "No. That's not what I'm saying."

To keep her fingers from untangling the wavy hair she struggled every morning to put into a strict bun, Kendal crossed her arms. "Okay, explain."

From his higher position, Tommy craned his neck and scanned the office over the top of the divider.

"You looking for someone?"

He dropped back down. "Not really."

"Then what'd you mean about a wrestler? I made it clear I needed to speak to anyone with a contact to any of the professionals. You didn't respond."

"I just found out I had one. And actually it's not me, it's Joe."

Kendal had only seen Joe Franconi a handful of times since she'd transferred to this office. On the verge of getting married and retiring, she assumed he had a short timer's attitude. Which was fine with her. She didn't need to invest a lot of time getting to know an agent who was on his way out. As a matter of fact, she hadn't invested any time getting close to anyone ever since she joined the FBI. A lifetime of moving from military base to military base had taught her how not to develop close friendships. "Joe didn't come forward either."

Tommy lifted a pencil and began to bounce it on the desk. "I don't think he knows."

"Boden, if you're trying to annoy me," she grabbed the pencil, "you're succeeding."

"A man called Python is an ex-NFW wrestler. He was in Joe's wedding party. All during the ceremony I stared at the back of his head and even though he'd covered it, I could see the tail end of a snake tattoo. It looked real familiar to me. It wasn't until I went to the reception that it clicked."

"You said *ex*. How's he going to help now? Even if he recommended who we should approach, we don't know who's turned, and who hasn't. How would he know?" The eraser end of the pencil in Kendal's hand made it into her mouth.

"I think we should use him."

Realizing she was about to start gnawing on the piece of rubber, she put the pencil down. "How? *Ex* means not on the circuit, right?"

"We can bring him out of retirement."

"Why would that do us any good? He wouldn't be part of the ongoing matches. We need to be in the thick of things if we're going to figure out who's filtering the money, and how the homeland radical group is getting it."

Shifting his legs, Tommy bent a little closer. "That's just it, he could step right back in. He was huge, a real face."

"A face?"

"That means a good guy. He started out as a heel, a bad guy. Then his fan base grew so large, they gradually changed his character."

She nodded. "Okay, I follow that. I'm not sure I see how this helps us get in."

"I guarantee the booker would give his right arm to have Python back in the ring."

"Sloan Rusen? Why would he be so excited about a wrestler who quit?"

"Python drew the biggest crowds ever in the NFW." Tommy threw his hands out wide. "He was a phenomenon like never before and hasn't been seen since. Unless Rusen is stupid, he'd jump at the chance to bring him back."

"Then why'd he walk away? Is he old?"

"No, he quit in his prime." Tommy hunched over slightly. "The last time he ever stepped into the ring, his opponent died."

The news made Kendal frown. "He killed someone?"

"Not on purpose," he said with force. "It was an accident, but Python never came back. Let me tell you, there was incredible mourning. Across the country tons of flowers and candles were brought to the coliseums and arenas where he had performed."

In reverence, she nodded. "For the dead wrestler."

He shook his head. "No, for Python." Her shock must have shown, because he held up his hand. "I mean, we were sad for Terror, the guy who died, but it was Python's leaving that really hurt."

When she saw the glazed look in his eyes, Kendal thought better of pointing out the use of the term *we*. Obviously he was a true fan of the sport, which gave him a great deal more insight into the wrestling world.

"I even have his action figure."

She reopened the drawer to find the notepad. "He gave you his doll? I didn't think he knew you."

"He didn't give me the action figure. I bought it. It's his."

"You just sai–"

"You know, it looks like him."

Behind her hand, Kendal coughed, hiding a smile at his adamant tone. "They actually made a doll of him? That's amazing. So, how's this supposed to help us with Stubb?"

"He can be the manager who brings Python back in."

The idea started her mind racing. This could be the big break. "And we could easily send in someone as a part of his team. This has definite possibilities. What do you think Wilson will say to having a civilian be a part of the operation?"

"Python's worked with Joe before. Since we don't have any other options, I think it's worth the pitch."

"Is Wilson in?"

Tommy stood. "Yeah."

Finally grabbing the notepad and a pen, Kendal joined him. "Let's go."

As she followed him, she pulled her suit jacket taut and checked to make sure the top button of her white shirt was securely fastened. After a perfunctory knock, they walked into Special Agent in Charge Wilson's office.

The commanding silver-haired man sat behind a substantial desk with numerous files spread across it. "Something important?"

Appreciating her supervisor's directness, she motioned for Tommy to relay all the information they'd discussed. If Wilson bit on this new idea, it'd probably mean she wasn't going to be the primary on the case. With Tommy's knowledge about wrestling, he was the logical choice.

After years with the bureau, she'd finally gotten the approval to go through the undercover in-service. Her covert cameo with an experienced special agent had been exemplary, and she'd been given the green light to accept an assignment of her own. When she experienced a twinge of regret at the loss of this operation, she readjusted her thinking. Didn't she have a dozen other cases just like all the other special agents? She just wanted this one so bad, she could taste it.

Money laundering wasn't uncommon. This time they'd linked the scheme to having its roots in funding a radical group rumbling about a standoff with the government. If they could catch who was cleaning the bills, then they could work back through the chain and arrest those who thought they had the right to brainwash innocents into suicidal, fatalistic missions.

"You think this is a viable option, Smart?"

Jerked back to the present, Kendal met her Wilson's direct gaze. "Yes, sir. I do."

With a curt nod, he looked from her to Tommy. "What type of position will the agent have?"

"There aren't many that won't draw undue attention," Tommy said. "Especially if the agent doesn't know much about the sport."

Real subtle, Kendal thought. If Wilson hadn't already been thinking about replacing her with Tommy, he sure was now.

"What would work?" Wilson asked.

"A trainer."

As Wilson leaned back, the chair creaked. "Why?"

"Because he," Tommy glanced at Kendal, "or she would then be with Python at all times. This way he's under constant surveillance. Reduces his risk and puts the special agent everywhere he needs to be."

"Okay. Who?"

Kendal couldn't believe Wilson was even asking. After all, it seemed pretty obvious who the choice would be. Thinking only of what's best for the case, she moved forward slightly. "Considering Boden has extraordinary, in-depth knowledge about wrestling, he seems to be the natural choice, sir."

Wilson nodded. "What do you think, Boden?"

"I was a big fan of the wrestling world when I was younger, sir. It wouldn't be difficult for me to fit in."

"Except maybe your G-man haircut," Wilson said.

"All I'd have to do is shave my head," Tommy said a little too eagerly.

"Good point. What about this Python? How hard will it be to bring him on board?"

"That could be a problem, sir."

All of Kendal's ill will at having felt excluded from the conversation was replaced with disbelief at Tommy's words. He was the one who'd brought up this option in the first place.

"Why?"

Kendal nodded, anxious to hear the answer to Wilson's question.

Tommy fidgeted. "He wouldn't even let me mention who he was at the wedding reception. It's going to take some convincing. I'm confident I can do it, sir."

Wilson let his chair fall forward. "Joe's wedding? He doesn't know you're FBI, does he?"

Tommy started to look uncomfortable. "*Uhm*, probably. Joe told him we work together."

Shaking his head, Wilson moved one of the files on his desk. A sure sign he was getting ready to dismiss them. "Rethink the plan. Give me other options."

Almost popping out of his seat, Tommy appeared barely able to contain himself. "Why?"

Wilson pointed a pen at him. "This is the same Python who helped with the Scalfone case, right?"

"Yes, sir."

Not knowing the details of this conversation, Kendal kept quiet. It wouldn't do to ask. Every operation, whether open or closed, was on a need-to-know basis. If it didn't affect a case you were working, then there was no reason to divulge the information.

Wilson frowned. "Didn't he take a hit?"

"Yes, sir."

Kendal straightened in her seat. The man had been shot?

"I don't like putting civilians in danger. Much less one that has already been injured."

"I know, sir. I have it on good authority that Python came through his surgery and rehabilitation with flying colors. He's had no relapses or difficulties."

"And you still think this is the most viable option?" Wilson asked.

"After years of getting nowhere, and knowing the radical group is ready to make its move? Yes, sir, I think this is our best shot."

Wilson rubbed his chin as he shook his head. "From what I can remember, he doesn't care much for the FBI. As a matter of fact, he'd most likely balk at the idea of having to work with an agent."

"You could be right, sir." Tommy's voice had a definite sullen ring.

Wilson leaned back once again. "So, what if we gave him an agent he didn't know?"

Her excitement growing, Kendal fought to keep perfectly still, waiting for him to finish his thoughts.

"Python's like a cowboy from the old days. Wants to be the one who saves the day. We convince him we need him to do that," Wilson continued.

She straightened. "I don't know if divulging the entire operation to a civilian would be wise, sir."

"You're absolutely right, Smart. We'll tell him it's drug smuggling. That way he won't be involved." Wilson turned to her. "That way he'll think you're a trainer Stubb demands he use, and he'll never know he's working with an agent."

Kendal couldn't believe it. She'd just been handed the case of a lifetime. The hard part was over. All Tommy had to do was convince Python, a man with a hero complex, to play a role it sounded like he'd jump at.

Panic, like a fast flowing river, coursed through him. How was he going to survive this time? His stomach pitched as the mammoth beneath him shoved upward.

Eerie, yet familiar, whistling echoed in his ears as the dark world blurred in front of his eyes. Suddenly, he was flying. Trying to control the flight, his body contorted and his legs scissored.

"Umph." *His lungs deflated as he landed face first on the hard ground. Bouncing once, he shook his head, working to gather his wits, knowing a second attack was imminent. Before he could pull it together, three hundred pounds of solid flesh crushed him.*

One mistake. That's all he needed for the attacker to make. The man might be good, but no one was perfect. One hairy hand reached back, probably to grab his leg. It was the break he wanted.

Using his torso, he flipped just as some of the weight lifted off, and the assailant tumbled away. On instinct, he rolled after him, wrapping his arms around the man's waist and squeezing. He had him now.

Angry at being here again–angry that he was forced once again to defend himself–he shifted to his knees. Yelling, he lifted the beast.

With power born of fury, he hoisted the swine above his head. Spinning, he grew angrier. This scum, this piece of trash thought he could come in and take him down? He was king, he was invincible, and it was time the world knew.

His mind began to chant and scream, demanding to see the attacker punished. The shouting fueled the wild bestial urge engulfing him. Enraged, he tossed the man as if he were a feather.

Flying through the air, looking like a gorilla searching

vainly for a vine, the heel soared past the ropes. The man slammed into empty chairs, his mouth open with an unheard scream.

Immediate silence as the body lay there, a grotesque contortion of arms and legs.

Harsh breathing roared through his ears as he forced air into his abused lungs. Sweat poured over his eyes. Still he stood transfixed, staring. Slowly the dark receded. Murmured voices grew, chanting his name.

A woman rushed to the prone form. Angry eyes filled with tears speared Python as she stabbed the air. "You killed him!"

Chapter Two

"Absolutely not." Python rubbed the top of his bald head. "I am not now, nor ever, going back in the ring. How the hell'd you find me anyway?"

"Megan." Tommy pushed the door and Python moved back. Glad that Joe's advice to use Megan's name had the desired results, he stepped into Python's cramped apartment.

"Mega thinks I should help you?"

Grabbing the single chair in what someone with a lot of imagination would call an eat-in kitchen, Tommy twisted it before straddling the hard surface. "She's unaware of the details, but yes, she thinks you should help the FBI."

Mentally, Tommy crossed his fingers and hoped Python never had the time to check out his story. Joe was supposed to talk to Megan, telling her only to back them up. Who knew if she would?

"She doesn't know I used to wrestle." Python dropped onto the only other piece of furniture in the one-room place, a decrepit sofa. The couch groaned against the weight.

"Really? How could she not know? You were huge."

Python glared. "Because I didn't want her to know." He shook his fist at Tommy. "And she'd better not learn it from you."

Could the man have handed him a more perfect opening? Tommy didn't think so. He shook his head. "I'm not sure I can keep that from happening if you don't agree."

"That's bullshit and you know it. If I go undercover, you aren't gonna want anyone to know what I'm doing. Where I'm doing it. Or why." Python shifted to the edge of the couch.

"To a point. We're talking about putting you back in the ring. Plenty of people are going to know what you're doing.

It's the why we're going to keep under wraps."

When the big guy's anger only visibly increased, Tommy hurried on, "What I mean is we need you. If it means letting Megan in on some of the details in order to convince you this is important, then we'll do it."

Falling back against the couch, Python stared up at the ceiling. "Why would the FBI want to go undercover in the NFW? I know there's drug use. I wasn't involved with it. How could I help now?"

Pleased that Python guessed the fictional cover they'd decided on, Tommy bit back a grin. "It's become a smuggling depot. Anything and everything selling on the streets is somehow coming through the matches. We need someone on the inside."

"I just told you I didn't use when I was there. I don't know the contacts."

Unsure whether he believed it, Tommy was unconcerned since it wasn't the actual goal. "You probably know more than you think. Besides, you can make the contacts now."

Python lifted his head. "The aging, comeback king would be a natural, looking for chemical stimulants to increase his performance abilities?"

Tommy held up his hands. "You said it, not me."

His eyes narrowing to slits, Python pounded one hand with a fist. "Don't push it, golden boy. I could take you with both hands tied behind my back."

Not absolutely sure if the man wasn't correct, Tommy curbed the automatic masculine rejoinder resting on his lips. "Okay, okay. We've got more important things to talk about than who can hurt who." He shoved out of the chair. "Are you in or not?"

"You don't know what you're asking."

Tommy took three steps, then had to turn in order to pace. "I don't understand your resistance. You were the best. The fans loved you. Why wouldn't you want to go back?"

"Not everyone liked me."

"So? You've got to be used to negative press. It's the

nature of the beast. Not all fans liked you. Get over it."

"It isn't the fans I'm talking about."

Swinging the chair forward, Tommy sat back down. "The other wrestlers? Who cares about them? I thought you guys weren't supposed to like each other anyway."

Python propped his arms on his legs, letting his hands dangle. "Yeah, we are."

"Then what's the big deal? You get back in shape, get in the ring, and do some storylines. We catch the bad guys and it's over."

Python's icy stare had Tommy wanting to squirm. A cold chill ran down his back. After seeing the ex-wrestler at Joe's, and knowing what he'd done for Megan, Tommy found his empty gaze disconcerting.

"That's it, huh?"

Shaking off the odd feeling, Tommy nodded. "That's it."

"And if we can bust the drug smugglers before I even have to go in the ring, then I can walk away."

The likelihood of Smart being able to break the case that quickly was highly unlikely. Yet Tommy had no guilt in answering, "Absolutely."

The thick smell of dirty socks and sweat choked the air as Python stared at his reflection in the locker room. There was much more to him this time. He sucked in his gut, sticking out his chest. *That's better,* he thought, nodding at himself. It'd be great, if he didn't have to breathe.

Exhaling, he scowled at his slight paunch. Of course, a little more weight wasn't the only thing new. His head now sported numerous tattoos instead of only the snake. He wondered briefly what the fans' reaction would be to his new colorful skull.

After Tommy had left, Python had reaffirmed to himself to crack this drug thing wide open before he stepped one foot back into competition. Needing to hear it aloud, he said, "It doesn't matter. I'm not getting in the ring, anyway."

"The hell you ain't! You're the biggest comeback ever.

And I'm gonna take you to the top."

Through the mirror Python watched as Stubb approached from behind. This part confused him the most. Why Stubb?

The man was the sleaziest manager on the tour, yet Tommy had said he was the best choice. Asking Tommy if the man was dirty and trading his services to keep his butt out of jail had only elicited a noncommittal grunt. Python felt pretty sure he'd guessed correctly.

Stubb slapped his back. "Boy, it's good to see ya. You've been sorely missed. The ride back up is gonna be great."

Of course, if Python wanted to look like a wrestler who used drugs, then having a shady manager would be a good choice. Maybe the FBI knew what they were doing after all. *What a thought*. "Yeah, great."

Stubb seemed oblivious to Python's sarcasm. With another slap, he headed out of the locker room. "Come on, boy, your trainer is waiting for you."

"A trainer?" Catching up to the stoop shouldered manager, Python huffed. "You hired someone else? I didn't think they'd let–" He cut himself off.

Per instructions from the FBI, he'd called Stubb to hire him as his manager. The man probably had no idea what was going on. Heaven knows what slimy friend he had hired to help.

"This piece of flab? This is what you expect me to get into shape?" The sharp female voice stopped Python in his tracks.

"Ease up, Big K. Python's the best there ever was. He'll shape right up."

As he slowly rotated his head, deep green eyes rimmed in thick black lines met his. Python wanted to groan aloud. *Unbelievable*. Stubb had hired a groupie to be his trainer. Could it get any worse?

In ankle-high black leather boots with ice-pick heels, the woman's blue metallic leggings were painted over muscular calves and thighs. Her shocking pink cropped top exposed six-pack abs any guy worth his salt would be proud to sport.

None of it reassured Python in the least. Her heavily made up face was framed by straight, parted down the middle, dark as midnight hair.

He'd had enough of groupies in his first go-round in the NFW. They'd invaded his life, come on to him, and all but showed up naked in his hotel room. Actually, they'd done that too. He hadn't been interested then. He wasn't going to be now.

He wanted a woman with something between her ears beside air and lust. Memories of his mother, strung out and smelling of sex, filtered through his brain. Shaking his head free of the distasteful recollections, he frowned. The groupies had only been attracted to him because he was a superstar. His mother had wanted any man willing to give her money or drugs. To him, there wasn't any difference between them.

Circling him, Big K surveyed his physique. He could feel her gaze as if it was scorching a path over his entire body. Observing her in return, Python wondered how she came to be called Big K. Of course *Big* made sense. That had to be in reference to her mouth.

"I don't know what you were thinking, Stubb. I can't see this tub of lard getting it together in time to make it to the top. He'd be lucky if he doesn't get tossed before the whole thing starts."

Her cutting words only solidified his first impression. Fisting his hands, Python pinned the woman with his most lethal glare. "Who are you t–"

"Who am I?" She punched his chest. "Who am I? I'm the person who's going to get your sorry butt back in shape in time to actually win a dance. I don't care what the booker says, if you got in the ring the way you are now, even a jobber would beat you just for fun."

Frowning, Python rubbed his offended chest. He didn't need some overdone, drag-queen-look-alike telling him he wasn't even good enough to beat a wrestler who was paid to lose.

Cocking his head, he checked her out more carefully.

Okay, she was definitely a she. For a minute he had wondered if maybe there was more to her than he could see. There had been a few of those who'd come on to him too. "Look, I don't need–"

"That's right. You don't need no more burgers, fries, or greasy takeout. From now on you're on a strict diet. We're scheduled to be on tour in a couple of weeks. It's time to get to work."

Expecting him to follow, Kendal walked away. If you could call what she was doing in these pitiful excuses for shoes as walking. Wouldn't her parents be appalled? Again they would've reemphasized how she should have followed in their footsteps like her older brothers and joined the Navy or Marines. No one would ever expect a soldier to be so inappropriately dressed.

She was seriously starting to doubt Tommy's insistence that this getup was appropriate for her position as a trainer. If Python's expression was anything to judge by, the sight of her had horrified him.

Of course, she'd horrified herself as well. Gone were the gray eyes she was used to gazing back at her in a mirror and her soft, wavy brown hair. Now, she looked brash, brazen, and shameless.

"Hey, Ho."

"You looking for a good time?"

"*Mmm, hmm.* You look like you could take it hard and fast from a real man."

She slammed to a stop as the catcalls from the men pumping iron continued. Turning slowly toward them, she stared.

"What's wrong, sex? You need an engraved invitation?" the ugliest one of the bunch asked.

"To do what?" she asked.

The loud idiot rubbed the front of his shorts. "Whaddya think?"

In two steps, she stood within three feet of them. "It's not what I think. It's what your mama thinks when she realizes all her hard work has created nothing but a two-bit, low-life, lazy jerk, who's got nothing better to do than sit around a gym all day."

The guy's face grew red as he stood.

Kendal stepped even closer so only he could hear her. "And I'd be real careful what I offer to someone I don't know. What you can't see in my pants are balls the size of Texas. You really want a piece of that?"

The man stepped back, mumbling as he stared hard at her pants. Turning and heading back, she rethought her earlier anxiety. Maybe Tommy was right. This outfit provided her a power necessary in this domineering environment. Reaching the mats at the far end of the gym, she planted her hands on her hips and waited, tapping her foot.

Python lumbered over with an overanxious Stubb in tow. "You've got a real way with words." His snide tone came through loud and clear. "What'd you say to him at the end?"

"You two need to stop bickering," Stubb interjected, saving her from having to reply. "We got matches to win." He hopped from one toe to another.

Python's sarcasm was not lost on Kendal, but he didn't need to know it. The more he thought she was only one step up from a bug in intelligence, the easier it would be for her to complete her investigation while he played wrestling. "We're going to start on the mat. Give me a hundred sit-ups."

"Give you?"

Stepping up until she was in his face, Kendal shoved her finger in his chin. "I'm not going to repeat and explain everything. I'm not your babysitter, your mother, or your girlfriend. I'm here to get you into shape. Now get your sorry, out of shape butt down on the mat and give me a hundred."

His face mottled, and Kendal was sure steam was going to come out of his ears just like in a cartoon. Instead, he shifted toward Stubb. "I'm not–"

"That's it!" Throwing up her hands, she pivoted and started away. "I'm not here to sweet-talk some has-been back into going for the gold. He's your problem, Stubb."

"Wait!" Stubb grabbed her arm, keeping his attention focused toward the mats. "Python, boy, you gotta listen to her. She's proven herself over and over in the amateur circuit. We need her and she's cheap. Now stop being such a horse's ass and git to work."

Playing the indifferent coach, Kendal shook off Stubb's hand. She was quite amazed at how much she was starting to enjoy her role. Being a ball-buster was going to allow her to let off some of the tension this case would create without blowing her cover. Preparing her expression, she faced Python once again with a scowl.

"I don't know why we have to use her. What happened to Hank? He and I worked well together." Python crossed his arms.

"Hank quit right after you left. He's married and has a kid. You don't think I didn't call him first?" Stubb whined.

Sauntering closer, Kendal dragged her finger down the front of Python's T-shirt. "What's your problem, tubbo? You got an inferiority complex?" She stopped halfway down and stabbed his stomach with the blunt edge of her fingernail. Tommy had wanted her to wear two-inch red fake nails. She'd drawn the line. "Can't take orders from a woman?"

Python knocked her hand away. "I don't have any problems, lady."

"Then you're just a lazy, good for nothing has-been, and it's not worth anyone's time to even try and get you back in the ring."

Pausing, she tapped her chin. "And now that I look at you, I'm surprised you ever even won a match. I bet the booker had to pay double to get you a win."

She put her back to Python and addressed Stubb. "I need someone with fire in his eyes. Someone who wants it more than this loser. You get one more chance to get me a real wrestler, or I'm moving on."

"Who the hell are you?" Python moved up behind her. "I was the best. You understand me? The best. You want fire, lady? I'll give you fire."

By the time she turned, he was on the mat. His sit-ups were fast and his eyes never left hers. Widening her stance, Kendal put her hands on her hips and started to count aloud.

At twenty-five, his breathing labored. At fifty, sweat beaded on his skin, and at seventy-five, his shirt stuck to him like skin on a banana.

"One hundred. Good. Turn over and give me fifty push-ups."

One glare and he did as she asked. This part of her assignment would be easy. After her own graduation, she'd spent her first three years as a special agent at the Bureau academy training the new recruits. They joined thinking they were in good shape. They left knowing the difference between in shape and physically fit.

What her roly-poly wrestler didn't know was that she was only putting him through a small part of her own daily routine. If Python didn't want to get hurt in the ring, even in these choreographed matches, he'd have to be in top physical condition. To make sure she had the maximum amount of time to find the radical group, he needed to be able to take the position of champion once again.

The well-defined muscles of his back flexed and bulged as he performed perfectly aligned push-ups. Not exactly hulk material, he reminded her more of that actor in *The Fast and Furious*. He turned his head and when his blue eyes bored into hers she tingled. A sexual tingle.

Huh? Who would've thought a man like this, with a head covered in tattoos, could elicit such a reaction from her?

"I'll tell you right now, I am not interested in having sex with you."

Startled, Kendal frowned. "Excuse me?"

He rotated and sat up. "I know that look." Using the bottom of his T-shirt, he wiped sweat out of eyes. "You think I haven't been around my share of groupies?"

With a grunt, he stood, then moved into her personal space. "I'm going to say this once and once only. I'm not interested in your kind. I never have been, and I never will be."

"You think I'm interested in you?" His uncanny guess at her thoughts stunned her, and she worked quickly to assimilate the information.

"It's pretty obvious, the way you were staring."

Would it be to her benefit to let him think her physically attracted to him, or would it be best if he knew she wasn't? She smiled. "Ah, sugar, I was just enjoying the view. Don't take it over personal. I've seen many men, and you're just one more."

"I just bet you have."

Happy with her choice to keep him guessing, Kendal motioned over to the free weights. "It's time to tighten up those muscles."

As he walked away, she could hear him grumbling under his breath. A hand on her arm kept Kendal from following.

"You almost blew it."

When she pointedly stared at his hand, Stubb let go.

"He could've said no. Then how would ya have busted the drug ring?"

Immediately she spun away from Python. "Don't ever talk to me like that again. The way I deal with Python and his training is my choice, and my choice alone. I don't ever want to have this discussion with you ever again."

Stubb stepped back. "Hey, I was just–"

"No, you weren't anything. Are you understanding me?" Could the scumbag be so dense as to not understand her second meaning? He was never to break cover. Never. He'd been told, and now he'd been reminded. She didn't have time for his inadequacies.

"All right, all right. I git it. Shit, what is it? Your underwear too tight?"

Letting herself relax, she grinned since he wasn't too far off base. Used to fashionable, comfortable underwear, she found this useless scrap of material called a thong pure agony.

"What're you guys doing? Figuring more ways to torture me?"

Raising an eyebrow, Kendal stalked to Python. "That's right, overweight wonder. You've entered the pain zone, and it's time for you to pay. Let's start with five sets of hundred pound curls."

He ached. Even after searching his brain, Python couldn't remember ever hurting this much. He had only himself to blame. Yesterday, whenever Big K made a sarcastic remark about his pathetic work ethic or the superior abilities of her former trainees, he'd pushed himself to surpass expectations.

On the bench in front of his locker, Python pulled his shorts up. *Damn, my body hurts.* As he sat, he slumped, breathing deep, loosening his muscles. Today's workout was going to be grueling. He was not looking forward to it.

He would not give in to her goads today, he reaffirmed in his mind. No matter how inferior she made him feel, he was only going to push himself as far as he knew he could go.

Straightening, he took another deep breath before heading for the battered door. Many a man had abused the metal with either his fists or feet. Unfortunately, Python also knew how it felt to have someone who said they loved you to use you as a punching bag.

The only place he'd allowed himself to hurt someone had been in the ring. And until that last time, it had never been more than a broken nose. Erasing the vivid memory of Terror's lifeless eyes out of his head, Python shoved open the door.

"'Bout time you made it out of there. What're you doing? Buffing your head?"

Big K's voice physically grated on his skin. How did this over-dressed femme fatale irritate him so effortlessly? Without sparing her a glance, Python stomped to the weights.

"Uh-uh. We're starting over there. I want to see if you got any moves."

With his stomach so tight from yesterday's workout, there was no way he was going back on the mat. Turning to tell her just that, he stopped. Gone were the slick pants and high-heeled boots. Instead skin-tight sweats and tennis shoes molded his trainer's body.

Continuing the perusal, he was somewhat surprised when

her face still sported the same amount of makeup as yesterday. He idly wondered if she slept in the gunk.

What the heck? What did he care what she wore in bed? *In bed*? He didn't care about her bed, or what she did in it, he frantically tried to convince himself.

Fingers snapped beneath his nose. "Hey, macho. What's with the daydreaming? We've got work to do here. You need to get a grip."

Stepping even closer, Big K peered intently into his eyes.

Python frowned, stumbling back. "Hey, back off. What're you doing?"

"I was checking your pupils. I wanted to make sure you aren't using. I don't train users. They're not worth my time."

"I'm not using." When she stepped toward him again, he held out his hands.

She put her fists on her hips. "Then stop spacing out on me. You need to be on your game. In the zone."

Not waiting for an answer, she started away. "Let's get to work."

He crossed his arms. "I'm not doing sit-ups."

Like slow motion in a movie, she turned, her brow arched. "I told you, I'm not your mama, so don't act like a spoiled brat. If I tell you to do sit-ups, you'll do them."

The stare down started, and Python was determined not to flinch. He didn't care if he did sound childish. A man could only be pushed so far.

"Hey, what're you two doin'? I thought you'd be working by now?" Stubb shuffled up, looking from Big K to Python.

Neither of them spoke. The only sounds were the grunts of the other men working out around the room.

"Why are ya just standing here?"

Without blinking, Big K smiled. "Your little boy here is trying to make a point. He has a need to establish dominance. What he doesn't realize is I'm not here to emasculate him. I'm here to make him better than he ever was. I'm here to take him to the top."

She broke eye contact. "Where you told me he wanted to

go."

"I can talk for myself." How dare she talk like he was incapable of intelligent thought.

"Fine. Then you tell me what you want."

"I want–" Python couldn't say what he really wanted–to find the drug dealers and get out before ever stepping into a ring. "I want to be number one again."

"Yeah?" She cocked her head. "That really sounded convincing."

"I don't need your sarcasm." Unable to keep his anger bottled up, he advanced, his hands flexing. "I told you I want to be number one, and I do. I don't have to establish dominance. I am dominant. I've been the best. I'll be the best again."

Instead of backing away, Big K nodded. "Good."

Adrenaline so high he wanted to crawl out of his skin, it took seconds for her words to register. He stopped. "What?"

"This is what I want. Raw emotion. If we're going to win, I need to know you want it." She shoved him. "Now get in."

Confused, Python looked over at the middle of the gym. "In the ring?"

She widened her stance and tilted her head. "Yeah, in the ring."

He knew she was testing him again to see if he wanted it bad enough. Damn, why'd he ever agree to this madness?

A niggling thought in the back of his head started to tell him his life needed closure. Although he'd complained and given Tommy a hard time, deep down he needed to slay this dragon in order to be free.

Mustering all the courage he'd ever claimed to have, Python climbed into the ring. Just inside he stopped and waited for the memories to overtake him. Waited for the paralyzing pain and fear he always felt in his nightmares.

When none occurred, he rotated his shoulders. "What now?"

"I want to see some moves," Big K said.

He leaned on the ropes. "Moves?"

"You know, the things you perform in the ring for the marks. The reason they show up in the first place."

The back of his neck tensed. With innate precision, she knew the exact buttons to push. "I know what moves are. I was only surprised." His jaw hurt from the force with which he ground his teeth. "What do you want to see?"

"Start with a flying snap kick to a roundhouse, ending with a leg lariat." Leaping up, Big K paused outside before bending over and slipping through the ropes.

After rolling his head and shaking out his arms and legs to loosen up, Python started with the first move.

"All right, boy. I knew you still had it in you." Stubb scrambled up, staying on the outside of the ring. "He's got it. You see it? He's got it."

Grinning at Stubb's overzealous excitement, Python went into the final move.

"*Oomph.*" His breath whooshed out as Big K smacked into his stomach. Automatically his arms wrapped around her waist. She used his instability to her advantage, continued her forward movement, and slammed him to the ground.

As soon as they hit, he rolled, pinning her arms with his knees, his hands on his hips. "What're you doing?"

"Getting you back in shape." Her chest heaved once, and he stared. She wore a v-neck sweatshirt giving him a tantalizing view of breasts.

From behind, suddenly her feet shoved through the inside of his arms up to her knees. She yanked.

Caught off guard, he fell back. Freed of his weight, she jumped up and stood in a crouched position a few feet away.

"Let's go, has-been." She wiggled her fingers. "Let's see if you can take me. Of course, I am only a girl."

Her sarcasm clearly said she thought that a joke. They started to circle each other.

"You could get hurt. This isn't scripted," he said.

Her brow lifted before her grin grew even wider. "Don't you worry about me. I can take care of myself. And I don't mind making it up as we go."

But she'd never been in the ring with a killer. Python reminded himself he was in control. This wasn't the past. He'd go easy–

"*Oomph.*"

Again she slammed into him. This time, though, he was better prepared. Flipping her, he wrapped his arms around her waist, her back to his front.

Heaving, he twisted her upside down, and her legs flew up. He spun once, prepared to drop her. She locked her feet around his neck. As soon as his hands moved to disengage the hold, she wrapped her fingers around his calves.

Her feet released his neck and fell to the ground. Shifting, she put her head through his legs and shoved. Off balance, he tumbled forward.

She's better than I thought she'd be.

As he fell, he gripped her leg. Twisting his body, he brought her around as he landed on his back.

She wasn't that good, he thought with unashamed male pride. He threw her over before following. Full body, he slammed and pinned her to the floor.

With their faces inches apart, he inhaled an intoxicating blend of heat and woman. Her green eyes sparkled, and he felt himself momentarily entranced by their depth.

"Are you satisfied?" he murmured.

"Satisfied?"

That mesmerizing emerald gaze held him spellbound. Her eyes widened, and her pupils expanded. Sure signs she was having the same reaction as him.

Knowing he shouldn't want it. Knowing being attracted to her was the last thing he needed. Python couldn't be more surprised at his sudden desire to kiss her.

She licked her cherry-slicked lips. He nearly groaned as he lowered his head.

Chapter Three

Pain!

Sharp and searing, the ache penetrated his entire body and Python rolled away, his groin throbbing. "What'd you do that for?" he choked out. Fortunately, he was wearing a cup, but it didn't protect him from everything. Especially a direct shot to his balls.

"Don't ever let your guard down." Big K advanced, and he rolled further away. "You just fell for the oldest trick in the book. Get it together or you're going to get hurt."

Sitting with his knees pulled up, Python took a deep breath. Why had he wanted to kiss her anyway? She was the same type of woman as his mother. Maybe not in the drug use category, but definitely in knowing how to hit him where it hurt the most. "That was a stiff shot."

"And you don't think you're going to have stiff-workers in the ring? You've got to be prepared for cheap shots from dirty players. You think the sport has changed? That everyone follows the script now?"

After climbing out, Big K dropped down to the ground. "Think again. If you're going to make it to The Brawl, you've got a lot of dances to win. I don't have time to coddle you."

Irritated with this woman he'd never heard of, even if she did seem to know about the wrestling world, Python heaved his still painfully pulsing body up. "I don't need to be coddled."

She looked back over her shoulder. "Yeah? You could have fooled me."

Much more gingerly than when he'd climbed in, Python stepped through the ropes, ignoring Stubb's outstretched hand. The two men followed her to the free weights.

Big K straddled the workbench. "We need to get on the

road, catch up to the tour, and get the plan made. Stubb, did you get in touch with the booker?"

"Yeah. Sloan's put us on in Roanoke in two weeks."

"Two weeks?" Python rubbed the top of his head. "I'm going to be in the ring in two weeks?"

Raising her eyebrow, Big K pointed her finger at him. "You sound surprised. What'd you think? We're going to take months to get you ready? Or are you having second thoughts?"

Her eyes narrowed, and she glanced between Stubb and him. "What's going on? I thought you hired me because you needed a win and wanted it quickly. I don't have time for wishy-washy has-beens who change their minds every other minute."

Tired of her calling him a has-been, tired of her constant attack on his abilities, Python shoved his fist in her face. "Listen, sweetheart. You've been on my case from the moment you met me. I'm sick and tired of it."

She stood. "Oh, yeah?"

"Yeah! I'm better than anyone out there. I need to get in shape. I know that. I'll get it done. What I don't need is you harping like a damn fishwife every time I turn around."

"A fishwife? You think I sound like a fishwife, let me tell you–"

"No." He stepped close. "Let me tell you. I was the best, I am the best, and I'll prove it to you and everyone else. Don't you worry about it. You just set the schedule, put me through the paces, and leave the snide remarks and nicknames out of it."

"Fine."

"Fine?"

With a shrug, she circled around the back of the bench. "That's what I've been waiting to hear. Now we can get to work." She pointed. "Sit your butt down. I'll spot you."

Kendal tugged at the bottom of the constricting bra pushing her breasts practically to her chin. How did women live in these contraptions? Her respect for comfortable lingerie was increasing every hour she spent undercover.

Today had been good. Thank heavens she had spent all those hours studying wrestling tapes and terminology. Even if you knew the exact next move of your opponent, your body was going to take a bruising every time you stepped into the ring.

Yesterday, she made a statement with her outfit. Today, she'd proved she had ability. She'd practiced as much as she could on her own, but until she stepped into the ring with Python she hadn't yet been tested.

Thinking about the ring had her mind replaying the almost kiss. She couldn't believe how her pulse had raced. She put her hand above her left breast as her heart kicked into high gear all over again. What would a real kiss do to her if only the memory of the almost kiss had her reeling?

This is not a professional attitude, she reminded herself. With both parents in the military, duty first was not just a motto but how you lived your life. There was nothing more important than allegiance to the United States and being a good soldier. Because of them, she'd learned to control her natural impulses to the point that she controlled her every reaction. She could definitely control this little hormonal effect. Besides, Python was only a man.

Getting her mind back on business, she focused on his breakthrough. His new determination to get back in the ring was a huge step. With Tommy's forewarning about his resistance, she'd known her work was cut out for her.

She had to admit, though, she'd gotten a little worried he was going to back out. That couldn't happen. She needed the inside track to get to the money.

Before grabbing the large, blunt handles of the heavy wood door, she threw her head up and got attitude. Thick smoke slithered out as she entered the dingy bar. Two steps inside, she kept her chin cocked at an arrogant angle.

Fighting the need to tug at her bra and the hem of the too tight, extra-short skirt, she searched the tables for Stubb and Python. Men of all ages and sizes turned to stare. Just like

Stubb to pick the most biker-plagued, testosterone-filled establishment to have a business meeting.

"Hey, baby. You looking for some company?" A burly guy with his front teeth missing waggled his eyebrows.

"Why? You think you know someone I'd be interested in?"

His brow knitted, and he scratched the side of his face. "I was thinking me."

"You shouldn't do that."

Confusion had his forehead creasing even more. "Huh?"

"I wouldn't recommend you straining yourself by trying to use your brain. It may cause you a seizure or something."

"Huh?"

You know better, she chastised herself. Something about wearing stilettos, skintight clothes, and make-up a clown could envy, gave her a real case of bitchy. Shaking her head, Kendal waved him off. "Never mind, cowboy. I'm meeting someone, and you aren't him."

"I was just asking," came his somewhat sulky answer as he shuffled back to the bar.

Watching him, she felt more than heard someone approach from her left. Whirling, her hand shot out. A direct hit to Python's chest.

"Hey!" He rubbed the spot. "What'd you do that for? Haven't you beat up on me enough lately?"

Unaffected by his fake wounded look, Kendal adjusted the strap of her purse on her shoulder. She chose to ignore the sudden increase in her heart rate. "If I were you, I wouldn't ever sneak up on me like that."

"I didn't sneak. You just didn't see me."

"Whatever." She shrugged. "How'd you know to come get me?"

"I just got here, saw Stubb, but before I could head over I heard your voice."

"Where're we sitting?"

"In one of the booths behind there." As he pointed toward a wall, he grabbed her elbow.

When they rounded the corner, she saw Stubb. He lifted his beer in a salute. Sliding in across from the grimy man, she looked up when Python hit her shoulder.

"Move over." He started to bend down.

"Why?" Too conscious of him from the physical contact, Kendal preferred he not be next to her.

In mid-squat, he stopped. "Because we're not going to sit in a bar with two men on one side while a woman sits alone on the other."

Such a logical reason gave her no recourse but to let him in. "Of course." Shifting further into the corner, Kendal gave Stubb a sharp glare as his gaze stayed glued on her chest. He never noticed.

"What can I get the two of you?" The waitress winked at Kendal and Python.

"Beer," Python said.

"I don't think so." Kendal leaned forward. "You can have soda or water. Take your pick."

The waitress laughed. "She keeps you on a tight leash, honey, don't she?"

Python ignored the waitress and faced Kendal. "I want a beer."

"And I want to win a match. My want outweighs yours." She looked at the server. "Make it two diet sodas."

The woman hesitated, waiting for Python to respond. Kendal pointed with her chin.

"Fine," he huffed.

Kendal snapped her fingers. "Wait a minute, make one orange juice."

Mumbling under her breath while smiling, the waitress left.

"You want juice at this time of day?" Python asked.

"No, it's for you."

"I didn't want soda, and I definitely don't want juice."

"Sorry. It's the way it's gonna be. As soon as you drop ten pounds, you can drink whatever you want." She poked his stomach. "Including beer."

"Gee, thanks."

Enjoying his sarcasm, Kendal eased back on the bench and grinned. "Don't mention it." From her large bag, she pulled out a notebook. "Okay, let's get down to business."

With a flip, she opened to a clean page. "We need to decide on the gimmick. I know we'll adjust as we go. We need something powerful for our first appearance in Virginia."

The waitress dropped off the drinks, placing the juice in front of Kendal. Quickly, she switched them.

Frowning, Python picked the glass up. "I thought the comeback would be a big enough draw."

"You would." When he playfully whacked her in the side, Kendal realized she could really like this guy.

No, no, not him. Being able to be herself that was what she liked. *Letting it all hang out*, she grinned inwardly as she glanced down at the exposed tops of her breasts. "We need it to be more. Stubb, what do you think?"

The man hadn't said a word tonight, which was odd. Finally tearing his gaze from her chest, he took another slug of beer. "Maybe he should come back as a heel."

"No way." Python shook his head. "I like being a face. I started out being hated, worked hard to move from heel to face, and I'm staying."

"Yeah, all right." Stubb nodded. "We can book him easier as a face anyway. Right now there are some solid heels. The break in will be easier as a face."

Not sure if Stubb was convincing himself or them, Kendal made a note on her paper. "Okay. I assume you'll still use the name Python, especially with the tattoo of one on the back of your head."

"That's the only one I had when I wrestled."

She circled his head with her pen. "You got all of these after?"

Her disbelief must have come through loud and clear. Python took a long drink of the juice, draining the glass. "I have a friend who owns a shop."

As if that explained it. "So? I have a friend who owns a

body piercing joint, you don't see me with studs and hoops sticking out all over the place."

"I don't have tattoos everywhere." He waved his empty glass at the waitress as she passed.

"Really?" Kendal eyed his colorful head, looking for unpainted skin. In front of his ears, his face and his neck were all free of any ink.

"I only went a little crazy with my head. I only have one tattoo on my arm."

"And your friend? Did he stop with his head?"

"No, none on his head. He's got them everywhere else."

Interesting, Kendal thought, that Python would only tattoo the most exposed part of his body. Something he couldn't ever hide, unless he wore a hat constantly. He'd wanted to stay in the limelight even after he left the ring. She bet he didn't even realize why he'd done it. "Back to business. You're still going to go by Python, right?"

"Right."

"So what's the gimmick?" She tapped her pen against the pad, started to stop, then realized she didn't have to curb her nervous habits. *Another bonus*.

After the server delivered his new drink, Python took a quick gulp. "I'm back to regain my title, since it was never actually taken from me. That angle will work every time."

"And the house will be bored stiff in two matches. You'll be no better draw than a tweener," she said.

He scowled. "I'm too well known. I'll never be a nobody that the fans don't know or even care if he's good or bad."

Pursing her lips, she shook her head. "No, we need something more. Something big."

"Then we use Terror's death."

"No!"

The soft-spoken words that had come from Stubb contrasted sharply with Python's angry outburst. Kendal eyed both of them. "Why not?" she asked Python.

"And how could we use it?" she asked Stubb.

"I said no."

Ignoring the vibrating man to her right, she put her elbows on the table. "How?"

"Everyone knows Terror's death was an accident–" Stubb started.

"Not everyone," Python grumbled.

Stubb darted a glance at him before focusing on Kendal. "Doesn't matter. Our angle will be Python scared the other wrestlers so much they forced him out. Now he's back to rightfully reclaim what is his. Only the meanest and baddest will dare climb in the ring."

Kendal could feel her excitement mounting as she scribbled furiously. "That's good. That can take us all the way to the top. I mean, we can spin the fear factor to fevered–"

"I said no!" Python slammed his fist on his table. "Aren't you hearing me?"

Stretching her arm across the back of the booth, Kendal tilted her head. "We heard you, we just don't agree. This is the angle of all angles. We've got to use it."

"I won't exploit Terror's death. It's not right."

"How is this exploiting his death? We aren't going to focus on that. We're going to focus on the results that action had."

"That action was a man dying," Python gritted.

Confused, Kendal could only stare. What was he so upset about? She'd watched the film. She'd seen the bout. Clearly the ropes had broken when the big wrestler had fallen against them.

If anything, the manufacturer should have been called to task if the ropes had been ruled defective. She hadn't taken the time to see whether the family had sued. "I know Terror died. I didn't mean to sound callous. Using your last match to promote your future is only logical."

"You don't understand."

The dejection in his voice and face confused her even more. And he was right, she didn't understand. She wished she had the time to ease him into this angle, but no one knew what the radical group was doing. The sooner she got the necessary evidence, the safer the nation would be. She turned to Stubb. "Get the word to Sloan Rusen. This should easily pack them in."

Python fisted the hand resting on the table. "Why aren't you listening? It's my match, my career. I have the ultimate decision."

"And if you were acting like an adult and not a teenager, I'd listen."

That brought his head up. "And you know what's best?"

"In this? Yes."

They stared at each other, neither breaking the contact even when Stubb polished off his beer and said he had to go. Once alone, Python faced forward. "You don't know what're you're doing."

"You've said that before."

His icy glaze speared her, and Kendal felt the chill stab her heart.

"Just know I don't like using this angle. If someone else dies, it's your fault."

Glad the two weeks were over, Python admired his trimmer, firmer physique. Big K might be brash and rude, but she was a damn good trainer. She'd held him to a strict diet, increased his resistance training daily, and fat pounds had melted away, replaced by lean muscle.

Lifting his arms over his head, he looked down at his emerging washboard stomach and couldn't help but smile. He felt good. Really good. The best he had since he left the wrestling world.

"It's almost time, Python. You need to git into costume."

His grin disappeared with Stubb's reminder that this was his first time back in the ring. "Yeah. I'm getting there."

"Well, you better git there a little faster or Big K's gonna come in and dress you herself."

Unable to stop his mind, Python's imagination ventured into forbidden territory. What if he did wait? Would she remove his clothes slowly, or tear them off in a rush? Would she rub her hands all over his chest, and then the rest of him?

The one thing that had become all too clear to Python was his definite attraction to his trainer. They'd continued to practice routines in the ring, especially after Sloan had called giving them the details of this first fight. Her sweaty, muscular, yet sweet-smelling body had been wrapped around him in ways he'd yet to try during lovemaking. After this week, he really wanted to try them now.

It'd been all he could do not to always have a raging hard-on. As if he could've prevented it every time. There had been a session or two when they'd been too intertwined, too close for her not to notice. She never acknowledged it or said anything.

"Hey, big guy. Get a move on."

Hearing Stubb again, Python snapped out of his reverie. "All right, all right. Keep your shorts on."

"I'm keeping mine on. You need to git yours off." Stubb sniggered as he strolled out.

Hustling, Python stripped out of his street clothes. He stepped into the legs of the sleek black spandex costume, then pulled the tank type straps over his arms. The thin material slithered over and covered him like a second skin. An intricate python decorated the front, matching the one etched into the back of his skull. An addition Big K had insisted upon.

The door of the men's locker room banged open. "You ready yet?"

Even her voice made his skin tingle. From a bench, he grabbed the black cape and swung it over his shoulders. "I just told Stubb to cool his jets. I'm coming." Rounding the corner, Python found Big K standing with one booted foot planted on either side of the threshold, holding the door wide open.

He stopped. His breath backed up and he had to make himself exhale. This was not the woman he'd been training with. Sure, she'd been wearing the thick make-up, but her hair had been in a ponytail and even though her sweats had been tight, they'd still ended in tennis shoes. But now...

"Come on, Python. We haven't got all day." The voice was the same, the look eye-popping. Not even the first time he'd seen her compared to now.

Big K was dressed in black leather from head to toe. Knee-high, patent leather spike-heeled boots, polished to a brilliant shine, were still quite a distance from a mini-skirt, which if it didn't show her cheeks in the back, he'd eat his cape. And they'd definitely only used the ear of a cow to make that halter-top.

"What'd you do to yourself?"

Her gaze darted about as if searching the hall. She looked back at him. "What? I didn't do anything."

He could've sworn a moment of panic flashed across her face. Crossing over to her, he waved his hand up and down her body. "This get-up. What the hell are you wearing it for?"

She planted fisted hands on her hips. "The same reason you're wearing that one. It's part of the show."

"But–" *Yeah, but.* What could he say? That he didn't like her wearing something so revealing? He didn't think she'd care about his opinion.

"But what?" Her eyes narrowed, and she tilted her head. "What's your problem?"

Shoving past her and all her free-flowing black hair, he stomped into the hallway. "No problem. I just don't see the need for it, that's all."

The clacking of her high heels on the cement increased tempo as she raced to catch up to him. "What put a bug up your butt? I would've thought you'd be the first person to want to use any means necessary to draw more attention to us."

Not sparing even a sideways glance, he barreled toward the curtain where they'd soon be introduced. "I didn't think you'd want that type of attention."

She grabbed his arm and pulled him around to face her. "What're you talking about? We want all types of attention. That's the point."

Stepping even closer, he moved nose to nose. "Do you know the kind of men who are out there? Do you know what they're going to think when they see that getup?"

"Aw, Python. Are you worried about my reputation?"

With a jerk, he moved back. "No. Of course not."

"Sure, you are. Let me assure you, I can take care of myself." Smiling, she sauntered to the curtain, then added over her shoulder, "No one will be messing with me unless I want them to."

That's what he was afraid of. Frowning so hard his head hurt, he was almost on top of her when the image across her rear end registered. "You have a snake."

"Not the last time I looked."

For a moment, confusion clouded his brain even as his eyes stayed glued to her backside. Then he got the sexual reference. He shook his head as he waved at her rear. "No, on your butt."

Glancing over her back and down at her skirt, she grinned. "Pretty cool, huh? I had them embroider your python. That way everyone knows I belong in your camp."

In his mind, Python finished that sentence differently. Like belong to *him*, period. Wanting to punch himself to knock off these inappropriate feelings, instead he stepped past her, then pulled back the curtain the tiniest bit and scanned the crowd.

"I'm not interested in groupies or groupie look-alikes. Never have been, never will be."

As she leaned to peer over his shoulder, Big K's sweet scent invaded his space.

"What're you mumbling about?"

"Nothing." The woman didn't even realize she was playing havoc with his senses. It didn't even make sense.

He wanted a normal woman, one who wore khaki pants and those cute cotton shirts with dainty collars and buttons in funny shapes. Like the women pictured on the front of magazines that talked about decorating. Someone like Mega, with a heart of gold, who wanted to settle down in a nice neighborhood and raise a family.

"You could've fooled me. I could've sworn there was noise coming out of your mouth," Big K said.

"LADIES AND GENTLEMEN," the announcer's voice

boomed, saving Python from having to respond. "THE MAN WE THOUGHT WE'D NEVER SEE AGAIN."

After slapping his back, Big K moved to stand off to his right. "It's show time. This is it."

"A LEGEND RETURNING TO CLAIM HIS TITLE."

Adrenaline and dread warred with each other inside him. He was about to go back into the ring. This wasn't a drill. This wasn't just him and Big K going through the motions.

"PYTHON," the announcer roared.

"We're on," Big K yelled as the curtain separated and the music swelled.

Spotlights speared them. Python instinctively went into character. Raising his arms, he strutted out onto the walkway as smoke billowed from the sides. The crowd screamed and chanted. He bobbed his head as he swaggered past. Men, women, boys, and girls reached out to touch him, offering encouragement or disparagement.

Keeping his distance, he paraded to the ring like a king in front of his subjects and hopped up. On the ropes, he waved to the crowd before jumping over and inside. There he turned a complete circle, and the noise surged once more.

Energy pulsed through him as he returned to his corner where Big K stood like a leather-clad warrior, her foot arrogantly propped on the bottom rope. Her face held no emotion, her features strong, most probably a match to his. As practiced, he made a dramatic turn, flinging the cape from his shoulders.

Just as dramatically, Big K caught it. She held it aloft as if it were a hunter's prize. The crowd went wild, stomping and cheering to a deafening thunder.

"AND THE BOLD, BRAVE SOUL DARING TO ENTER THE RING WITH A MAN WITH A KILLER'S INSTINCT...DOOMSLAYER!"

As boos permeated the dome, a silver dressed wrestler marched his way to the ring. He jeered back at the crowd. They responded in kind.

"You can take him," Big K shouted above the din.

Nodding, Python wasn't worried. He was scheduled to win. Some wrestlers though, stiff-workers, played dirty and intentionally hurt the person they wrestled. The Doomslayer was one.

Suddenly, Big K clutched the back of his neck. "Watch him when he comes on your left. From the tapes, that's where he likes to strike outside the script."

Her face close to his, their breath mingling, the crowd cheering, all actions seemed to be pushing him to do it. Like lightning, his hand snaked out and forced her head the rest of the way.

For a fleeting second their lips met. With a push, Big K pulled back slightly. "What're you doing?"

Unashamed, he grinned as the crowd noise swelled again. "Giving the house what they want."

"Well, from now on check with me first before you decide to ad lib."

"Whatever you say, boss."

A slight, warm smile broke across her face. "How come you never say that in the gym?"

Feeling good, he laughed aloud. "Because I know better."

"LET THE MATCH BEGIN."

Turning back to the center of the ring, Python's entire body went on alert. Doomslayer's face contorted, and he pointed his finger. "You going down, Python. You going down."

Being on the sidelines wasn't as easy as Kendal thought it was going to be. With another almost kiss added on top of everything else, she felt she could explode. As the two wrestlers circled each other, her eyes stayed glued on the Doomslayer.

He was a jobber. She'd heard he had bigger dreams than just being paid to lose. What Kendal didn't want was for him to try and break out of the role by screwing up this match.

As scripted, Python and Doomslayer lunged. The routine went smoothly from the jumping powerbomb to the hanging kneebreaker. Kendal began to relax as the cheering could be physically felt whenever Python made a particularly good move.

Python put Doomslayer in a bulldog headlock and the silver wrestler went down. The ref fell to his knees. He slapped his hand on the mat. "One." Another slap. "Two." Kendal held her breath. The last slap. "Three."

"Yes!" Pumping the air with a raised fist, she shouted along with the crowd. A huge grin splitting his face, Python strutted and played to the fans.

Kendal felt proud. The same pride she had when one of the new recruits made it through her rigorous training program. Or so she tried to convince herself. As Python circled in front of her, she surveyed him carefully, looking for any injury.

The most important thing was to keep him healthy and winning. The reasoning sounded good. And if it gave her the opportunity to constantly scrutinize his body, then that was just a side benefit.

"He did it!" Stubb appeared next to her, vibrating with excitement.

At least she hoped his nervous energy was excitement and not chemically induced. "Yes, he did. What's next?"

"He'll do some interviews, make a lot of noise about being the best and baddest, and then he needs to git back where the marks can't git to him."

"Good. I'll meet you both outside the locker room in about twenty minutes." Kendal pivoted to hop down.

"Where're you going?"

Pausing, she smiled tightly. "I need to get everything in order." She raised her eyebrows, hoping the thickheaded twit would get a clue.

"Oh, yeah." His eyes darted away, flitting over the crowd. "That's fine."

"Glad you concur," she muttered as she jumped off the edge and strode for the restricted wrestlers' area.

Even in her state of outrageous dress, the fans paid her little attention. As she made her way back behind the curtain where she and Python had emerged, she thought back on

Stubb's reaction. He was probably doing drugs and was scared that when she busted the ring he was going to get caught. If only she were here on a drug bust, she'd love to take in the smarmy guy all over again.

Bumping into hard muscle, Kendal looked way up. "Oops, sorry."

"No prob, sweet-thing." The obvious steroid using, muscle-bound hulk patted her shoulder with thick, blunt fingers before ambling on down the hallway.

Watching his retreating back, she was glad Python wasn't an overblown, too bulked-up wrestler like so many she'd seen in the tapes and now in person. Yes, Python was muscular and larger than your average guy, but he didn't look like his head was growing out of his shoulders.

No, she'd have to say he was definitely one of the best-looking wrestlers, or men for that matter, she'd ever met. If you liked the type, that is. Which she didn't, she reminded herself again.

When the giant stranger looked over his shoulder and found her still watching him, he wiggled his brows and flexed his back muscles. She blinked. Flexed his back muscles? What other body parts did he have that much control over?

Laughing at herself for even thinking about it, she gave a slight wave before spinning and heading in the opposite direction. This was her first chance to infiltrate, and she wanted to make the most of it.

She gave a momentary thought to changing to make herself less conspicuous, then realized her existing outfit made her blend in. Anything more demure and she'd stick out like a sore thumb.

Rounding the corner, the number of people hanging around and mingling began to dwindle. Good, the fewer people who witnessed where she went, the better.

Her target was a temporary office for the booker during the event. There she hoped to find documentation that could possibly lead to the laundering scheme.

After a quick check over her shoulder, Kendal shoved

open the door leading to the stairwell and ducked inside. Waiting, she listened for sounds of anyone else climbing or descending the stairs.

Silence.

On her toes to reduce the sound of her heels, she rapidly ascended the two flights. Once on the second floor, she held still, listening. She cracked open the door to a dimly lit corridor.

No one was on this floor. Everyone was involved in the activities downstairs. It would be tomorrow before the staff came up here to complete the accounting process before moving on to the next show in a different town.

Stepping into the hallway, she closed the door as quietly as possible. This part of the arena was carpeted, allowing her to move much faster. She only had a limited number of minutes before Python and Stubb would start wondering where she was.

"Oh! No! Stop!"

The woman's piercing shriek froze Kendal in her tracks. Someone was being attacked. She rushed forward.

"Shut up! I told you not to make noise!" a man growled as something crashed.

"Oh, God! I can't–"

Kendal could still hear the woman, but the sound was now muffled. He'd somehow gagged her. Anger like nothing she'd ever felt pumped through her blood. On reflex, she snatched at the small of her back.

Crap, no weapon. More muted sounds of a struggle. Without thought to her cover, Kendal slammed into the room.

"What the–" A massive, naked man scowled back at her. Two fishnet stocking-clad legs stuck out on either side of him, while one of his enormous hands covered the mouth of a woman, her eyes as wide as half-dollars.

Chapter Four

"Step away from her." Kendal crouched, ready to take on the wrestler hand-muzzling the woman.

His mouth quirked. "Hey, babe. Wait your turn. I've got enough for you too."

Could the man be more arrogant? "I said step away."

The woman squirmed and thrashed.

"Ow, you bit me." His hand jerked away from her mouth.

"You're damn right, I did."

Kendal looked from the wrestler calmly inspecting his hand to the woman who'd crossed her legs at his back.

"Why'd you go and do that?" he asked in a sulky tone that only a three year old could master.

"You're offering to do someone else while you're still in me. And you're asking why I bit you?"

This bizarre scene began to click into place, and Kendal loosened her muscles.

"You were the one that offered a threesome. I just thought your friend was late." Over his shoulder, he winked at Kendal as he started to thrust his hips. "And jealous."

The woman on the desk speared her with a lethal look that turned provocative when she gave Kendal the once-over. "Yes." Her eyes closed as the wrestler shoved harder. They reopened and she licked her lips. "Come join the fun, sugar. I ne–oh, yeah–I need something to do with my mouth."

Unbelieving that this was happening in front of her, unbelieving that she was still standing here, Kendal decided no answer would be best. Turning, she hightailed it out.

Once back in the hall, she realized the woman's hose must have been crotchless, because they definitely weren't thigh highs.

Not wanting to waste the chance to check the office, Kendal stopped at a door marked PRIVATE. Her hand on the knob, she put her ear to the door and heard voices inside. Erotic screams erupted from down the hall and she jerked away. Cursing her bad luck, she rushed back down the stairs. Out on the first floor once again, she slowed her pace and headed toward the locker room.

She rounded the corner and bumped into Python.

He grabbed her arms. "There you are." Dressed in jeans and a T-shirt, he still sported a huge smile. "Where've you been? I've been looking all over for you."

His touch felt too good. She shook off his hands and started down the hall. "I wanted to find Rusen and talk about the next bout. Someone said he was upstairs." Tossing her hair over her shoulder, Kendal tried to appear nonchalant. "All I found was a wrestler and his girlfriend needing some privacy."

"Girlfriend? Privacy?"

With an exasperated sigh, she punched his shoulder. "Privacy. As in wanting to be alone."

Giggling rolled from behind them. The two sex fiends from upstairs sauntered past.

"Hey, babe. Anytime, anywhere. Just say the word." The now dressed wrestler cupped his crotch. Draped over his arm, the woman licked her lips. Her thin, almost transparent tank top clearly showed she was braless.

Both leered at Kendal.

Python swiveled, putting himself between her and them. "What was that all about?" All remnants of elation gone, his voice and face were harsh.

"They misunderstood why I came into the room. They thought I wanted to join the party."

He stepped closer. "And did you?"

"How could you even say such a thing?" Indignant, Kendal jutted her chin, and black hair swayed in her peripheral vision.

Oh, yeah. I look like the type of person who might. She

glanced again at the woman. *At least my shirt doubles as a bra.*

Python swiped his hand over his rainbow colored head. "You're right. I know you better than that."

His instant support, even if he didn't know the real her, gave her immense pleasure. "I'm glad you do. Besides, why would I want to be with someone who's already involved?"

"Yeah, why would anyone?" Python turned back toward the departing couple.

Just before they rounded the corner, the woman looked over her shoulder and gave a finger wave before throwing her head back and laughing.

Abruptly, Python spun around. "Do you still want to find Sloan?"

Her mind swimming with all the bizarre happenings and Python's strange behavior, Kendal shook her head. "No. I'm going to let Stubb handle it. I'm beat and want to head back to the hotel."

"Good. I'll go find Stubb and let him know we're out of here."

Pacing the small room, Python was antsy. He hadn't wanted to call the number, but felt it was his duty.

"Special Agent Boden."

"Uh, Tommy?"

"Python. What's wrong?"

"I thought you should know something."

"You got a break in the case already?"

Shaking his head, he stopped when he realized Tommy couldn't see him. "No, no. Nothing like that. I think Stubb is using."

"You have evidence?"

"No. He's anxious all the time. It may be the way he is. I don't know."

The phone crackled in the silence of Tommy's pause. "Do you think we can use him to lead us to the main dealer?"

How the hell should I know? It sure did seem as if the FBI was letting him do this his way. They hadn't given him anything concrete on how to arrest these guys. "I don't know. I just wanted you to know."

"That's good. Let me know the minute you learn anything else." Pushing the end button, Tommy grinned at Kendal. "Your choirboy wrestler just snitched on his manager. Did you know Stubb was using?"

Three blocks from the hotel, Kendal sat in the nondescript rental car. She tugged at her skirt. "I suspected. I don't have actual evidence to say for sure."

"Yeah, that's what Python said." Tommy nodded at the hand still holding her hem. "Nice getup, by the way."

"Stuff a sock in it."

He held out his hands. "No. I'm serious. This is a good look for you. If for some reason you decide to leave the bureau, I think you have a future in the NFW."

"Haven't I warned you before about your penchant for making fun? Now, let's get serious."

"Fine, spoilsport." Tommy hunched over the steering wheel. "There's new evidence that the drop is being made during an event."

Kendal shifted, propping her shoulder on the door. "That's too risky. The intel's wrong."

"I think that's what they're betting on." He looked at her. "Make the transfer right under everyone's noses. Nobody's the wiser."

"This doesn't sound right, Boden. You don't have to be so open for money laundering." Kendal gazed unseeing out the front windshield. "There are a dozen ways to get the money to the booker without being so noticeable."

"Don't forget they are criminals, you know. That means they're not so bright to start with."

With a chuckle, she tapped her finger on the dashboard. "I'll concur on that point. It still doesn't make sense, though. Something isn't right."

"We got three verifications. It may seem unlikely, but–"

She waved her hand. "Okay, I get the picture. I'll be able

to snoop around at the next match. Knowing this win would start the draw, Rusen put us on a televised match in Hershey, his hometown. I should be able to get into his office."

"I told you it'd go down like this."

His smug attitude had her hiding her smile behind a hand. "Yeah, okay. There's going to be several matches and Python's fighting last. The promo's going as planned. Tonight they had the largest crowd ever for a dark match."

When he opened his mouth, she held up her hand. "Yes, I know, you told me. Anyway, the stakes are going to be higher with it being on TV."

"I don't think you have to worry about anyone recognizing you," Tommy said in obvious sincerity.

Another chuckle escaped, surprising her probably as much as it did Tommy. "You did look a little green when you thought I was soliciting you."

He puffed out his chest. "You just surprised me, that's all."

"What'd you expect? You were the one that recommended the look." Kendal was even more astonished at her defensiveness. She'd blended well with the wrestling crowd at the arena.

"I know it. I guess I just didn't expect it to fit so well. I mean, you know, tight, I mean. . ."

His discomfort restored her pride, so she took pity on him. "All right. I get the picture. My cover is very effective."

"Yeah, effective."

"Anything else?" She reached for the door handle.

"Nope."

When she opened the door and the interior stayed dark. The first thing any decent agent did was disable the dome light. "Okay. I'll check in as scheduled."

"Get Smart?"

Hesitating, half in and half out, she gritted her teeth and resisted the need to scream. "Yeah?"

"Be careful getting inside tomorrow."

His concern thawed her irritation. "Aw, Boden. Keep this

up and I might actually start thinking you care."

"I wouldn't push it that far. Besides, you haven't heard our new code name."

She paused, almost afraid to ask. *Almost*. "Spill it."

"Operation: Stiletto."

In spite of herself, she laughed as she looked down at the outrageous pair of spike heels she was wearing.

"You heard me, right?" Tommy's confused tone made her grin.

"Yeah, I heard you. Was it your idea?"

If the interior of the car had been lit by anything more than a street lamp, she'd bet he was blushing.

"I helped."

Another laugh, and Kendal closed the car door. The kid might be young, but he was a good agent, and she was glad he was covering her back. At a fast pace, she ate up the sidewalk with long strides, looking forward to getting out of the thick makeup and tight clothes.

As she neared the door to her motel room, she could practically feel the hot water of a shower pounding out the day's tension.

"Where the–"

Swirling in the direction of the gruff voice, Kendal lashed out with her foot.

"*Oomph*."

In a crouch, she hesitated. She knew that *oomph*. "Python?" Squinting into the dark corner, she could just make him out, doubled over.

"Yeah," he huffed.

"What're you doing out here?"

Straightening, he came out into the light. "Looking for you."

"Why?"

"You didn't answer your phone when I called your room."

Arrogantly, she tilted her head. "That would be because I was out."

"Where'd you go?"

"I don't think that's any of your business."

Grabbing her arm, he pulled her close. "Yes, it is. We're partners."

"In business." Without real force, she shoved at him. "What I do on my private time is just that, private."

"It's not safe for a woman to be wandering out late at night. If you wanted something to eat, I would've gone with you to get it."

This overprotective demeanor of his could become a problem if Kendal didn't watch it. She worked to ignore the small, very wrong, feminine thrill it gave her. "I think of all people, you'd have firsthand knowledge that I can take care of myself."

Releasing her, he rubbed his head. "Yeah. What is it with you and knocking me in the balls? Don't you ever aim anywhere else?"

Her key in hand, she headed once again to her door, already missing his touch. "Nope. When something works, you stick with it." Twisting the lock, she grinned over her shoulder. "How about if I'm ever hungry again, I'll call you before wandering the streets?"

"That's what you were doing? Getting something to eat?"

Donning her most innocent expression, she widened her eyes. "What else could it have been?"

"Uh, well, nothing." He pointed at her. "You promise you'll call me from now on. That you won't go out without me?"

"I promise." The door edge now between her and Python, she felt no remorse at having to lie. It was for his own good. The last thing she needed was to have a civilian hurt, or worse, killed on her case. "Did you need me for anything else tonight?"

His eyes gleamed briefly, making Kendal wonder if she'd imagined it.

"I was hoping we could, um, talk."

"Talk?"

"Yeah, I'd like to go over the match."

With her body longing to be cleaned, then dressed in comfortable clothes and not this leather harness, she still pushed away from the door. "Sure, come on in."

As she plopped onto the edge of the bed, she immediately took off the stilettos. At least she could get out of these contemporary torture tools. Her feet throbbed, but she fought her overpowering desire to massage them.

Python took the only seat, a single chair near the window. He scanned the room. "It's just like mine."

"Since you're right next door, it doesn't surprise me."

"Uh, yeah, right."

Something was wrong. Python had never been nervous around her. "What's up? What'd you want to talk about?"

He frowned before he rubbed his head. "You know this was my first time back in the ring, right?"

His sullen tone had her answering slowly. "Right."

With his head bent, he put his elbows on his knees. "I thought I'd freeze up."

"You didn't."

He lifted his gaze to hers. "Yeah, I didn't."

His hesitant answer concerned her. "That bothers you more than if you had?"

"Yeah, it does."

"Why?"

He stared at her so long she thought he wasn't going to speak, then he looked at the floor. "I should've hated it. The memories should've made it impossible."

The pain and anguish ringing through his voice drew Kendal to him. Kneeling, she placed her hands on his knees. "You're angry that you were able to fight."

His eyes mirrored all the pain she'd heard. "I lost control before." His gaze fell. "I killed a man. How do I know I won't do that again?"

"Two reasons." She waited for him to look at her. "One, you did not kill Terror. And two, you're a different person now." Unable to stop herself, she stroked his cheek. "You're older, wiser, and much more in control. It's time you realized it."

With sudden shock, she felt the roughened skin beneath her fingertips. The heat of Python's intense stare throbbed through her, and their close proximity screamed at her logical self to move away.

This isn't smart, Smart. *I cannot, repeat, cannot get involved with a civilian while on an operation. It is unethical, immoral, and just plain wrong. My parents never let their emotions interfere with duty. I could lose everything I ever worked for.*

But she didn't budge even as Python leaned forward. Didn't pull away even as his eyes closed and their lips touched. His firm mouth was amazingly gentle. Her own lids grew heavy, and she let herself succumb to the wondrous feeling flowing through her.

Before taking the kiss deeper, Python pulled back. "Big K."

His use of her undercover name snapped her out of the madness. Scrambling, she got up and tugged down her skirt. "I don't think this should happen."

A look she could only describe as a mixture of confusion and lust clouded his eyes until they cleared. "Yeah," he agreed, the tone gruff.

"It would mess up our working relationship. It wouldn't be right."

His head cocked, Python's mouth opened as if he was about to argue. Then he rubbed his hand over his brow. "Yeah, I suppose."

She nodded. "Good, I'm glad you agree." Fighting back the ridiculous dejection she felt since she was the one who stopped everything, she tried to smile. "Now, if you don't mind, I want to take a shower and go to bed. I'm beat."

To her amazement, his eyes blazed again, and a responding heat surged through her. They stared at each other, neither moving. And even after all her successful arguments, it didn't stop her tongue from slipping out and licking her suddenly dry lips. "So, I'll see you in the morning."

Python blinked, effectively banking the heat in his eyes. "Yeah." He started toward the door that connected their two rooms. "See you in the morning."

"Isn't that locked?"

He stopped. "Not on my side." Without looking back, he pulled open her door, then pushed open the one behind it that led directly into his room.

As soon as he crossed the threshold, Kendal closed the door on temptation. She heaved a sigh the size of Niagara Falls and sagged against the door. Who would've ever figured a man like Python could tie her up in knots? Man, she needed a shower.

"What the *hell* are you doing in here?"

Kendal snapped to attention when Python's harsh words reverberated through both doors. Jerking the first one open and slamming the other one against the wall, she surged into his room.

Python and a cheerleader, with her legs wrapped around his waist, froze. Surprise etched their faces.

Kendal could feel her own face warming. Was she destined to interrupt people having sex during this entire operation? "I'm sorry. I didn't mean to interrupt."

Ignoring her inappropriate disappointment, Kendal backed toward the door. How could he have kissed her like that, knowing he had a girl barely past eighteen considering her uniform, in here waiting?

"Wait!" Python shook the girl's shoulders and she giggled. "Get off of me."

"No. I want to be here with you." A pout that would've been appropriate on a baby only made Kendal realize how old this girl really was. The woman gyrated her pelvis. Definitely past the age of consent.

To Kendal's amazement, Python, hands wide, walked toward her as the appendage began to assault his neck with her lips. "Can't you give me a hand here?"

"A hand?" Kendal held back a smile.

"Yeah. I want her off." His new accessory made

obnoxious kissing sounds.

Curious to know if he was only saying this because of what almost happened earlier, Kendal asked, "How'd she get in here?"

"The same way they all do. Bribed someone, slept with someone, or picked the lock." He gave Kendal the most exasperated look she'd ever seen. "How should I know? I just want her off."

High pitched, sick cow moaning punctuated Python's words. Kendal tried not to laugh, then gave up, and let it rip. Python leaned toward her, and the back of the woman's bobbing head came within sniffing distance.

"What's so freaking funny?"

"You do understand that this person," Kendal swept her hand up and down the back of the cheerleader, "wants to have sex with you."

"I'd say that's obvious. It doesn't exactly strike my funny bone."

"I'm–"

"Could we continue this conversation," he spread his arms even wider, "after you help get her off of me?"

"Of course, of course." Kendal grabbed the woman's ponytail and yanked.

"Hey!" Her head snapped up.

Still holding the hair, Kendal tugged sharply.

"Stop it, bitch." The cheerleader tried to pivot around without releasing her leg hold on Python. Long fingernails, sharpened to lethal points, searched blindly for something to scratch.

"I don't think you're getting the message." Kendal yanked once more. "He wants you off."

"That's it." The overage pompom girl popped off Python. "You're going to pay for that."

Large hands grasped the cheerleader's shoulders, and she stilled a feline smile spreading across her face. "You see, bitch. It's all a game. He plays like he don't want me, and I play the lusty virgin."

Kendal raised a brow and peered over the woman's shoulder.

"Get out," growled Python.

The cheerleader smirked. "See. I told you. Now get out of here."

"I'm not talking to Big K. I'm talking to you, Dina." Python propelled her to the front door. "Leave and don't come back."

"But–"

After jerking open the door, he shoved Dina out, then slammed it closed. The room felt electrified in the ensuing silence.

"You knew the cheerleader?"

Rubbing his head, he sat on the edge of the bed. "Yeah."

"Old friend?"

"No. She's a groupie. She was running the circuit back when I was here the first time. Her goal in life is to sleep with every wrestler there is. She takes a souvenir from each one."

Crossing her arms, Kendal smiled. "And what'd you give her?"

In two strides, Python was up and inches from her face. "She has nothing of mine and I've never had her." He backed away a bit. "I told you, I don't do groupies."

Kendal tried to squelch the elation his adamant statement made her feel. It wasn't like he was saying he was a monk. But in this world where sex was available around every corner, she found it impressive that Python held himself to a higher standard.

Not that his sexual nature had any bearing on this case whatsoever. "Okay. Well, if we're done with the excitement, I think I'll call it a night." She walked toward the connecting door.

"Thanks, Big K."

With a shrug, she slid through the opening. "No big deal."

A hand snaked out and caught her arm. "It is a big deal. They're relentless." His face grew haggard. "I get real tired of fending them off."

She placed her hand over his. "It's that bad?"

"Yeah."

On impulse, she touched the side of his neck smeared with lipstick. "Well, sleep easy, big guy. I've got your back now."

He glanced at her hand, then back to her face. She jerked away. To cover her impulsive response, Kendal feigned a yawn and hurried through the doors. "I'll see you in the morning."

Once she was safe on her side, she leaned against the cool wood. How could a man topping the scales at over two hundred pounds make her think he needed her for protection? But he had.

Dropping his forehead on the door, Python repeatedly bumped it lightly. How could he be so attracted to a woman like Big K? *Big K*. Hell, he didn't even know her real name. Of course, she probably didn't know his either, so at least in that they were the same.

Who was he trying to kid? They were the same in a lot more ways than that. Maybe it was all a pipe dream. A normal woman, a normal life. A wife, white picket fence home, two point five kids and a dog. Wasn't that the all-American dream?

Or was he destined to repeat the life his mother had led? At first he'd been worried that Big K was out getting it on with someone else, or worse, getting high. But he had a good nose for scents, and he'd smelled neither sex nor drugs when she got near him. Could her looks be that deceiving?

If he pursued his feelings for her and fell in love, he'd be stuck here forever. In a life where drugs and sex played a predominant role. Would Big K be able to resist it forever? Something told him she couldn't. Not in the long run. Leaving the door, he turned off the lamp before plopping down on the bed. He spread his arms.

Fall in love? How had he made the jump from being mildly attracted to his overly made-up trainer to being head over heels for her?

A shower started and he rolled his head in the direction of her room. Suddenly, the picture of her naked, water pouring over her soft skin, filled his mind. He could see her hands caressing the soap before they moved on to her body, touching herself everywhere. With a groan, he twisted and his *johnson* reminded him why he needed to stay on his back.

"You come to attention now?" He looked down at the front of his tented pants. "I have a willing woman wrapped around my waist and you just lie there. I only have to think about a naked Big K and you're ready to shoot bullets?"

Putting his hands beneath his head, Python grinned. He might not want to stay in the wrestling world, but he definitely wanted to get to know his trainer a lot better. "Maybe it's time I figure out a way to get closer. Yeah. That's what I need. A plan."

The shower stopped and images of a glistening Big K grabbing a towel crowded out all other thoughts. A fantasy bloomed as he drifted off to sleep.

Darkness swirled and a crowd chanted, "Python, Python." Pride swelled his chest as he tried to lift his arms. They wouldn't move. Confused, he tried again, but nothing.

Why couldn't he move?

The chanting grew, "Python, Python," as colors in the dark swirled. Wanting, no, needing to get away, he tried to run. His feet felt cemented to the ground.

A spotlight infiltrated the gloom.

He didn't want to see! He tried to lift his hands to cover his face. They stayed fastened to his sides.

Dull, lifeless eyes appeared, floating in the spear of light.

"No, not again," he wanted to scream, but the words were silent. Even the chanting died away and the spotlight grew until the only thing left was Terror's dead, contorted body.

Unable to stop, unable to move, he stared. A woman with long, flowing black hair rushed into the small beam of light. She skidded to a stop in front of the body. Python's heart stopped, waiting for the moment of accusation.

She turned, her green eyes hard. "Murderer!"

Big K!

Python woke, face down on the bed, still dressed in his

jeans. Shaking, he rolled over, staring up into the dark. Why the change in the nightmare?

How could he have become so callous? He'd started to believe the hype. He'd thought no one could beat him, no one was better, and he dared anyone to try. And when they did, he considered them fair game. Men sent by God above for him to conquer and squelch. Just like the gladiators of old. It was his purpose in life to prove over and over again that he was superior.

This time it had to be different. This time he had to stay in control. If anything, the dream had shown him he didn't belong in the wrestling world. As soon as he could, he needed to uncover the drug ring and leave.

All his fanciful thoughts of Big K and a life together were implausible. The lure of drugs and sex would be too much and she would become his mother, a drugged up prostitute that he'd find one day dead from an overdose. He was never going to go through that again. It was time to get back on track and focus on getting out of here.

"Python? Are you all right?" Big K knocked as she entered.

"I'm–" His throat closed and he coughed. "I'm fine. Why?"

She came closer. "You screamed for me."

Had he yelled out in his sleep?

"Did someone else get in?"

A light scent of soap wafted over him when she halted at the edge of the bed.

"No." She needed to leave. He needed for her to leave.

"Do you need me?"

Need her? Damn right he needed her. Not the way she was thinking, though. "Not in the way you want me to."

"What?" Comprehension must've dawned because she backed away. "I see. Are you sure you're all right?"

Sitting up, he rolled his shoulders. "I'm fine. I must've dozed off. Why don't you go back to bed? I'm going to take a shower."

She hesitated in the darkness, and he could imagine her narrowing her eyes. Something she did quite often in his presence. "You'll call me if you need anything?"

Oh, he'd like to call her all right. He doubted she'd really be interested in taking care of him the way he wanted her to. "Yeah, I'll call. Now, unless you want to see me naked, I suggest you get your tight little butt out of here."

Still she hesitated, before slowly walking to the door. "I've got your back, Python. Whether you like it or not."

The door closed behind her and he stripped off his jeans as he headed to the bathroom.

Space.

That's what he needed right now, space. He couldn't feel the things he was starting to feel for her. He didn't want to feel the things he already felt.

Turning on the water, he adjusted the temperature before climbing in. The hot water beat his neck and back. A long, gruff sigh escaped as the last images of the nightmare swirled down the drain, clearing his head.

Just as he started to close his eyes, movement caught his attention. A slender hand slipped between the curtain and wall, blindly searching.

"Big K?" Even as the question left his mouth, he knew it wasn't her. Bright fluorescent pink nails clacked on the shower tiles. Clearly not Big K's.

A bleached blonde, pink-striped head poked around the edge. "Hi!"

The candy slick voice sank into his brain and Python saw red. Would he never be left alone? Why did they keep coming?

"Get out." His words reverberated, increasing the tension within the stall.

"I came to play."

"Get out!"

No other words could form as his anger grew. Shutting off the water with a violent twist, he stepped out of the shower. He advanced on the woman. "I said get out."

Her eyes wide, she backed away. "I heard you. Boy, you aren't at all like the others."

"Good." He kept advancing, and she retreated to the door. "Tell everyone."

Her hand on the knob, she pointed a shaky finger at him. "You're a freak. You know that? A freak."

"What's going on now?" Big K's voice came from behind him.

Python ignored her for the moment. "That's right, I am. Make sure everyone knows that too."

The bleached pink zebra looked from him to Big K before snatching the door open and fleeing.

As it slammed closed, Python snapped around to face Big K. "You're a hell of a lot of help."

"Excuse me?" Her eyes traveled down his front and then back up. "I see that you used to be a brunette."

Disregarding the inane remark, he strode to her. "You said you had my back. Where the hell are you when these freaking groupies show up? What the hell good are you?"

"What the hell good am I?" Her hands fisted at her sides, and she took a step toward him. "I'm an excellent coach. If you think for one minute that I'm going to be an around-the-clock bodyguard, you've got another think coming!" Within striking distance, she poked his chest.

"You said you'd watch my back. I can't even take a damn shower without being attacked. I'd think the least you could do is be there when I'm vulnerable."

She threw her hands in the air. "You didn't ask me to stay while you showered. All you had to do was ask."

"Now I have to ask? You should know. You know how the circuit is."

Her brow furrowed, and somewhere in the rational part of Python's mind he knew he was being unreasonable. He didn't care. He was fed up, tired, and horny as all get out. And the reason for most of his problems was standing right in front of him.

He grabbed her forearms, jerking her close. "You know

how it is." And crushed her mouth to his.

Chapter Five

"Did you think about me last night?"

Kendal blinked at the sex fiend female who she'd interrupted in the office after that first match. The woman stood too close for comfort. "Excuse me?"

The acrylic tip of a long fingernail caressed Kendal's cheek. "Did you think about me? I thought about you. Like how hot we'd be together." Her tongue slid around the bottom of her teeth. "How good it's gonna be."

Stepping to the side, Kendal brushed the woman's hand away. "You've got the wrong gal."

In a quick move, the leather-clad woman blocked her again, edging even closer until their breasts touched. "I don't think so." She shifted, rubbing against Kendal. "You and I will be good together. It's what I want."

"Listen, either you back off or I'm going to make you. It's your choice." Kendal's body tensed, ready to make good on her word.

"Hey, Shockra! You found our plaything." The male side of the duo joined them and crammed Kendal into the corner, blocking any escape route.

"You see, even Jammer wants to play," the woman purred as her lips moved dangerously close to Kendal's cheek.

Kendal jerked her head away. "Back off."

A hard hand grasped her waist, and she was yanked up against Jammer's hard chest. "Don't be testy, babe. Me and Shockra, we just wanna have some fun."

Tilting his head, he eyed Kendal's electric blue halter-top.

"And you look like you know exactly how to give it." His fingers found their way to the bottom edge of her diminutive shirt and started inching underneath.

"Either let me go, or you're gonna pull back a nub instead–"

"Get away from her!"

Never had Kendal been so glad to hear Python's voice. After her hasty retreat from his room following their intense kiss, the drive here to Hershey, Pennsylvania, had been tense, with little conversation. Which had been fine with her. She'd needed the time to reinforce her resistance to Python and lecture herself on staying in control.

But right now, she could use his help. Even though she was confident she could take care of these two bozos, she didn't want to tip anyone's hand to her fighting abilities. It might be her only surprise weapon when she got close to the radical group.

Jammer released her. Ducking his head, he took a step back. "Aw, come on, Python. Share." He sounded like a teenager who'd just had his privilege to drive revoked.

Reaching in, Python snagged Kendal's hand. "No."

Shockra gripped them both with hers. "Uh-uh, sugar. We're in the middle of something here. You need to go play by yourself for now."

Kendal went on alert, prepared to fight, when Python let go of her hand. He turned toward Shockra. "You stay away from Big K. We're not interested."

Dragging her fingertip down Python's chest, Shockra edged in close, just like she had to Kendal. "You don't mean that, lover."

Snatching Kendal's hand again, Python wrenched her away from the couple and put her behind his back. "I do mean it. Stay away from us."

Twisting, he pushed Kendal quickly down the hall. With his hand at the small of her back, she worked to stamp out the small flare of jealousy she'd felt when Shockra called Python *lover*. What was wrong with her? It didn't matter who the man had slept with. So what if he'd melted every bone in her body last night. He wasn't hers.

"Did he hurt you?"

Never slowing, Kendal shook her head. "No."

"Did he touch you?"

That stopped her. "What?"

Anger vibrated off him like the unseen seismic waves of an earthquake. "Did he touch you?"

Confused at the intensity of his ire, Kendal frowned. "No more than she did."

Visibly relaxing his tense muscles, he rubbed his head. "They tag teamed you."

"Tag teamed?" She glanced down the hall. The couple was gone. "You mean they planned it that way?"

"Yeah, and if I hadn't come along, they'd have done a lot more than just touch."

"I don't think so."

Bracing himself with a hand on the wall behind her, Python leaned in. "You couldn't have taken both of them."

"You wanna bet?"

"You're good, Big K. But not that good." When she only raised an eyebrow, he shook his head. "They're seasoned wrestlers. It would've been two against one. You didn't stand a chance."

Indignant, she lifted her chin. "You wanna bet?"

He sighed. "Okay, tough guy. You could've taken them, and I just happened to come along."

Feeling a bit foolish and glad that this episode might dissolve last night's tension, Kendal smiled. "All right. I appreciate you helping me out of the tough spot."

"You need to be careful. Don't get cornered by them again. You were lucky yesterday and today."

Her defenses popped right back in place. "Don't push it, Python. I'm not scared of a couple of over-sexed, steroid-popping freaks."

His eyes took on a sad, faraway look. "You should be."

"You miss her?"

His gaze shot back to Kendal. "Shockra?"

Kendal nodded.

"She was never mine to miss." Again he looked away.

"Not that she didn't try."

Immediately, she squelched the reemerging inappropriate jealousy that reared its head with his words. "Something that happens quite often. Why is it more personal with her?"

She thought he wasn't going to answer when he started to walk away. He hesitated. "She was involved with Terror."

Hurrying to him, Kendal placed her hand on his arm. "The wrestler that died during your match together."

"Yeah." They started walking side by side. "She was the first one to realize he was dead. She accused me of killing him." He paused and stared accusingly at Kendal.

Unsure why he was staring at her like that, she blinked. "And now it bothers you when she comes around?"

Reaching the door to the men's locker, Python halted. "Not exactly."

"What exactly, then?"

He looked up and down the hall as if to make sure no one was in hearing range. Unconsciously, Kendal found herself copying his actions.

His voiced lowered as he bent forward. "It bothers me because after accusing me of murdering her lover, she showed up in my bed that night naked."

The earlier banked rage flared in his eyes, making Kendal take an involuntarily step backwards. "I'm sorry." Even though she knew the words were trite, she didn't know what else to say.

"Yeah, so am I. Terror didn't deserve to die." The anger dissipated as quickly as it appeared. Python reached for the door.

"Wait."

He stopped, but didn't face her.

"Python, you didn't kill Terror. I've watched the tapes, the ropes broke. It wasn't your fault."

Slowly, he pivoted. "What do you mean the ropes broke?"

"Exactly what you heard. You did not kill Terror. It was an accident."

He shook his head. "I threw him over the ropes."

"Only in your memories. The ropes broke when Terror hit them. It could've just as easily been you."

Moving away from the door, he hustled her across the hall. "What'd you say?"

"Can't you hear today?"

"Just repeat what you said."

"I said–the–ropes–broke."

"No, the other part."

"The other part?"

"Now, you're the one with the hearing problem."

Playfully, she punched his stomach. "That it could've been you?"

"Yeah." Scowling again, he rubbed his head.

With sudden understanding, she grabbed his arms. "It could've been you! In the script, were you supposed to be the one who hit the ropes? That's what you're thinking, isn't it?"

"I'm beginning to wonder."

"Wasn't there an investigation on the quality of the ropes?"

While shaking his head, Python continued to rub it until his forehead wrinkled. "I don't know. I left the next day and never looked back. For the first few months I waited every day and night for the phone to ring or a knock on the door."

"You thought you were going to be arrested?"

"Yeah, wouldn't you?"

The seriousness of the question didn't escape Kendal. She took the time to carefully consider her answer. "If I had misinterpreted the situation like you had, then yes, I would've assumed I'd be arrested."

"I didn't misinterpret anything. Terror's dead, and I threw him out of the ring. That makes me a murderer."

"In your mind."

"That's the only place that counts."

Not wanting to argue, Kendal refocused on the new angle. "You know, you could've been the one to hit the faulty ropes. That makes it an accident without anyone to blame. Even you."

From the expressions flitting across Python's face, Kendal could only imagine the battle warring in his head. How hard it would be to assimilate the idea that the guilt you've harbored all these years was wrong. "Give yourself some time to let it sink in."

She hit his arm. "Right now we've got a dance to win. Personally, I can't think of anyone more deserving of some whup-ass than Jammer."

At the mention of the touchy-feely wrestler's name, Python's body went rigid under her hand. With a nod, he headed for the locker room. "You're right."

He disappeared, leaving Kendal staring at solid metal. She thought about her earlier conclusion that Python had tattooed his head to keep attention on himself. Now, she reconsidered. Perhaps, he'd done it to punish himself for murdering another wrestler, giving himself a self-imposed lifetime sentence.

Python's intensity continued into the ring. Kendal had never seen him more focused, and it made her concerned.

What was the matter with her? She needed Python intense. She needed him winning, and she needed to find out more about the inner workings of these matches.

The personal anxieties of the civilians she was working with were not her concern. If her supervisor knew of the distraction, he'd pull her out so fast she'd think she was CIA. Or so she'd heard him say to other agents on more than one occasion.

Tonight she'd get into the main office and get pictures of everything she could. It wouldn't be evidence they could use in court, but it could put them on the right track. The money being funneled to the radical group had to be identified, and it was her job to find the clues.

Python hit the ropes and she sucked in a breath. There was nothing to be concerned about, she reminded herself. She'd personally checked every part of the ring. The ropes were solid, but after this afternoon's revelation, she still felt uneasy. Jammer hit the mat, and his gaze met hers and held.

Grabbing Jammer's leg, Python jerked it backwards. "You ever touch Big K again, you son of a bitch, and I'll take you apart piece by piece."

"Dammit, Python, lay off. You're breakin' my damn leg."

Twisting, they broke apart. Python charged, and they clashed head on, grabbing each other's shoulders. "That's not the half of what I'm gonna do to you if you don't stay away from her."

"What's got you so hot? She yours?"

Out of the corner of his eye, Python could just make out Big K's black hair and form. Last night hadn't gone the way he planned, like her in his bed, but that was only a matter of time. "Yeah, she is."

Breaking apart again, they circled each other. Attacking, Python slammed into Jammer. They hit the mat, rolled with Jammer ending on top. Returning the favor, he jerked Python's leg. "Tough, we ain't an exclusive kinda club, so you better learn to share."

He yanked even harder, and Python gritted his teeth.

"Shockra has her sights set on getting that piece of ass. No one, not even you, is gonna stop her."

Red colored Python's world. "No!" Flipping Jammer, he jumped to a crouch.

All the common sense in the world hadn't prevented him from wanting Big K, and he wasn't about to share her now. The kiss had been hot, and she'd all but climbed him. It hadn't been until that point that he'd realized he was dripping wet, naked, and she was in a bathrobe.

Things would've progressed right then and there, if the phone in her room hadn't rung. Who the hell was calling her anyway? She'd closed the door and hadn't come back. That's when he'd decided they were going to be together.

Without waiting as scripted, Python smashed the other wrestler into one of the corner bars.

"What're–"

Grabbing Jammer's arm, he swung him across the ring.

As he ricocheted, Python grabbed Jammer's head, thrusting him to the ground, and then fell full weight onto his back.

The next time he'd seen Big K, she was being mauled by this piece of trash and Shockra.

Rolling off, he squatted, and with a strength born of anger, lifted the Neanderthal above his head and spun. How dare this piece of scum think he could touch Big K. How dare he put his filthy hands on her. He needed to be punished. He deserved to be punished. And it was his job to inflict the pain.

Using every muscle, Python threw Jammer. Through the air the man soared, arms and legs flailing as if searching for something to grab to stop the flight.

Thwack. The wrestler hit the corner bar, then slumped.

Motionless.

Sweat poured down Python's face as Jammer didn't move. The referee crouched beside the body and started to count.

One.

Two.

Three! Standing, the ref rushed over to Python, grabbing his hand and raising it high.

All Python could do was stare. Was Jammer dead? Had he killed another man?

Jammer shifted. It was slight, but he definitely moved. The relief Python felt was immense, and his knees almost buckled from the release. The oblivious referee maneuvered Python around the ring, allowing him the chance to search for Big K.

She wasn't in his corner.

Unnoticed, Kendal had left Giant Center and made her way to the office building across the parking lot. Surprisingly, getting into Rusen's office hadn't been hard. A little suspicious, since he was laundering money. Then again, as Tommy had said, criminals were known to be stupid.

Pulling out the tiny camera from a secret pocket in the bottom of her leather bra top, she spread the papers she'd withdrawn from the filing cabinet. The pencil-thin camera made no noise as she clicked off picture after picture.

"*Shh*." Giggling filtered through the wall. "We're not supposed to be here." The voice cracked.

In a rush, Kendal shuffled the papers into a pile. *Great, this is just what I need.*

"Oh, Benny. Why can't we be here?"

The girlish shriek had Kendal wondering just how old these two were. *Don't come in. Don't come in*, she repeated mentally as she scrunched under the desk, pulling the swivel chair back in behind her.

The door creaked. "Because my uncle'd be mad. I left the door unlocked. He'd kill me if he found out."

"Ohhh, you're so brave, Benny." Feet scuffled on the floor as the two obviously young people started to make out.

"Oh, baby. Let's get it on."

Now, that's romantic, Kendal thought with enough sarcasm to fill the room.

"You'd better make it good."

Kendal could hear the pout. She wouldn't have thought that possible. She'd bet her next paycheck the girl's bottom lip was stuck out like a plum ready to be picked.

"It'll be good." More rustling.

Clothes must be coming off. Kendal rolled her eyes. *Not this again*! Was she destined to hear or see every person in the wrestling world doing the horizontal mambo?

"I'm missing that rad Python for this. If I don't come, I'm gonna be mad."

As half of Kendal's brain applauded the young woman for making sure she'd be pleasured, the other half screamed she didn't have time for this. She should just stand up and scare the crap out of these two. Prevent everybody from having sex, especially since she was at the moment being as celibate as a nun.

"I told you, it'll be good."

"Ohhh, Benny, you're so big. Where we gonna do it?"

No sound. He must be casing the office, Kendal thought. *Not the desk. Not the desk*, she mentally shouted.

"How about the desk?" the girl suggested.

Good heavens, am I ever going to catch a break on this case?

"No, we can't do it there."

Yes!

"Why?" The pout again, loud and clear.

"That desk has important stuff on it. We better not mess it up."

Thump. "I wanna do it here." *Swish*. "You want to do it here too, don't ya, Benny?"

"Uh, yeah." What had to be his adam's apple clicked, and Kendal knew he was having a hard time swallowing. "You ain't, uh, you ain't got no underwear on."

A louder thump. "That's right. And I'm already ready. Can you see that? Watch my fingers, do you see how slick I am?"

Swallowing hard herself, working to keep her earlier dinner from coming back up, Kendal recalculated the girl's age. She was no teenager. This woman had come up here to seduce this young man, and it made her wonder why.

"Uh, yeah, I see it." His eyes had to be the size of half dollars because his voice came out in a squeak.

"BENNY! BENNY! Where the hell are you, boy? I saw you coming over here."

"Ah, shit. It's my uncle." His voice cracked, washing away all trace of arousal. "You gotta get up. Come on. If he finds us here, he'll kill me."

"Take a pill, Benny. It's no big deal." From the sounds above, Kendal guessed the woman had slithered off the desk.

"The shit it ain't."

"BENNY!"

"Come on. There's a back way out of here."

Kendal's ears perked. A back door? There was no other way out. She'd checked for possible escape routes as soon as she arrived.

Something rolled.

"The bookcase moves? Oh, Benny. What a cool thing to

know." The woman's voice became almost indistinct as it trailed away.

"BENNY?"

Kendal quickly calculated her odds. Would the two who left be far enough away for her to follow? Or should she sit tight and hope Rusen didn't come and sit at his desk. She looked down at the papers she still held. *Crap*.

It was time to get the hell out of Dodge. Scrambling out, she saw the silhouette of a man approaching the half smoked-glass door. Heading straight for the only bookcase, Kendal pushed. To her immense relief, it slid easily. She slipped behind and started to roll it back in place just as the outer door opened.

Bam! The door rattled from the force of the knock.

"Big K?" Python pounded again. "Big K? You in there?"

Shoving the weapon she'd snatched from the bedside table under the pillow, Kendal pushed the hair out of her bleary eyes. *What time is it?*

Another *slam*. "Big K? *Whereinthell* are you?"

"Shut up, you big oaf," she yelled as she flung open the door. She ducked when Python's fist came flying at her. He stumbled inside, carried by the momentum of his missed knock.

"T'ere you are!"

"What's wrong with you?" When he lurched forward, Kendal took an immediate unwanted sniff. "Whoa," she waved her hand in front of her nose. "You drink the beer or bathe in it?"

"I drank it." His exclamation was combined with an inflated chest.

"And this is a fact you're proud of?" Shaking her head, she went back to the bed and sat down.

"Yeah." He staggered. "I tied one on." His silly grin had her grinning right back.

My eyes! Had he noticed her gray eyes?

My clothes! Wearing a mock-turtleneck sweater and

stretch pants weren't the norm. Unable to make any changes with him standing, well, more like leaning, right in front of her, she'd just have to hope he wouldn't remember anything in the morning.

My gun! She checked to make sure it was completely hidden by the pillow.

"And to what do I owe the pleasure of having you visit me after you drank your way just this side of oblivion?"

"You weren't there," he pouted.

Somehow, to her, his pout was much more endearing than the one Kendal imagined earlier on the woman in Rusen's office. "I wasn't where? At the bar?"

"No. I mean, yeah." He scratched his head. "Ya weren't at t' match," he slurred. "Where'd you go?"

Feeling a devilish need to tease, she smiled. "Did you miss me?"

Python lumbered over and slumped on the bed beside her. "Yeah."

Something in his tone, even in his drunken state, made her worry. She laid her hand on his bicep. "What's wrong?"

"Ya weren't there."

"You said that. You needed me, why?"

"It happened again."

"Another groupie attack?"

"Nah."

Irritated, she squeezed his arm. "What happened? Stop talking in circles, Python. Tell me what happened again."

"I wanted to kill 'im. I wanted it just like when I killed Terror." Red, bloodshot eyes bored into hers. "I wanted it 'cause he touched you."

"You did not kill Terror."

He grabbed her shoulders. "It doesn' matter. I wanted to kill 'im. That's all tha' matters."

"He didn't hurt me."

"He touched you."

"That's not what made you go and drink."

Releasing her, he hung his head. "I can't go back in the

ring."

Alarm–pure unadulterated fear–flooded her system. Was she going to lose her way inside so soon? "You have to!"

His head popped up and the saddest expression she'd ever seen stared back at her. "Is that all I am to you? Your ticket into the wrestling world? Just another wrestler?"

What was she supposed to say? *No, you're much more than that? You're the FBI's way to demolish a radical group that's gaining way too much power. Or, better yet, I'm attracted to you and want to be around you like no one before? I don't think so.* "I thought we'd also become friends."

"Only friends?"

She took a deep breath. "What do you want me to say?"

He rubbed his head, a sure sign he was flustered. "I thought, I guess, I hoped–"

She waited, even after the silence became uncomfortable.

"I think more about you." His voice was harsh, yet husky.

Even though his sentence was worded strangely, she knew this conversation was headed into dangerous territory. Territory she'd avoided last night, thankfully because of a call from Tommy. She wasn't sure she wanted to face it now and definitely not with a drunk Python. "Why don't we talk about this in the morning?"

"No." His sharp answer jerked her gaze to his.

"No?"

"I wanna talk now." Two hands wrapped around her shoulders. "I need t' talk now."

"You're drunk."

He laughed. "Yeah, so?"

"I don't think this is the time to have a serious conversation."

"Can I stay?" His fingers began to flex on her arms.

"Excuse me? Stay?"

"I need to be here with you."

His tone reminded her of little boy begging for permission to crawl into bed with Mommy and Daddy for safety. "Why?"

Again, he released her and hung his head. "They followed

me."

She tensed. "Who?"

"Women."

Kendal rolled her shoulders. "More groupies?"

"Yeah, from the bar. They'll try all night. Please, you gotta let me stay, Big K."

If someone had told her forty-eight hours ago that this mountain of a man couldn't keep a sex-starved groupie out of his room, she wouldn't have believed it. But after witnessing Dina's relentless pursuit, the other cotton candy haired groupie, and her own run-ins with Shockra, Kendal knew he had reason to be concerned. If any of the groupies had a tenth of Shockra's intensity, he was in trouble. "I don't know–"

He grabbed her hands. "Big K, I really need a good night's sleep. You gotta let me stay."

She had a mission to complete. If she didn't get back to the booker's office tonight, she'd never get those papers back into Rusen's filing cabinet, or snoop around for more evidence. She shook her head.

"You're tossing me out."

The despondency in his voice struck deep inside her. Part of her job was to keep Python in top condition and make sure he got his rest. With that reasoning rolling around her brain, she said, "Okay."

"Really?" The excitement in his voice was unmistakable.

"To sleep."

His head bobbed. "Yeah, I know."

"Do you want to take a shower?"

A strange look crossed his face as he glanced over at the bathroom door. "Here?"

"Since you had a visitor in yours last night, I think it might be a good idea."

"Yeah. I'd like that."

"Help yourself. There are fresh towels in there." And while her impromptu guest cleaned up, Kendal needed to make some changes. Like putting her green contacts in, changing her clothes, and putting away the gun.

When Python came back out, she needed to look more like Big K. And less like a federal agent about to embark on a midnight caper.

Hot, blistering water pounded his back. It felt good. Somewhere in his fuzzed brain, Python knew he shouldn't have drunk so much.

When he couldn't find Big K, it hadn't taken much coercing from Stubb to get him to go to the bar. That it turned out to be a gentleman's club, without any gentlemen and lots and lots of naked women, had only been icing on the pisser of a day it had already been.

So, who could blame him for pounding down the beers? And no matter how drunk he got, what did he do? Compare every single female to one dark-haired, green-eyed vixen who had started him rethinking all his previous opinions about women. What if he really didn't want a woman from the suburbs?

He leaned into the spray and the stream hammered his face. He wished he could blame his feelings on the alcohol. Or believe this was a passing fad. He knew beyond a doubt that neither was true.

He'd never wanted groupies, female wrestlers, or any woman dressed one step away from a prostitute. Having spent his childhood evading his mother's drunken fists had cemented his beliefs. Yet here he was, all but falling in love with Big K.

Shutting off the faucet, he wiped his body with his hands to get rid of any excess water. He didn't want to use two of Big K's towels, and when you were as large as he was, you learned to be the driest you could before you grabbed one.

After drying off, he stepped back into his boxers. He picked up his pants, then promptly dropped them. Man, they stunk. Had he spilled his last mug? He shrugged as he left the room. His head swam as he stepped out, and he braced himself with a hand on the wall.

"Did you forget some of your clothes in there?"

"They stink." He wasn't sure, but he suspected he sounded sulky.

"I see." Her beautiful black hair swayed around her shoulders when she nodded. *God, she's gorgeous.*

"You'd better lie down. You don't look so good." She patted the bed where the spread had been pulled back to expose white, crisp sheets.

"Yeah." With a swagger he just knew was sexy, he strutted over. His heart pitched when she didn't move away as he got close. Her hand reached out for him. *She wants me.*

"Let me help you."

Grinning, he couldn't think of anything more desirable than her touching him. "Yeah." Supple hands enclosed his wrists and he let her lead him to the edge of the bed. Like cool silk on his heated flesh, she felt like heaven.

"You need to take some ibuprofen."

"No."

Her brow rose.

"You are so cute when you do that."

"Do what?"

Reaching up, he traced the raised eyebrow with his fingertip. "Make this go up. You have good muscle control."

"You need some sleep."

"That's not all I need."

"Yes, I think it is."

In a lightning fast move, he grabbed for her arms. Stepping incredibly slowly, she somehow evaded his high-speed attack.

"Uh-uh. You don't need any more help tonight. It's time for beddy bye."

How'd you get away?

"Because you're drunk, genius."

"I said that out loud?"

"Duh, yeah."

Flopping back onto the pillow, Python exhaled in a gust. He peeked out from around his elbow to see what Big K would do. She circled around the edge of the bed. "Where're you going?"

"I need sleep too."

Hiding beneath his arm again, he waited, like a snake. Yeah, like a python. Although it was hard, he kept himself from grinning. The bed shifted as she climbed in on the other side. A king-size bed might be big, but he took up more than his fair share. His flop had put him over the middle easily. With less flair, Big K settled on her side, facing away from him. "You asleep?"

"I just laid down, Python."

"You wanna talk?"

As he hoped, she turned over. "You need to talk some more?"

"I've had a hard day."

One of her sleek hands tunneled through the sheets coming to rest on his shoulder. "It wasn't your fault. You didn't murder Terror, and nothing happened today that wasn't supposed to." Her long fingers started massaging his muscle. "You didn't hurt Jammer, Python, and that's all that matters."

His eyes drifted shut. "*Uhmm*, that feels good." As if he'd ordered off a menu, her other hand joined the first. In perfect harmony, her hands began a symphony of pleasure. "Oh, yeah."

Moving in closer, she adjusted to the back of his shoulders. "Is this helping?" Her breath feathered across his face as she leaned over him slightly.

"Yeah." It was time for him to make his move. She was exactly where he wanted her. Now, if he could only open his eyes. *Come on! Wake up*!

"It's going to be all right, Python. We're on our way. This is what you're supposed to do."

Finally his eyes popped open. "I want you."

Startled, she yanked her hands away. "What?"

Using her immobility, Python clutched the nape of her neck. "I want you."

"What're you doing?"

"Kissing you." With a tug, she landed on his chest. Like her eyes, her mouth was wide and round. He wasted no more time.

The minute their lips met, he felt an electric shock. His tongue slipped between her teeth where a rich, tangy flavor filled his senses.

After a slight hesitation, she relaxed and her tongue joined his in a duel. Thrusting and retreating, they parried and clashed, reveling in the taste of each other.

"Python," she muttered against his lips.

This is so good. I could do this forever. It's…

Chapter Six

Kendal sat up and stared down at Python. He was smiling, his lips pursed, his head tilted as if she was still there. And probably to him, she still was. Thinking herself crazy, she shook her head. How could she have given in like that again?

A loud snore erupted. His lips smacked and his smile widened as he pillowed his head on his hands.

"Great, our making out put you to sleep." As soon as the words left her mouth, Kendal cringed. "Who cares? Get a grip." She needed to get back to the office building and into Rusen's office.

Another snore and smack.

"I don't suppose I have to worry about you waking up and finding me gone, huh?"

"*Humph*," was his answer.

"Yeah, that's what I thought." Going to the dresser, she tied back her hair. In the mirror, his reflection caught her attention.

How strange to see him lying in her bed. Not sure why she felt it necessary, she went to him and pulled the covers further over his shoulder. "Sleep tight. You're safe here."

"*Humph*."

With a grin, she patted his arm. "I can see you were worried." Resisting the urge to lean down and kiss his cheek, she tugged on a cap. It was time to go to work.

Because of the intel, Kendal knew the patterns of the night security guards and slipped into the two-story office building unnoticed. She chose to enter Rusen's office from the hidden passageway. Inside the darkened hall, she felt her way to the far wall and searched until she found the edge. The bookcase was already cracked open.

"What're you're doing here?"

Kendal froze.

A murmur around shuffling feet was the answer. Taking a silent, thankful breath, Kendal held perfectly still.

"Why? Everything's decided." The booming male voice must be Rusen. Kendal had yet to meet or even see the man.

More murmuring, but Kendal was unable to make out the words or the voice. The footsteps stopped, so she assumed they were both seated.

"No one here but us." Innuendo oozed out of Rusen's voice, telling her the other person in the office was a woman. Standing behind the bookcase, Kendal wondered if she had stumbled into the twilight zone. The situation was too reminiscent of when she'd been hiding under the desk.

When another murmur began, Kendal pressed her ear to the crack in the door. She still couldn't decipher the woman's words.

"They're not walking the floor tonight. I told them I didn't want to be disturbed."

More murmuring.

"Business? I told you there's nothing more to say." A tremor of irritation rang through his words. "Besides, I can think of something better to do." His tone sounded drenched in oil.

The low voice sharpened.

"There's nothing left to talk about." Impatience and irritation returned to Rusen's tone.

Slam. Something hit, most likely, the top of the desk.

"Listen, bitch. You know the drill. If something better comes along, you go with the flow."

A chair screeched. Rusen must be leaning back.

"You just gotta sit back and relax."

More low talking in response, but again Kendal couldn't make out the words.

Rusen laughed. "Yeah? How're you gonna stop me?"

Whamup.

At first Kendal's brain refused to identify the sound.

"You," Rusen sputtered, "how–"

Whamup.

A silencer! The minute it registered, Kendal tensed, her adrenaline starting to flow. Hideous laughter erupted from the room, wrapping around Kendal like seaweed in a rough sea. The walls started to close in, making her claustrophobic as she yanked out her gun.

With the element of surprise on her side, Kendal prayed the bookcase would move silently as she pushed. Cautiously, she inched her head out.

The woman's back was to her, blocking the dim light coming from the lamp on the desk. Frizzy hair exploded in all directions from her head and down her back. Other than the assailant's height, Kendal couldn't determine much more about her.

The shooter waggled the gun in front of Rusen's dull eyes, then started to turn. Kendal ducked back behind the case.

A quiet click, and footsteps moved away. A door opened and closed, and Kendal knew the woman had left. Slipping inside, Kendal found the room in shadows. All lights had been turned off. Going straight to Rusen, she checked for a pulse.

None.

Unable to do a visual check of the room, she scurried back to the bookcase. As quietly as possible, she felt her way down the short hallway. Keeping her hand at waist level, she bumped into a knob and let herself out into the corridor. After a quick check both ways, she headed for the stairs.

The escape route ended in the hallway around the corner from the office. She knew it was by design. Rusen wanted a way out in case someone showed up that he didn't want to see. Too bad he hadn't realized who was a real danger to him.

Down the stairwell Kendal crept, not making a sound. Every so often, she would stop and listen. She needed to get out and alert Tommy. Easing out onto the first floor, Kendal scanned the area backlit by the red light of the exit signs.

A thunder of footsteps rumbled. With quick resolve, she

darted across the hall and into an unlocked room.

"Code red, code red. Second floor," squawked a walkie-talkie. "I'm on it," announced a male voice as he pounded past and into the stairwell.

The need to get out unnoticed intensified. Being here jeopardized the case. With her ear to the door, she listened. No new footsteps. The door creaked as she cracked it open making her cringe. Without hesitation, she slid out, staying close to the side of the hallway.

The best escape route would be out the back where it was the darkest. She knew her time was limited. As soon as the guard found Rusen's body, all hell would break loose. With the threat of the operation being exposed heavy in her mind, she started to run.

Coming to a corner, she slowed to peer around it first. A guard stepped inside a door. She popped back, her hand on her heart. Rushed, she searched for a new hiding place.

Where? He'll be checking every room. She spied an exhaust screen.

Of course! Heading back the way she'd come, she returned to the unlocked room. Quickly, she found another screen. As quietly as possible she climbed on top of the desk.

She opened her backpack, pulled out a Swiss army knife, and went to work on the bottom screws. When she had enough of them undone, she shoved a gloved hand inside and pulled the gate open. After putting the gun, knife, and screws in her pack, she tossed it into the shaft.

Sucking in her stomach, she squeezed through, careful to let the screen fall back into place without sound. She let her eyes adjust to the darkness.

With little room around her shoulders, she shoved her pack with her face as she belly crawled. Her mouth filled with dust, forcing her to breathe through her nose. Coming to an intersection, she turned left, hoping she was guessing correctly at the layout of the ventilation system.

"We need an ambulance. He's been shot," a muffled voice echoed through the vent.

"Call 911. Get the police here, now. Seal off the area. No one enters, no one leaves."

Dammit, she needed to get out. The only thing she hoped was that the killer hadn't been fast enough either. If she wasn't going to make it and her cover was going to be blown, she wanted the frizzy blonde assassin to pay for that too.

Turning right this time, she continued to slither through the tight tunnel.

"Suspect sighted! Suspect sighted! West entrance!"

Sounding like a monsoon, rushing footfalls pounded at Kendal from all directions. Her internal navigation in place, she knew she was headed north. This was her chance.

As fast as she could, she crawled to another screen as the footsteps receded into the distance. Peering out, she saw no movement. There was no time to worry about noise, so she backed down to an intersection, dragging her pack by the strap held in her mouth. Going left into the T, she then scuttled backwards to the screen.

When her feet hit resistance, she kicked. Kicking again, this time she felt the screen give. A third kick had the bottom edge cracking off.

She forced her way out, bending the screen in the process. Half in and half out, she dangled. A deep breath and she dropped to the ground. A twinge sparked up her legs when she landed. In a crouch, she listened. Not hearing anyone, she ran for the end to the corridor.

The exit door loomed in front of her. Grabbing the knob, she jerked it open, excited with the prospect of getting out. One step through, she halted, anchoring the door with her hand so it would close quietly. The fresh air smelled sweet after the stuffy vent. Hugging the brick building, she headed for the dark area where she planned to escape into the night.

Men yelling from inside had her searching once again for a hiding place. Two steps away she found an alcove and slipped in.

"Well, well, well. What have we here?" A gravelly whisper asked as cold metal rimmed Kendal's ear, shutting out all other sounds.

"Big K?" Python searched the space next to him for the woman he'd made passionate love to.

At least, he thought they'd made love. He frowned when he found nothing but empty, cool sheets. He sat up and his head throbbed. He grabbed it with both hands.

"Big K?" From his room, he could hear a phone ringing. That must've been what woke him up.

Jumping out of bed, he swayed and braced himself. With a hand to his head, he trudged through the connecting doors, then lunged for the phone. "H'lo?"

"Python." An excited voice bounced into his brain. "You won't believe what's happened."

His head pounding, Python tried to hear Stubb's words around the pain. "What?"

"There's been a murder in Rusen's office."

"What?"

"I said–"

"No. I heard you." Stretching the cord, Python went to the sink. "Who?"

"They haven't released any names. All I know, it's not Rusen."

"How–when did it happen?" Python found a bottle of pain medicine and popped a few pills.

"Seconds ago. They're searching for the guy who done it now. They thought they'd gotten 'im, but he got away."

"How'd you know so fast?"

"I've got connections," Stubb said with clearly heard pride.

As Python's mind cleared, he thought about Big K. "Where are you?"

"I'm here at the hotel, why?" Stubb answered.

"I wasn't asking you."

"You just–"

"Forget it. Is tomorrow's schedule changed?"

Stubb cackled. "Nope. The cops are roping off Rusen's office, and I can tell you he's not happy about that. The show must go on, you know."

Yeah, Python guessed so. Besides, the wrestling world would only use this to their advantage. "I gotta go. Call me if anything changes."

"Sure. You want me to call Big K?"

"No," Python said a little too sharply. "I can knock on her door."

"Sure. See you guys in the morning." As soon as he hung up, Python headed back next door. He went immediately to the bathroom. It was empty.

Where the hell was she? Or the better question was, had she left him to go to someone else? Could she have done that after what they'd shared?

He scratched his head. Of course, that's if they'd shared anything at all?

"We can do this the hard way or the easy way. It's up to you."

Unable to see behind, Kendal wanted to memorize the voice. Her captor continued to whisper, making a positive ID more difficult. The one thing Kendal wanted to make certain, if she didn't take this killer down, she could definitely identify her.

"I don't know what you're doing down here, but with the black knit hat and clothes, I'd say you've been pretty naughty. Now, we either both get out of here without being caught or you die. You choose."

Remembering the woman had a silencer, Kendal knew her choices were limited. *Damn, I wish she'd talk above a murmur.*

"Uh-uh. Relax those muscles. Don't even think of trying to get away. You'd be amazed at my ability to pull a trigger even while I get hit."

The arctic laughter chilled Kendal to her bones.

"You want to feel what it's like to have a bullet crack open your head? This isn't a puny twenty-two that'd only circle around that little skull of yours. No sirree, this sucker will blow the side right off. You want to test it out?"

Kendal had witnessed madness in the slammer. She'd interviewed hardened criminals who'd just as soon break her neck as give her information. She'd been in a standoff with a drugged, frightened teenager waving a gun, swearing to kill her. None of them had ever frightened her as much as this one woman.

Evil personified, she was psychotic, the one thing that discounted all reasoning. The one attribute that rendered Kendal almost defenseless. "No."

"Good answer. Good answer. Now, let's try another one." Her hot, sticky breath blew into Kendal's ear. "How do we get out of here without being seen?"

"Over there. That dark patch leads to a small wooded area."

"You think so, huh?"

"Listen, you've got about two minutes before this place is swarming with so many cops you're never going to get away. Either we get out of here right now or you're going to get caught."

"Not just me, honey, you too."

The gloved hand shoved the barrel deeper into the tender flesh below Kendal's ear.

"What we're going to do is this. Together we're going to slide out of this little hidey-hole, and then right down the side of the building. Then we're going to run like the dickens. If at any time I think you're a nuisance, I'm going to shoot."

Another shove into her ear.

"You got that?"

"I got it."

"Good, let's go."

As instructed, Kendal led the way, and the gun moved from her ear to the small of her back. She needed to take back control of the situation. If she looked back, then stumbled, she felt pretty certain it would provide the opportunity she needed to gain her freedom.

Ready, she checked over her shoulder and found herself

staring at a mass of blonde, frizzy wig. Kendal struck out and slammed the woman's head into the brick wall. Face down, the killer slumped to the ground.

Crouching, Kendal started to turn the woman over.

"Over here. Someone went out this way."

Kendal jumped up, hearing the security guards so close. In a sprint, she left the woman's body, confident it'd be found. Having prepared for a discreet getaway, she'd parked the rental car five blocks away. She skirted through the private yards of tree-lined streets.

Once safely in the car, she snatched off the cap and finger combed her hair. The one thing she was pretty certain of was that Python was going to know she'd been gone. Driving one-handed, she fumbled with the backpack until she found her cell phone.

After punching in a number and adjusting the earpiece, she drummed her fingers on the steering wheel, waiting.

"Boden," Tommy answered on the second ring.

"Smart here. There's been a murder."

"Are you hurt?"

"No. Meet me at the store."

"I'm on my way."

She disconnected. Flipping on the blinker, she swung into the parking lot of an all-night convenience store a block from the hotel. Driving to the back of the store, she parked in the darkest area.

Grasping the bottom of her mock turtleneck, she pulled off the black shirt exposing a bright green halter. Headlights spotlighted the side of the car making her duck until she was sure it was Tommy.

Out of his car like a shot, Tommy slipped into the passenger side seat. "What happened?"

"Someone killed Rusen."

Tommy grabbed the dashboard with his right hand. "Are you a witness?"

"Yes and no." Kendal pulled down the visor, checking her makeup. "I heard the confrontation. Then I had a collision with the killer myself. I left her for the authorities to find."

"You left her?"

She glanced over at him. "It's a long story. One we can enjoy over a beer after this thing is wrapped up."

Even as he smiled, he shook his head. "I'm going to want to hear this one."

"What's got me concerned is the operation." After one last look at her reflection, Kendal flipped the visor up. "With Rusen gone, the laundering might go underground. Depends on how high up in the chain this guy was." She pulled off her socks and tennis shoes, replacing them with stilettos.

"Will that matter? The more time you have, the deeper you'll be able to infiltrate."

"Except we're limited with Python. I don't know how long we can keep him in the ring."

"He's still balking at that?" Tommy turned forward. "I thought for sure with his early success, it'd get in his blood. Make him realize he can't live without it."

She opened the car door. "The one thing I think Python will always be able to live without is the wrestling world. And after I've been here a bit, I can see why."

Tommy got out and spoke over the roof. "I'll call my contact with the locals and see what I can learn about your perp."

"I'd appreciate it. I'd like to know the name of the woman who may have ruined our operation."

"You'll make the next contact?"

"I think that's best, unless you know for absolute certain Python isn't with me. Then you can ring the cell."

"Good." He slapped the roof, then walked to his car.

Kendal went into the store to buy an assortment of goodies. Five minutes later, carrying the bag, she hurried as best she could on the five-inch heels back to the hotel.

At her door, she tried to turn the key. The door flew out of her hand. An irate and fully dressed Python stood in the entry.

"Hey, you're up." Kendal edged her way past. "I was

kinda hoping you'd still be sleeping."

After closing the door, he crowded behind her. "You were?"

"Well, yeah." She held the plastic bag out like a prize. "Then this could've been a surprise."

"A surprise?"

Tilting her head, Kendal touched his face. "Are you all right? Does your head hurt? You had a lot to drink."

His expression softened. "It did. I took something."

"I was gone that long? It must take longer then I thought to walk to the store." She placed the bag on the bed. "Are you hungry? I thought you might be. It sounded like you didn't eat before you drank."

As if in response, his stomach rumbled, and he rubbed it. "I guess I am."

"Then it's a good thing I got you some chicken."

"Is that what I smell?"

"They'd just fried up a new batch." Pulling out the steaming box, Kendal handed it to him, heaving a huge mental sigh. *Thank God.* The last thing she needed was for him to be more suspicious of her activities.

Python sat at the small table with the food, then bit into the fragrant meat. How was he going to find out if he and Big K had done it? Was there a polite way to ask a woman if they'd made love without hurting her feelings? Never having been in this position before, he wasn't sure.

He decided to start on safer ground. "I guess you haven't heard the news?"

"The news?" Her back was to him, but he thought she tensed slightly.

"Someone was killed tonight in Rusen's office."

She spun, frowning. "Someone?" Joining him, she picked up a plastic fork, then put it down. "Not Rusen?"

"So you've heard." He finished off the chicken piece and went for another one.

"Yeah, I heard something at the store on the news." She fidgeted with the napkins. "I guess I assumed it was Rusen.

They didn't give any names."

"Stubb called. He said the same thing." A mostly bare chicken bone in one hand, Python rummaged through the box of meat with his other. "They hadn't released the name, but he's talked to Rusen."

"What about the person who did it?"

He chose a drumstick, then paused before taking a bite. "He didn't say."

She nodded. "What about the match?"

Python swallowed his mouthful. "As in the words of Stubb, the show must go on."

"That about covers it in this world, doesn't it?"

Setting the chicken bones in the trash, Python wiped his fingers clean. "Is that what you've always wanted to do, Big K?"

"What do you mean?" She went to the sink and wet a washcloth.

"Wrestle. Is this the life you always dreamed of, or deep down, do you want something else?"

After handing him the wet cloth, she sat. "What else would I want?"

"Yeah, what else." With an unusual amount of attention, Python cleaned his fingers.

"I don't understand the question. I'm a trainer. It's what I do, train wrestlers to be the best." She held out her hands. "Do I look like I could be anything else?"

"You could be anything you wanted to be. Looks don't mean that much."

"Is that right? And how's that been working for you in the regular world? You got other job offers coming out of the woodwork since you left?"

Her words cut like thousands of tiny knives into his heart. "No, they weren't."

"This is where we belong, Python. This is who we are."

The saddest part, Big K had no clue his comeback wasn't an option either. This was only a temporary arrangement, one where he'd hopefully, finally, conquer his inner demons and expose a major drug ring at the same time.

How angry was she going to be when she learned the truth? Even if they did become the couple he wanted them to be, could she ever forgive him for his deception? "Can I ask you a question?"

"Of course, you can."

"Earlier, when you and I, *uhm*, when we were in bed. Did I, I mean, did we, uh–"

The phone rang in his room. Their heads jerked in unison toward the sound.

"You going to get that?"

Without answering her, he got up and rushed to his room. "Hello?"

"Did you tell Big K?" Stubb asked.

"Is that why you called? Just to ask me a question?" Not turning, Python could feel Big K's eyes on his back.

"I wanted to know what she thought."

"Why?"

"I just do. Did ya tell her?"

Python twisted to face her. "Yeah, I told her." Big K cocked her head.

"What'd she say?" Stubb asked.

He continued to stare at her. "Not much."

"Do you know if she's still awake? I think I'll call her."

Python looked down at the phone. "No."

"Why not? She won't mind if I wake her up."

Looking back up, their eyes met. "She's not asleep, she's right here."

"Let me talk to her." The excitement in Stubb's voice bubbled through the wire.

Python frowned at the phone. "Why?"

"What's your problem?" Irritation colored his words. "Put her on the phone."

Shoving the handset in her direction, Python growled, "Stubb wants to talk to you."

With wide eyes, she took the phone. "Stubb?" Big K visibly tensed, and she turned halfway away from Python. "I don't know. All I care about is the match."

As if the rug had been pulled out from underneath his feet, Python sucked in a breath, and Big K turned back to face him, a curious look on her face. He'd hoped she'd wanted more. He'd hoped they could move on from here, but this was the life she wanted, probably needed.

"Have they caught the person who did it?" she asked while staring at Python. She scowled at whatever Stubb said.

"I can't speculate and it doesn't matter. We've got a big day ahead of us tomorrow and we need some sleep. Why don't you let the police handle this and mind your own business?"

Something in her tone confused Python. He couldn't put his finger on it. Somehow it was different.

She hung up. "Python, are you all right?"

He focused in on her. "You've been saying that a lot lately, haven't you?"

"I have?"

Waving his hand, he dismissed the train of conversation. "You were right when you told Stubb we needed some sleep."

She stepped over to him, paused, then continued to the connecting door. "Python?"

Weary, he sank down onto the bed. "Yeah?"

"About earlier this evening?"

He perked up. "Yeah?"

"I think your dreams were a heck of lot better than anything that happened between us." With a wink, she closed the door.

Jumping up, he crossed the room in four strides and stopped short of the door. What'd she mean? Had he only dreamed kissing her? Or was she talking about the lovemaking?

He lifted his hand to knock, then lowered it. It was late, he was tired, and tomorrow was an important day. Satisfied that all would be revealed then, he pulled off his shirt with a smile. Forever might not be in the stars for him and Big K, but who said they couldn't enjoy a few trips to the moon in the meantime.

* * *

Police swarmed the arena as Kendal and Python arrived. They had a grueling workout and practice session scheduled, and Kendal wanted to make contact with Rusen. Especially since she knew he was still alive.

What bothered her was that the police hadn't captured the woman she'd left lying in the grass. She'd been out cold. How'd she get away? Kendal needed a break in the case, and it was time to take a few chances.

"IDs, please," a uniformed officer asked as they entered the west entrance.

Both she and Python pulled out the plastic coated IDs they'd been issued when the competition started. The young officer inspected them carefully. Then he directed them to the two officers taking statements.

Kendal gave an abbreviated version of last night, leaving out any mention of her being at Rusen's office. She hadn't even tried to coordinate stories with Python. If the cops starting sniffing around too much, she'd have Tommy disclose just enough information to clear her.

When she finished, she found Python leaning on the wall waiting. She frowned. "That was intense."

"Yeah, I guess it's necessary with a murder."

Staying in character, Kendal shrugged. "I suppose you're right."

They rounded the corner and spotted Stubb at the same time he saw them.

"Hey, I thought you guys would never get here." He scurried over to them and lowered his voice when he neared. "You wouldn't believe who bit the bullet."

She and Python waited without comment.

"Bernard Cook."

Her heart fell to her stomach. The dead man whose pulse she'd checked had been the same young man whose voice had cracked earlier in the evening. That didn't make sense. She'd heard the man talk before the shooter fired, and he hadn't sounded the same.

"His son Benny is really shook up. He's taking it hard."

Relief washed through her, and Kendal had to look away. Not that one person's life was more important than another. It was just that she'd developed a connection with the unseen Benny. "Is he here?"

"Who?" Stubb asked.

"Benny," she said.

"Yeah, he's in the locker room."

"I'd like to go talk to him." The kid might know more than he realized.

"When did you meet Benny?" Python asked.

"I haven't." A moment too late, Kendal realized her mistake. Thinking fast, she anticipated Python's next question.

"Then why do you want to talk to him?"

Bingo. "He just lost his father. I want to make sure someone is thinking about his loss, that's all."

Her answer seemed to appease Python.

Stubb shook his head. "The cops are with him right now."

Kendal cocked her hip. "So?"

He hopped from one foot to another. "They might not like you sticking your nose in."

The little idiot had learned nothing from the conversation last night. The idea of her being undercover at all times just wasn't sinking through that thick skull of his. She popped him in the shoulder. "You of all people should know I don't give a rat's ass about what the cops like or don't like."

Scowling at her, he hunched as if to protect himself from a second attack. "Fine, go on in, then. I don't care."

"I will." Wanting to hear all she could of the interrogation, Kendal hurried to the locker room.

Python caught up and grabbed her arm. "You think this is a good idea?"

Shaking loose, she continued. "Why wouldn't it be?"

He matched his stride to hers. "Stubb might be right. They might not like you being in there."

Undaunted, she opened the door. "Then they can tell me that, can't they?" The rancid smell of sweaty clothes and bodies wafted out on the draft she had caused.

Python followed her in.

The two detectives, sitting on either side of a pimply, skinny teenager, looked up.

"That'll be all, son," the detective closest to Kendal said as he stood. He pulled out a card. "You think of anything else, call me." The other detective stood as well, and both nodded at Kendal and Python as they exited.

Python stepped in front of Kendal and went to sit next to Benny on the bench. "You all right?"

The young man's head was bowed and his hands dangled between his knees. When he lifted his head, red-rimmed eyes peered out from behind thick glasses. "I guess."

Slipping past, Kendal sat on his other side and patted his knee. "Is there anyone here for you?"

His head drooped as he shook it. "My uncle."

Obviously Benny didn't feel his uncle was going to be much support. She looked over the top of the boy's head to Python and mouthed the word mother.

Python shook his head.

Glancing back at Benny, then again to Python, she raised an eyebrow.

Python shrugged.

She made a face clearly expressing her desire for him to say something.

Python shrugged again, this time with a frown.

She was ready to hit him behind Benny's back. Then the boy suddenly raised his head. Kendal smiled.

"Uh, Benny, if you want to talk or something, you can," Python stammered.

Benny scratched his ear. "Okay."

"I mean with me, you know, talk."

Benny scratched the side of his neck. "Okay."

Python put his hands on his knees. "Well, then, good. You know where to find me." He stood.

Kendal all but rolled her eyes. What was it with testosterone and feelings? Did they cancel each other out? She patted Benny's knee again. "How're you doing now?"

Benny dragged the back of his hand under his nose. "I'm okay, I guess."

Python sat back down.

"Are you going home? Is there someone to take you?"

He looked at her strangely. "I'm staying here. There isn't anywhere else for me to go."

"What about school?"

"I'm eighteen. I already graduated." He thumped his chest. "I don't need no more schooling."

Apparently so, she thought a bit sarcastically. "Were you close to your father?"

"I guess." He shrugged.

Another male phenomenon, the nonchalant shrug. "How about you and your uncle, are you close?"

"Not really."

This was surprising news. "Hasn't he come to see you?"

"Nope."

"Oh." She tapped her chin. "Then I guess you haven't spent much time in his office."

Benny's head jerked up. "No. Why'd you think I had?"

Guilt. "I hadn't. I was just asking. I know this is a difficult time."

The young man's eyes filled and he ducked his head.

Python cleared his throat. "Let's give Benny space."

Wanting to ask about the woman, wanting to figure out how much the boy knew about why his father had been in his uncle's office last night, Kendal curbed her intense need to ask. "Yes." She touched Benny's arm. "We're here for you."

Without raising his head, Benny nodded.

After a last squeeze, Kendal rose. A slight tremor shook the boy's shoulders, and she knew he was fighting back tears. Her heart went out to him and she wanted to sit back down and hug him.

Python grabbed her arm, pulling her to the door. "I'll be out in a minute."

"But–"

"I'm here." Python's eyes said more than his words. It was a man thing again.

She nodded. "It's going to be a tough day." She opened the door and stepped out.

Python looked back over his shoulder. "Yeah, it is."

The door closed on the teary scene. Kendal drew in a deep breath as she started down the hall.

A woman's high-pitched squeal bounced off the walls as she pointed at Kendal and screamed, "FBI!"

Chapter Seven

Immobilized, Kendal could only stare.

"FBI," the woman shrieked again.

Kendal's heart raced. How did she know? Who was she? Her cover couldn't be blown. Kendal took a step toward her accuser.

"It's them." The woman shimmied and continued to point. "The *F*ull *B*odied *I*talians. I can't believe they're here."

Understanding the intent seconds after hearing the words, Kendal slowly turned. Three men strutted up the hallway. Her knees almost buckled from her immense relief.

She knew of the wrestling trio and their nickname. But with the woman pointing at her, and all the other things that had gone wrong in the investigation, Kendal assured herself any special agent would've made the same mistake. Thank heavens none were around to witness her snafu.

Skirting the wiggling woman, Kendal walked to the locker room. She needed some space herself. Once inside, she rested back against the door and inhaled deeply. Musky smells lurked beneath the fruity, flowery scents of the many hair and body products women used, very different from the seemingly permanent stench of the men's locker room.

After a quick search of the shower and toilet stalls, Kendal knew the area was deserted. Happy to have the place to herself, she plopped down on the bench and put her head in her hands.

She needed to call Tommy and give all the information she could about the woman who'd killed Cook. Her supervisor would want a report on the ongoing investigation soon. Up to this point, she had nothing.

Zilch.

"I couldn't have ordered up a more perfect situation, if I'd had a menu."

A groan from deep inside Kendal rolled out. "Shockra, I don't have time for this." Weary of this woman's constant pursuit and angry at herself for not hearing the woman enter, she lifted her head.

Damn. Shockra wasn't the only one who'd entered. With her stood the three largest women Kendal had ever seen.

"Block it. We need this chat to be private," said the redheaded amazon to Shockra's left. The other two women, both sporting spiked dog collars that matched their blue and green spiked hair, dragged a bench and shoved it against the door.

Kendal jumped up. "Listen. I don't need trouble, especially today of all days."

Shockra sauntered close. "What's the big deal about today to you? You're too new to care."

"I do care. Python and I–"

"Don't even say it like that!" The redhead rushed forward, hands fisted and raised.

In immediate defense, Kendal dodged left, shielding her face.

"Stop, Flame," Shockra shouted, yanking the back of the woman's shirt, halting her. The other women crouched slightly in ready attack mode.

With fire in her eyes, Flame thrust her fist at Kendal. "He isn't yours."

Shockra didn't loosen her hold on the redhead. "That's not what we're here for."

Flame threw her intense look at Shockra. "It's what I'm here for."

Kendal's mind raced with exit possibilities. It didn't matter to her why these women were here. The only thing she cared about was finding an escape route.

"Not now, Flame."

Shockra's adamant tone must've sunk in, since Flame dropped her hands. Then she pointed a finger at Kendal. "He's mine, and you need to learn that." She pounded one fist into her other hand. "It's a lesson I plan to teach you."

What was it with all these women wanting Python? As the thought filtered through, Kendal already knew the answer. He was a rarity even in the regular world, a nice guy with values, and a real caring spirit.

Here, he stood out like a sore thumb. The one they all wanted but none could entice into their beds. Kendal felt real pride, as if she was somehow responsible for his attributes.

A fingernail traced the inside edge of Kendal's orange halter-top. She knocked Shockra's hand away.

"You need to learn how to play the game, Big K."

"I don't need to learn anything. All I have to do is take Python to the top."

Flame lunged. "He's not yours!"

Kendal bobbed left, slamming her shoulder into Shockra. Together they tumbled to the floor. Entangled, Kendal fought to get free when Flame smashed into her. Kendal fell, squashed between them.

With her knee in Kendal's back, Flame yanked her hair. Kendal gritted her teeth. Flame twisted her hand, tightening her grip, and wrenched. Kendal's head snapped back.

The redhead loomed over her. "You gonna learn, he's mine."

A hand caressed her breast. Kendal jerked.

"And you're gonna learn that there's more to life than men," Shockra purred from below. A tongue licked Kendal's bare abs.

"That's it!" Kendal punched backward with her elbow as she shoved to her knees, smashing Shockra in the mouth.

"*Umph*," Flame whooshed as she released her hold.

"*Aagh*," Shockra spat.

Two of the most satisfying sounds Kendal had ever heard. She leapt up, spun, then crouched. Blood spurted from Shockra's nose, while Flame sat doubled over on the floor. The other two women advanced.

"I wouldn't even think about it if I were you," Kendal

warned as she backed away.

"I need a damn rag." Shockra wiped her nose with her arm, smearing blood everywhere. "Get me something, now!"

One of the women dashed over to a pile of towels. Grabbing a handful, she hurried to Shockra. Bright red splotches grew on the pristine white terrycloth.

"Ya shouldna ha' don' tha', Bi' K," Shockra's voice was muffled by all the material.

"Yeah, you stupid dike." Flame got up off the floor, still holding her side.

Shockra threw the bloodstained towel against the lockers. "You need a lesson. And we're just the women to give it to ya."

"Hey, who blocked the damn door?" someone yelled as they battered the door with what must've been fists.

A crash, and the bench screeched against the floor. "Whoever did this better have a fucking good reason for it."

Slam. The bench shifted a few inches. "I hate getting sweaty if ain't got nothin' to do with sex or a match."

Another *slam.* "Someone in there is gonna pay."

"Hold yourself, would ya?" Shockra motioned at the two lackeys. "We're getting to it."

The women wrestlers heaved the bench out of the way.

"Don't think this is finished." Shockra glared. "You're mine."

"What're you guys doin' in here?" Another massive woman, with a haircut most male Marines preferred, entered.

After one more glare at Kendal, Shockra turned. "We weren't doing anything that concerns you. Stay out of it."

Amazingly, the big woman cut her eyes to the side. "I didn't realize it was you."

Shockra laid her hand on the woman's arm. "I know you didn't. If you had, you would've waited."

The woman only nodded. Shockra snapped her fingers. In response, her entourage fell in step behind. A crowd had formed outside the door, and they parted to let the women pass.

"Big K?" Python peeked around. "Big K, are you in

there?"

The concern in his tone rang loud and clear. She stepped quickly into view. "I'm here. Are you ready?"

Python surveyed Big K from head to toe. She didn't look hurt. "Yeah, I am." He hadn't liked it when he saw Shockra and her cohorts leaving the locker room. When Big K emerged into the hall, he took a closer look.

"We have the ring for the next hour. I think we need to run through routines three, five, six, and ten." Without stopping, she walked past him. "They're the ones that need the most work."

Falling in step, Python waited until they made it into the arena before putting his hand on her arm. "Did she attack you?"

She stopped without looking at him. "Who?"

"Don't play dumb with me. I saw Shockra and her band of thugs. Were you in there alone with them?"

"It doesn't matter." She waved her hand in his face. "We've got more important matters to be concerned with."

Her indifference infuriated him. Grabbing her shoulders, he shoved her against the wall. "There is nothing more important than your life." He braced his arm beside her head. "Why can't you see I care? Why are you so blasted hardheaded about this?"

Several emotions flickered across her face. Python wasn't sure what they were. He could only hope he was getting through.

"They wanted to teach me a lesson."

The words were softly spoken, yet their power sucked the air out of his lungs. He dropped his forehead to hers. "Did they hurt you?"

"I can take care of myself."

He rolled his head against hers. "That's not what I asked."

"No."

He leaned back to look into her eyes. "No?"

"They tried. They didn't succeed."

"I'm sorry, Big K. I'm so sorry."

Her hands encircled his face. "It's not your fault, Python. It's not your fault."

"Yes, it is." He placed his hands over hers. "They're after you because of me."

"No. They're after me because of their egos. They can't stand the fact that we aren't interested in them."

"How about me?" He trailed his hands down to her shoulders.

"What?" She let go of his face.

Never breaking eye contact, he stepped closer until their bodies touched. When his thumbs pressed the tender flesh inside her collarbone, he felt her shiver. "Are you interested in me?"

"I'm attracted."

"Is that all?"

"It's all I have to offer."

"And if I want more?"

"You'd better find someone else."

Not the answer he wanted. No, needed. Yet he still couldn't prevent himself from crowding even closer. "How attracted?"

Her nipples hardened against his chest. "You have to ask?" She licked her lips. "Can't you tell?"

"I want you." He lowered his head until their mouths were centimeters apart. "Do you want me?"

"Yes," she breathed.

When their lips met, he felt a jolt so strong he ached. She opened her mouth, and he delved inside. Her scent and taste invaded every one of his senses.

Her knees spread, and he took the silent invitation, nestling his growing erection. She responded with a slight gyrating motion. Python groaned.

Leaving her delectable mouth, he kissed his way down her throat. "You taste good."

Her tongue swirled around his ear. "So do you."

"They're in the arena." Python heard Stubb announce from behind the curtain separating them from the hallway.

Emotion overwhelmed him, and he grabbed her face. "We will finish this later."

With swollen lips, wide eyes, and flushed skin, Big K only stared.

Smiling, Python showered off the sweat and grime of his match. Big K had shown no mercy during their practice session that afternoon. He'd enjoyed it more than any other. Excitement and anticipation had mounted with every routine, every move. His *johnson* bobbed as if in agreement.

"There you go again. Just the mere thought of Big K, and you're dancing a jig." Turning the water to ice cold, Python let the arctic temperature take the spark out of his plug. Once he was hanging again, he shut off the water and stepped out. He grabbed a towel and slung it around his hips.

Tonight's match had gone smoothly. Another win, just as planned. He was well on his way to being put into the largest match the NFW had ever seen. This comeback gig was becoming the biggest draw pro wrestling had ever seen. Fans were clamoring to get near him. Their excitement reminded him why he'd joined the circuit in the first place.

Lips pursed to whistle, he glanced over and caught his reflection in the grubby locker room mirror. Stopping, he struck a pose. His body looked good, trim, shaped, solid. Flexing, he moved into another dramatic display of muscles. "You are one good looking guy."

"Is that what you think?"

Python scowled at Shockra in the mirror. "What're you doing in here?"

"What do you think, lover?" She strolled toward him.

Instinctively, he tightened the towel. "Not interested." Ignoring her, he walked to his locker, then opened the door.

She followed and leaned against the opposite bank of lockers.

"Get out."

"Why?" She dragged the tip of her tongue along the bottom edge of her teeth.

"I need to change."

"So? It's not like I haven't seen it all before."

"Not mine."

She waved her hand up and down. "Seen one, seen 'em all."

"Not mine."

"I'm not leaving."

He put his hands on his hips. "What do you want?"

"You know what."

"You're not getting her."

"This is a share and share alike world, Python. Or have you forgotten?"

Uncaring of his barely dressed state, Python stalked forward until his knees hit the bench between them. "No, you've forgotten I don't play that way. I'm not telling you again. Stay away from Big K."

Shockra sneered even as she backed up. "You're gonna wish you never said that. One day soon someone's going to take you and your bitch down a peg." She pivoted. "I'd watch my back if I were you," she said as she left the room.

Python sat heavily on the bench. This was not good. He needed to expose the drug ring and get himself and Big K out of here. She thought this was the life she wanted. He'd just have to convince her it wasn't true.

He grabbed his shorts. But first it was time to strike a deal. He knew just where to start.

"You thinking you need some stuff, Python?"

Not liking even the hint that he needed chemical stimulants, Python swallowed his pride. "Yeah."

"Feeling sluggish in the ring." The crew cut young man nodded. "It happens, especially at your age."

Again, Python swallowed, but this time it was in irritation. "Yeah."

The guy looked left, then right, as though checking to see if someone had somehow sneaked up on them out here in the middle of a deserted lot. "All right. Meet me here in three hours. I'll have what you're looking for."

"Three hours?" Python shook his head. "No. Won't work."

"Hey, you don't want the stuff–"

"I said I want it. Just not tonight. I thought you'd have it with you."

"What'd you think? That I walk around with the stuff on me? Are you crazy?"

Python seriously began to wonder the same thing.

"That's the deal, man. Tonight, or nothing."

Tonight. He'd planned to start where he and Big K had been forced to stop earlier. How could he make love to her, then leave?

"Hey, if you don't want it, it's no skin off my nose."

Not liking being manipulated, Python growled, "No. I'll be here."

"That's more like it."

The kid's smug smile irritated him even further. At least he'd started the ball rolling, he reminded himself. Leaving the dirty lot, Python dialed Tommy's number.

One ring. "Boden."

"I've set up the first deal."

"Python?"

"Yeah." The pause was so long, Python thought he lost his connection.

"With who?"

"The local pusher. I'm making the buy tonight. It shouldn't be long before I set up a meet with the supplier."

Another pause. "Okay. Where and when?"

"The deserted lot at Second and Main. Three hours."

"Sounds good. Call me after the deal goes down."

"Fine." Python ended the call. He wasn't overly familiar with FBI protocol, but it sure did seem they had a sloppy structure when it came to a civilian doing the investigating.

Pulling into the motel's parking lot, he mentally shrugged. They probably knew with his background, he could take care of himself. Hell, he was probably in better shape than most agents.

Out of the car, he looked from his door to Big K's. She'd left the arena without him. Should he go straight to her now, or to his room? Maybe he should call first.

He pulled out the card key. Yeah, that's what he'd do. Call her.

As soon as he entered, he went to the phone. The anticipation he'd felt earlier came back with a vengeance as he dialed.

Busy.

He held the phone away. "Who're you talking to at this time of night?" he asked the beeping receiver, then hung up.

He paced over to the connecting door and put his ear to it. A muffled voice. Lifting away, he looked around and spied a plastic cup. That's what he needed.

He grabbed it off the sink counter, then marched back. He placed the cup between his ear and the door.

Silence.

He leaned harder, straining to hear.

Nothing.

He'd heard her before. He shoved harder and the cup crushed.

A hard knock on the door vibrated his bald head. He stepped back.

Two more loud knocks. "Python? Python? Are you in there?"

Opening the door, he bobbed to miss Big K's pounding fist. "Who were you talking to?"

Her hand still in the air, Big K cocked her head. "Excuse me?"

He crossed his arms. "I just tried to call you. The line was busy."

"I was ordering a late night dinner. You feel like Chinese?"

"You ordered enough for me too?"

"Yes. I assumed you'd be hungry."

Contrite, Python ducked his head. "Chinese sounds good.

Thanks."

"I'm glad your highness approves."

"You are, are you?" He lifted his head, grinned, and started toward her.

With her hands held out as if they could stop him, she retreated. "The food's going to be here soon."

"Yeah?" He advanced until the back of her knees hit the bed. "You want to see how I work up an appetite?"

She laid her hands on his chest. "This isn't a good idea, Python."

"No."

She lifted her chin. "No, what?"

"You're not pulling back now. Not after what we did this afternoon at the arena."

"All we did was kiss." She shoved. He didn't budge.

"I told you we'd finish later."

"And you think that means we will? Because you say so?"

Python dropped his forehead to rest on hers. "This is not a war, Big K. We're attracted to each other. Why can't you just go with the flow?"

"It's not that simple." Her eyes closed. "There are things I can't get over."

"What can't you get over? I got over who you are."

She jerked away. "Excuse me? You got over who I am? What's that supposed to mean?"

Frustrated, he stepped back. "I told you, I don't do groupies or groupie look-alikes." He gestured up and down her body. "You dress like a damn drag queen. If I can see past all that, and still have feelings for you, then what the hell can't you get over?"

"Feelings for me?" Her brow arched. "Don't kid yourself. You've got a bad case of lust. That's all. You want in my pants. Once you're there, you'll be done."

Angry, he advanced until their noses were inches apart. "Is that what you think?"

"Do you think I'd have said it if I didn't think it?"

He grabbed her upper arms. "You've got a big mouth, Big

K."

"And you've got a bald head." She shook her shoulders, but he held on. Heat poured from her body as she visibly vibrated. "Let me go."

"Yeah? Whatcha gonna do if I don't?"

Her eyes narrowed to slits. "You don't want to know."

Yanking her close, he crushed her mouth to his. She shoved at him again. "No." His lips vibrated on hers as he spoke and he liked it.

She wrenched her mouth free. "What're you doing?"

"I'm kissing you." He pursed his lips and made another stab.

Her head bobbed back even farther. "We're fighting. This is not a time to start making out."

Without loosing his grip, Python frowned. "Why not? This is the best way to make up."

Bu–I–how–" She shook her head. "You don't make up if you haven't settled the argument."

"We settled it."

"We did?"

"Yeah," he said, pursing his lips again.

With hands braced on his chest, she kept a small distance between them. "You just said you're not attracted to women like me, but you still want to have sex. Exactly what part of that is settled?"

"That is not what I said."

"Really? It's what I heard."

Irritated with the turn of events, and how out of control this entire episode had become, Python threw Big K backwards onto the bed. He followed quickly, pinning her down. "You heard wrong."

"Then why don't you explain it to me."

Unable to help it, he rolled his eyes. "You're definitely too complicated to be a groupie."

"Is that supposed to be a compliment?"

"Take it any way you like."

She shifted beneath him, and her soft curves infiltrated his consciousness. "Dang, you feel good."

Their eyes met and held.

"I didn't mean it the way it sounded, Big K. Against all rational thought, I really like you. A lot. Can't you see that?"

Her hand traced the side of his face. "Against all rational thought, I like you too, Python."

He smiled as he lowered his head. "Good. That's good."

The minute his lips met hers, he lost himself in their heat. She opened and he thrust deep. Their tongues sparred much like their earlier argument, each searching for an edge to be able to penetrate even deeper. Tilting his head, he achieved a better angle.

"*Mmmf,*" she mumbled around the intense kiss. She spread her legs as her hands dragged his shirt over his head.

He dropped inside, then rocked, pressing his growing erection between her thighs.

"Oh, yes." Her head rolled to the side, and he took advantage, suckling her neck.

Following the edge of her leather halter, he kissed and sucked her flesh, enjoying the plumped up cleavage. "I need more."

She became still, then pushed his shoulder. He rolled away, throwing his arm over his eyes. "What's the matter now?"

No answer.

He waited a little longer. When she still didn't respond, he propped himself up on his elbows. "Why–"

He wasn't sure, but he felt certain his tongue had fallen out of his mouth, hanging somewhere around his stomach. There sat Big K in all her naked glory.

Well, at least from the waist up. Which at the moment was quite enough for him. "You, um, I thought you'd changed your mind."

"You said you wanted to see me." She opened her arms.

Staring at the glorious breasts protruding proudly from her chest, he reached out to touch the tip. The nipple hardened, and he circled it with his finger.

Her head fell back. "More."

He attacked, taking her down, landing with his mouth fused to her breast. Using one hand, he pumped up the side, covering the entire orb with warm, moist kisses. With his other hand, he fondled her other breast, concentrating on its responsive nipple.

"Oh, Python."

He raised his head. "Owen."

She lifted off the pillow. "What?"

"My name is Owen Brandt."

Dropping back down, she grinned. "Owen?"

"What?" He nuzzled her neck. "You think my name is funny?"

She arched. "I just never would've guessed, that's all."

Lifting up again, he kissed her lips. "What's yours?"

"My what?" With her eyes closed, her voice sounded dreamy.

"Your name."

She stilled again.

"You do have another name besides Big K, don't you?"

"Of course."

"Well," he kissed her neck, "unless you want us to sound like a couple of circus people, I'd like to know your real name."

She stared at him without emotion, then closed her eyes. When she inhaled deeply he didn't think she was going to respond.

"Kendal."

"Kendal." He let the name roll around in his brain. "I like it."

"I'm happy you approve."

"Yeah?" He suctioned onto the side of her breast, then popped off with a loud smacking sound.

She laughed and grabbed his head, pulling him even tighter. Taking her nipple between his teeth, he bit lightly, then teased the tip with his tongue. Leaving the tempting mound, he traveled up, taking her mouth in a searing kiss.

The fire within exploded. His searching hand found the

tab of her shorts and snapped them open. Plunging inside, he burrowed past a small scrap of silk to the warm, moist skin beneath. Like a heat seeking missile, his finger delved between her smooth folds with a direct hit to the soft center.

"Owen!"

Smiling, he sucked her lips, releasing them with a pop. "You like that?"

"I–"

Loud knocking.

His hand stilled, making Kendal wish she hadn't ordered food. As Owen rolled to her side, she closed her eyes, calming her breathing. "Lousy timing."

"Yeah."

More knocking, louder this time.

"Just a minute!" he yelled.

Sliding off, she wrapped herself with his discarded shirt. "You want me to get it?"

He jerked her onto her back, leaned over, and seared her with a hot kiss. "Absolutely not. If you think I'm going to let some pipsqueak delivery boy see your hot, sexy body, you got another think coming."

"The money's on the dresser." She pulled the shirt over her head.

With a smirk, he jumped up from the bed. Kendal enjoyed the view of a half-naked Owen. His unbuttoned pants rode low on his hips, a definite bulge straining the front.

"Prepared, were you?" He gathered up the bills.

"Girl Scout."

He threw her a grin over his shoulder. "I just bet you were."

He opened the door and there stood a teenager, but not a pipsqueak boy. A young girl, who had to be all of nineteen years of age, stared at Owen, her eyes growing as big as dinner plates. She took two steps back and held out the bag at arm's length.

"How much?"

The question came out gruff. Kendal knew he wasn't

trying to sound mean. The poor girl looked like she was going to cry. "They'd said eleven twenty on the phone. Just give it all to her."

As soon as the shaking girl grabbed the money, she threw the bag at him and fled.

Kendal dropped back, laughing. The bed dipped, and Owen loomed above her, his hands planted on either side of her head. "You think that's funny?"

"No." She giggled.

"What about that did you find so humorous?" he growled good-naturedly.

"You scared the poor girl to death."

He made no movement, but his face showed his pain. He moved off of her. "You hungry?"

"Owen?" She sat up, grabbing his arm. "What did I say?"

"Nothing."

She tugged. He didn't budge. "It wasn't *nothing*. Look at me."

His back to her, he still didn't move. She climbed over and sat next to him on the edge of the bed. "We can sit here all night and let the food get cold. Or you can tell me what I said that hurt you so much."

He looked away. "You didn't hurt me."

Reaching around, she brought his face back toward her. She waited until he looked into her eyes. "I did, and it's the last thing I'd ever want to do. Now, tell me what I said."

"You wouldn't understand."

"That's a pretty big jump you just made. Why don't you let me decide?"

He blew out a breath as he shook his head. "I don't want to scare girls."

"Why would one little girl's reaction mean so much to you?"

"It's not just hers."

"I'm confused." She kissed his neck, and he tensed. She leaned back. "It's me?"

"No, not you. You won't understand."

"Whether you're meaning to or not, you're hurting me by saying that." She started to move away.

Python grasped her to keep Big–Kendal close. "I'm sorry. I didn't mean to."

"Tell me."

"I want to be normal."

She frowned. "Normal?"

"Yeah, where people don't stare."

"You tattooed your head." Her fingers caressed his skull.

Indignant at her tone, he shifted. "So?"

"I mean if you'd wanted a chance not to stand out, you should've chosen some other place. Unless you plan to wear a hat the rest of your life, you're going to always stick out in a crowd."

Dejected because he knew that in more ways than one she was right, he dropped his head. "Yeah, it was a pipe dream."

"That's not what I meant." She lifted his face with her hands. "You're as normal as the next guy."

"Normal guys don't send delivery girls running."

"Yes, they do, if they show up at the door practically naked with a hard-on the size of Mount Vesuvius." Caressing his stomach, she laughed. "If there's one thing I can guarantee, it's that young girl didn't even notice your face, much less your head."

"Really?"

"Really."

With a light touch, Kendal traced her way up his stomach to his chest, stopping at a scar. "How'd you get this?"

"I was shot."

Her eyes widened. "You were shot? By who?"

"Awhile ago I got caught in the crossfire between the police and a mob guy." He shrugged, not wanting to talk about that day. "It's no big deal."

She looked for a moment as though she wanted to ask more, so he kissed her hard, then held her away. "You ever think about the future?"

She broke out of his hold and went to the bags of food

sitting on the small table where he'd left them. "You mean like winning the Brawl title?"

Not liking the distance, he joined her at the small table. "No, more than that. Like buying a house and settling down."

"How can I buy a house? As a trainer, I'm constantly on the move, and the pay isn't all that great. You know how the tour is. Until I get established, I have to be anywhere and everywhere."

"Don't you want more? A husband, kids?"

She opened a white carton. "Where're you going with this? What're you really trying to ask me?"

"I want more, Kendal." Grabbing her shoulders, he turned her toward him. "I want a home, a wife, and kids. I want to go to the grocery store and shop for food for the family. I want to attend PTA meetings. I want neighbors who I talk to over the fence bordering our yards. I want a minivan."

She stared at him for a moment before shaking out of his hold. She turned back and opened another carton. "Why are you telling me all of this? I'm training you to be the best. How does that mesh with what you just told me?"

Reality reared its ugly head, and Python remembered her dream. She couldn't see herself in the regular world. She thought this was the only place where she could find acceptance. He opened a carton of fried rice. Maybe she was right.

"How about we pull the table over to the bed? It'll be easier to share that way."

All Python could do was nod as he helped lift. His throat had tightened as a tremor of what he could only classify as fear coursed through him. What if Kendal really wouldn't leave the circuit for him? Could he stay for her? He shook his head.

"You didn't want kung pao chicken?"

He focused on the carton he was staring into. "No, I mean, yes. It's fine."

"Owen."

He raised his gaze to hers.

"It's going to be great. Once you have the title, you're

going to see that." She patted his arm. "I know you want it. It's what we're working so hard for. You think you want the other things because the road to the top is so hard. Once you're there, you'll forget all about this silly dream you think would be so great."

Not wanting to discuss this now, knowing he still had a drug deal to make tonight, he smiled. "You're right. We've got a title to win. Let's eat."

She handed him chopsticks, and he dug in. Shoveling food and chewing prevented him from having to talk. Questions swirled in his brain.

Could he stay in this world? Was it an option he wanted to even consider?

"Isn't the food good?" Her hand held the chopsticks midway between the box and her mouth.

"It's fine." Stuffing in another mouthful, he smiled at her. He needed to keep his mouth full if he wanted to prevent a discussion.

After another large bite, he handed the box to Kendal and took the one she offered him. He polished off the contents, then began to gather up the empty cartons.

Dropping them into the trash, he stretched and faked a yawn. "I'm beat."

"Oh, okay."

She didn't seem as surprised as he thought she'd be. Maybe she was hurt. "I'm sorry. I guess the day has caught up to me."

"No apology necessary." She tossed the carton she was holding into the trash. "This is better. You need to get your rest, and so do I."

Heading for the connecting door, Python wondered at the choices he was making. He didn't want to leave her. He didn't have any answers, but he didn't want to go either. "I'll see you in the morning?"

"Okay."

Halfway through the door, he halted, then looked over his shoulder. "You okay?"

"I'm fine." She settled on the edge of the bed. "How about you?"

"I'm all right."

"Good."

"Yeah, good." He shut the door, then leaned back against it. Whoever thought falling for a woman could be so convoluted?

Standing at the closed connecting door, Kendal listened to Owen hustling around the room. Tommy had called her, informing her of Owen's plan to expose the drug ring. She'd given him all she had on the woman who'd murdered Cook.

Great, this was all she needed on top of everything else, Owen out there putting himself in danger. Quickly, she changed into an all black outfit. She reached over to grab her cap just as she heard a door close.

Owen was on the move.

Tommy had said they'd cover it. She couldn't just lie low and wait. After Owen pulled away, Kendal hurried out to the car behind the convenience store. Luckily, she knew where the buy was going down.

Two blocks from the site, she parked. Staying in the shadows, she hurried to the edge of the deserted lot. Two vehicles sat, a hundred yards between them, facing away from her. Owen got out, rounded the front of his sedan, and stalked toward the dark van.

The tinted window rolled down as he approached.

Why wasn't the guy getting out of the vehicle? The man's face appeared just as he lifted his hand.

A gun!

"No!" she screamed, running, pulling out her weapon just as a shot blasted the night.

Chapter Eight

Owen got up, slowly brushing off his pants. Kendal slammed to a stop, then darted behind a rusted barrel. Breathing hard, she fought to calm herself.

He was okay. Owen was okay. Somehow he hadn't been hit.

What the hell was she doing? This was not like her, jeopardizing a case. Resting back against the barrel, she closed her eyes. This was not good. She had to get her emotions back under control. Letting them influence her decisions could get her and everyone else involved in this case killed.

She peered around the edge as Tommy stood next to the car pointing his Glock. Shattered glass was all that was left of the passenger side window. Tommy had told her he'd take care of Owen. He'd meant it. It was time she got her mind back on the case. Not on Owen and how much she was starting to care for him.

Sneaking back the way she had come, Kendal headed for the hotel.

"How'd you know?" Python stood staring at the almost decapitated man sitting in the car.

"It didn't feel right."

Python transferred his stare to Tommy. "Didn't feel right?"

"The deal came too easy for you." With his weapon aimed at the dead man, Tommy reached in and checked for a pulse. It was procedure even when the guy was missing most of his face.

"They knew I was working with you?"

Tommy shook his head. "I don't think so."

"I'm not going to be any good for you if I can't set up deals."

It was time for some fast thinking. Tommy knew Python would jump at any reason to bail. "Like I said, I don't think he thought you were working with us. If he had, he'd been more careful, like staking out the place, searching for us."

"And if he had?"

"He wouldn't have found anything. But we'd have known he was on to us."

Python scratched his head. "Then why'd he pull a gun on me?"

Tommy noticed he didn't say, try to kill me. "That's something I'm going to spend some time figuring out." Even though this was his first kill, Tommy forced his emotions to the back of his mind. He slapped Python on the back. "Go on back and try to get some sleep. Tomorrow's a big travel day."

"Yeah, it is."

"We need you in the game, Python. You going to be able to hold it together?"

"Yeah, I'll be fine." He suddenly grinned. "I've got one hell of a trainer."

"Really?" Tommy jumped on the change in topic. "She's that good, huh?"

"More than good, she's a prize."

Tommy hid his surprise. "A prize? Sounds like she's becoming much more than a trainer to you."

Python stared at him, his eyes going cold for only a moment before they thawed. "I guess I can tell you, since you aren't involved with the tour."

"Sure, you can tell me anything." Tommy hoped his voice wasn't shaking. He also hoped Python hadn't noticed he'd yet to alert the police about the dead body.

"I'm going to convince her I'm a better bet than the tour."

He sounded so confident that Tommy felt sorry for him. What was the guy going to think when he learned about the real Kendal? Suddenly, Tommy wished he hadn't wanted to know. Sometimes ignorance was bliss. "Ahem. Well, good luck. Convincing a woman of anything is a chore."

"You've got that right."

"You okay to drive?"

"Yeah." Python looked over at the dead perp. "You gonna call the police."

"Yes."

"You don't want me here."

It was a statement, not a question. Tommy answered anyway. "It's better if you're not involved. Keeps your cover intact."

"You think so?"

"I know so." Clamping him on the shoulder, Tommy urged Python back to his car. "Don't speed. The last thing we need is for you to get pulled over by the police."

After a short, nervous chuckle, Python started to leave, then hesitated. "Uh, Tommy?"

"Yeah?"

"Thanks."

Aware of Python's antipathy toward any law officer, Tommy knew his expressing gratitude was probably one of the hardest things he'd ever done. He nodded. "Anytime."

An answering nod and Python was gone. Tommy dialed the authorities, then made the more important call.

"Smart," Kendal answered after one ring.

"We had a problem."

"I saw."

"You saw?" Tommy shook his head. "Of course, you did. Then you know we have a dead body."

A pause. "You okay, Boden?"

"Hanging in there." He didn't want to talk about it.

"You might get pulled out of the investigation."

"Not going to happen." He was prepared to take it all the way to the top to make sure he stayed active on the case.

"Listen, if you need–"

"I know, I know."

She paused again. "Locals on the way?"

Kendal must've finally got the message that he didn't want

to discuss it. "Yes. That's not our real problem."

"What're you talking about?"

Even through the phone, Tommy could hear her concern. A concern that could get a special agent killed if they weren't careful. "The attack was deliberate."

"What're you saying?"

Smart was becoming too personally involved, Tommy thought as he rubbed his nose. She didn't even try to extrapolate the obvious. "Someone wants Python dead."

Ten hours on the road and Kendal was ready to spit nails. During this entire drive to Huntsville, she'd had no time alone in order to make contact with Tommy. She wanted to discuss their next move and find out how he was. No agent went unaffected from a shooting.

She glanced at Owen's profile as he drove. How about him? How was he handling witnessing a kill?

Knowing his torment over the first death he blamed himself for, was he doing the same with this one? She wanted to scream at her inability to ask any of these questions.

Now, someone wanted Owen dead. Who? Shockra came to mind, but Kendal hadn't a clue as to motive.

That's why she needed a brainstorming session with Tommy. How did all the pieces connect? And what about the murder she witnessed? Did Cook's death have something to do with it too?

Her eyes focused on Owen's strong hands turning the steering wheel, and memories of last night pushed out all other thoughts. The way he'd caressed and kissed her, she knew she shouldn't be thinking about him like this. It was becoming increasingly more difficult not to, since they spent so much time together.

"Are you hot?" he asked.

"Excuse me?"

Owen gestured at her. "You're fanning yourself. Are you hot? You need air conditioning?"

"We might be in the South, but it's not that warm." She

waved him forward. "I'm fine."

"Are you sure?"

She laughed, trying to ease the tension she felt. "Yes, I was only thinking."

"About?"

Wouldn't you like to know? "*Um*, nothing in particular."

He waggled his brows. "Nothing?"

"Okay, you got me." Giving in, she said, "I was thinking about last night."

"Yeah?"

"Yeah."

"Me too."

Her gaze jerked to his. "Which part?"

He looked back at the road. "What part were you thinking about?"

Were they in kindergarten? "You've got to be kidding."

He threw her the most innocent look she'd ever seen. "What?"

"You tell me first." Maybe she *was* reliving her youth.

"I was thinking about how hot and wet you were when my finger was inside of you."

His low, husky voice washed over her, overriding the shock she felt at his words. *Okay, definitely adult.*

"I was thinking how soft your breast was when I sucked it into my mouth."

Heat flooded her entire system, making Kendal squirm slightly in her seat.

"I was thinking how hard and tight your nip–"

"Okay, okay. I'm getting the picture." Happy that he didn't seem overly affected by the shooting, she took a calming breath, trying to bring her racing system back under control.

He grinned.

Remembering her role, she shifted in the seat to face him. "So, why'd you leave me last night?"

His fingers whitened on the steering wheel. "I had an appointment."

She crossed her arms. "With another woman?"

His head jerked toward her. "No! How could you even think that?"

"Isn't that always your assumption when I'm out at night?"

He focused on the road. "It was nothing like that."

"Where'd you go?"

"Stubb wanted to meet with me."

"Anything I should know?"

"No. We just went over the schedule."

"Okay." Kendal wasn't going to push Owen to lie any further. All she wanted to do was show the appropriate amount of curiosity and move on. She had to talk with Tommy, which meant she had to be alone.

Seeing a blue sign, she made a quick decision. "I have to use the bathroom."

"This rest area?"

"Uh, yeah. As if I would say it only to have you drive past."

Owen muttered something under his breath.

Kendal laughed.

"What's so funny?" Sulking, he put on the blinker and pulled off the interstate.

"You are. You remind me of a two year old, and I think it's cute."

"Cute, huh?" His brooding gone, he parked.

"I'd love to stay and enjoy the moment, but nature calls." She grabbed her purse from the back seat. The benefits of being a woman paid off at the most convenient times.

At a fast pace, she ignored the many stares that her outrageously tight, short leather outfit garnered, and scurried into the women's restroom. She entered the first stall and pulled out the cell.

"Boden," Tommy said.

"Smart, here."

"How close are you?"

"About an hour away." She flushed the toilet. "We need to meet tonight."

"Face to face?"

"Yes."

"I'll scout out a location," Tommy said.

"Text it to me."

"Okay. Get Smart?"

Couldn't he give the nickname a rest? "Yes?"

"Be careful."

Alert, Kendal immediately forgot her annoyance. "Have you heard more?"

"No, just keep your guard up."

"Always." As she hung up, she frowned.

"How'd you get away?" Tommy asked from the front seat, looking at Kendal in the rearview mirror.

Sitting in the back, she made a face. "It wasn't easy."

"Python getting possessive?"

Her eyes met his in the mirror. "What're you saying?"

Tommy threw his arm over the back of the seat and turned to look at her. "I know about the two of you. I don't think it's in our best interest for you to try and hide it from me."

"How'd you find out?"

"Python told me."

"He told you?" She shook her head. "Why in the world would he say something to you?"

"I was safe."

"Safe?"

"You know, someone he can talk to and it won't get back to you."

"I see."

"He's serious about you, Smart."

"You think so?"

"Yes, and I'm worried about your objectivity."

"Well, don't."

Tommy held up his hand. "Hey, don't cop an attitude. It's not like I'm going to Wilson with the information."

Incensed, she sat forward. "Are you implying you might?"

"No."

"Well," she leaned back, "that's good, since there's nothing to go to him about."

"We're doing good here. We're in, and everyone's buying the cover. If it's become too personal..."

Knowing silence to be the best reaction, Kendal only stared as his words trailed away.

Tommy dragged his hand through his hair. "We make a good team. I'd like to think we could work together in the future. That means we both have to live through this one."

Needing to ease the tension, Kendal smiled. "Aw, and here I thought you were going soft on me, Boden. Now I know you only want to save your own skin."

An answering grin spread over his face. "What can I say? My true colors shine through."

"Okay, I'll be careful. What's the latest?"

"The rumor is something's going down during the Brawl."

"The Brawl? That's way too public. Something's not right. There's no need to launder so openly. I don't like it, Boden. I think we're looking in the wrong direction."

"I agree. All we can do is stay in and see where it leads."

"Do you think it's connected to the assassination attempt on Owe–Python?"

"That's a good question. On the surface you wouldn't think so. It could be, though."

Grateful when Tommy didn't comment on the name slip, Kendal tapped the seat. "Terror's murder keeps intruding every time I start trying to piece everything together."

"Terror's death? Why?"

"Something about it doesn't fit." She placed her elbows on her knees. "Maybe it's the fact that Python was supposed to hit the ropes. Were they ever checked?"

"The ropes?"

"Yes."

Tommy pulled out a small notebook. He flipped through the pages. How he could see in the dim light, Kendal wasn't sure.

"I don't know."

"Find out, will you?"

"I can do that." His shoulders bent as he jotted a note. "You're thinking it wasn't an accident. That even back then Python might've been the target."

"Bingo."

Tommy paused, then snapped around to face her. "If that's the case, then we've just handed him on a silver platter back to the killer."

The Von Braun civic center buzzed with the excitement of the night's bout. Hours before the competition was to begin, the parking lot filled as faithful marks came to cheer their favorites or jeer the hated in the ring.

Kendal watched the participants' entrance. Where was Owen? She craned her neck to see around the mass of wrestlers and workers pouring through the gate.

A dot of color bobbed at the back of the crowd. *Finally.* Keeping him in sight, Kendal worked to relax her tense muscles. Not an easy accomplishment, knowing someone wanted Owen dead.

As he came closer, she moved over to the side. Now, she had double duty. Not only did she need to expose the money laundering, she had to keep Owen alive.

"Hey." He reached out, and knowing she shouldn't do it, she still put her hand in his. "You didn't have to wait here."

"I know. Was your cup in the car?"

"Yeah." Like a teenager, he swung their clasped hands. "I guess it rolled out of my bag, because it was under the seat."

"Then you better make sure you wash it off before putting it on."

Bending over as they walked, he got close to her ear. "Why? You worried about the health of my *johnson*?"

One finger on her bottom lip, Kendal made a deliberate leer. "I'd say that's as an important part of you as anything else. I want you to stay very healthy."

He laughed and hugged her. "Yeah, me too."

"Owen, you need to promise me something."

He maneuvered them over to the wall. "Anything."

"Don't leave the civic center without me, ever."

"Why?" His forearms framed her head on the wall.

"After Shockra and her thugs cornered me in Hershey, I don't want to press my luck."

A smug smile on his face, Owen pulled her to him and put his arm around her shoulders. "You got it."

Kendal felt no shame in using his hero complex to get what she wanted–him in her sight at all times whenever they weren't at the civic center. "Good. Now about today."

"What about it?"

"How are you feeling about scene seven?"

He squeezed her. "Good."

"Are you sure?" Kendal halted and faced him. "The guy you're scheduled to fight is a stiff worker."

"As if you haven't prepared me for every cheap shot there could be."

She grinned and started down the hallway. "I have, haven't I?"

"Yeah."

They reached the men's locker room. "Ten minutes?"

"I'll be right here."

He tilted his head. "You're going to wait?"

She crossed her arms. "Yes."

"You're that scared?"

Playing the needy woman wasn't going to be easy. "I'd just prefer to wait here."

After a quick hug, he disappeared into the locker room. Kendal paced over to the other side of the hall, then back. They needed more undercover agents on the case. There were too many times Owen wasn't going to be within sight, and she still had an investigation to complete.

Taking a chance, she pulled out her cell.

"Boden," Tommy answered.

"Smart, here. We need UCAs, now."

"Problem?"

"Hunch." With a snap, Kendal returned the phone to the

duffle bag.

"Hey, Python."

"Hey, Benny. What's up?"

The boy motioned him over. "Well, I appreciate your, uh, you know, talking to me after my dad was killed."

"No prob. You doing all right?"

"I'm okay."

"Well, that's good. I guess."

"Yeah, I guess." Benny bounced from one foot to another. "Listen. I don't know if it's my place, I mean she was nice to me and everything. I was just thinking you should know."

Confused, Python held up his hand. "What're you trying to say?"

Benny looked right, left, then back at Python. "I didn't think it was her at first. Then she got out of the car. That's when I knew it was her. Man, I'm sorry."

Still puzzled, Python knocked Benny in the arm. "Spit it out."

"I saw Big K last night."

Python frowned. "What do you mean you saw Big K?"

"I'd had a hard time, you know. So I went for a walk. It kinda hit me again about my dad and all, so I had to stop."

"It's okay, Benny." Python put his hand on the boy's shoulder. "Where'd you see Big K?"

"Getting out of the back seat of some guy's car."

The information refused to process in Python's brain. "Say again."

"I wish I was wrong, man. I really do. Like I said, she was real nice to me and all. I just thought you'd want me to tell you."

"You were right." Python rubbed his head. Kendal had said she needed girl stuff and didn't want him to tag along. She'd said she'd had to go to two different stores to find the brand she used. It had all been a lie.

"You ain't mad at me, are you? I mean–"

"No. I'm not mad." The last thing he needed was for

rumors to start. "That was a friend of ours. Did you see him too?"

"Well, that was the kinda strange part of it."

"Why's that?"

"Unless there was two of 'em, the guy was in the front seat while she sat in the back."

"How long did you watch them?"

The boy blushed deep red. "Not long."

"I'm not accusing you of anything." He bumped the boy in the shoulder. "I just want to know."

Benny shrugged. "About ten minutes, I suppose."

"Thanks for telling me." Python threw a blatant look at the wall clock. "I've got to run."

"You're sure you're not mad?"

He ruffled Benny's hair. "Not at all. I 'preciate your watching my back." Containing himself, he walked out instead of running.

Kendal stood against the far wall. She smiled as he emerged. "You didn't change."

"We need to talk." He took her by the elbow.

"Owen, what's wrong?"

"Private. I need to talk in private."

Her eyes grew round. "Did something happen?"

He steered her into what he hoped was an empty room. It was. Letting her go, he locked the door.

She tilted her head at him. "What is it?"

"Who were you with last night?"

Surprise flashed across her face, so brief Python wasn't sure if he hadn't imagined it. She put her hands on her hips, a definite defensive posture.

"Last night?"

"Don't play dumb with me, Big K. You were seen getting out of a man's car."

Think, Kendal, think. "I told you I needed tampons. I was walking and this guy offered me a ride. I took it."

"Then why were you in the back seat of his car for over ten minutes?"

Damn, who saw us? "He wanted information."

"Information?"

She threw up her hands. "All right, you caught me. This blond guy's been paying me for information about the circuit. He wants to know who's dealing."

When he stared at her without comment, she knew he was putting the pieces together, hopefully the way she wanted him to.

"Kendal."

Good sign, he used her name again.

"Who is this guy?"

"A cop, I think. He showed me some kind of ID. He approached me the first day, offering money for information." She hugged her elbows. "You know trainers don't get paid much. I can use the cash." Striding to the other side of the room, she turned her back to him. "I know what you must think of me."

He laid his hands on her shoulders. "Why didn't you come to me if you needed money?"

"Right. Isn't that one of those kettle, black things? I mean if you were rolling in the dough, you sure wouldn't be here putting up with all this bullshit, would you?"

His mouth blew hot breath across her ear. "You could've come to me."

She turned. "I didn't *need* the money, Owen. I wanted it. I didn't even have any real information. Still, I met the guy, answered his questions, and took the cash." She broke away. "No better than a common whore."

He spun her around. "No, you're not. I don't ever want to hear you say anything like that again."

The guilt stung fast and hard. She hated doing this, hated lying to Owen once again. She had to. She and Tommy had gotten sloppy, and now she was paying the price.

The only saving grace was that Owen made the connection. She had to make sure Tommy got the details before Owen contacted him.

"Do you hear me? You're a good, honest person. You

took advantage of a legitimate offer and made some money." He paused and stared at her for a moment. "I don't want you meeting with him again."

Thankful her cover was saved yet again, Kendal nodded. "I don't think he'll be calling me again anyway. I didn't have anything new this time."

His arms enfolded her. "I'll take care of you, Kendal. Don't you worry about the future. I'll take care of you."

Not feeling good about herself, she said nothing. Dreams of being with Owen were just that–dreams. When he learned how much she'd deceived him, he was going to run as far and as fast from her as he could.

"There you are."

Not now. Kendal ignored the feminine purr as she emerged from the women's restroom. A sharp grip grabbed her arm.

"I'm talking to you."

Slapping the woman's hand away, Kendal curled her own into a fist. "I don't have time for your nonsense. Back off."

Shockra blocked her way. "Don't you ever learn? Why fight the inevitable?"

Fed up with Shockra's constant abuse, weary of lying to Owen, and frustrated with the dead-end this investigation had become, Kendal closed her eyes.

"That's better. Relax. Let me show you the way to paradise." Shockra's hand touched Kendal's bare belly.

Reopening her eyes, Kendal purposely softened her gaze.

A look of confusion crossed the wrestler's face, then she stepped closer. "That's better."

Reaching out with both hands, Kendal framed the sides of Shockra's head.

The woman licked her lips, leaning slightly forward. "I knew you'd come around."

Snatching Shockra's ears, Kendal head butted her. Shockra went down with a thump.

Pleased with her quick thinking, Kendal smiled even as

she made sure the corridor was still clear. "That felt good. Real good."

She squatted at the unconscious woman's side and whispered in her ear, "You'd better think twice before you take me on, witch. I've put up with your sneak attacks and warped thinking long enough. It's going to stop, now."

After checking Shockra's pulse, a procedure she couldn't ignore, Kendal stood, rolled her shoulders, and cracked her neck. She'd needed that. She definitely felt better.

Over her shoulder, she smirked at a reawakening Shockra and rounded the corner. She bounced back when she hit soft flesh. "Oh, sorry."

The short, pudgy man reeking of cigarettes waved his hands. "No, no. I wasn't watching."

Kendal stepped right just as he stepped left.

He laughed. "I don't believe we've met." He held out his hand. "I'm Sloan Rusen."

The booker. After all this time trying to make contact with the man, I literally bump into him in the hall. She shook his hand. "Big K. Python's trainer."

"That's who you are." He pointed a stubby finger in her face, while stroking his chin with his other hand. "I've heard excellent reports about you. You open to other opportunities?"

Not too eager. Remember, I need to close this, not scare him off. She put her hands on her hips. "Depends on the opportunity."

His oily smile exposed a top row of gold teeth, the middle one boasting a dollar sign. "Good." He started away. "I'll be in touch."

She watched his retreating back and wondered, why now? So much could've been avoided, if she'd gotten inside earlier. Owen could've left, and she wouldn't have had to hurt him.

From around the corner she heard, "Shockra? Are you hurt?"

"No! But that bitch Big K is gonna be." Shockra's voice dripped with venom.

"Big K, huh?"

Kendal could imagine him rubbing his chin again and decided now was the time to get out of there. Determined, she walked briskly, suddenly needing to find Python.

I'm worried about your objectivity. Tommy's words came back to haunt her. He was right. She needed to get back on track.

If Rusen offered her the in she needed, they'd cut Owen loose. Then he could get out, move on with his life, and not be in danger.

Once he was out of harm's way, she'd be able to concentrate on the investigation. Gain back her objectivity. Nothing could supersede her dedication to the nation's safety.

"Why didn't you tell me you contacted Big K?"

Grateful for the text message from Kendal, Tommy adjusted the phone on his ear. "What're you talking about?"

"Don't play games with me. She said some blond guy was paying her for information. I know it's you."

"It could be someone else."

"Listen–"

"Okay. We work on a need to know basis, Python." Tommy decided to give in and keep Kendal's cover solid. "You didn't need to know."

"You knew I was close to her. Having her meet you late at night puts her in danger. Don't approach her again."

Properly chastised, Tommy grinned, since Python couldn't see him. "She wasn't much use. I was done with her."

Silence.

Python probably didn't care for how he'd phrased that. Tommy grinned even wider.

"I'll try and make another deal," Python finally said.

"Why don't you hold off on that? Give me some time to come up with a plan. After the close call, I want to have as much information as we can before you go back in."

"Is that why you contacted Big K? To try and help make a deal?"

"Her and others."

"Who else?"

"Need to know."

Python muttered something.

Tommy stifled the need to laugh. "You're going to be seeing me around. Be prepared."

"Here?"

"Yes. I'll be introduced to you. Be surprised." Hanging up, Tommy turned to the group sitting around the conference room. "That was Python, our wrestler."

"He thinks we're after a drug ring, right?" asked a middle-aged Special Agent.

"Right, and we want to keep it that way."

"Boden, explain the basics," the local Special Agent in Charge directed.

Tommy stood, nodding to the SAC. "We're going to need undercover agents for the rest of the operation."

"With the logistics constantly changing, how many UCAs are you predicting?" a female special agent asked.

"The number of undercover agents needed will depend on the location. The tour heads to Knoxville next. The arena holds close to twenty-five thousand, twice the number here. We'll contact the local police departments. Preferably, we'll use officers who've gone through our National Academy."

The petite female scrunched her nose at him.

Unsure why the woman gave him such a strange look, Tommy continued, "The big news is they've rescheduled the Brawl to Indianapolis. Python has created the biggest draw ever. To accommodate the increase in fan base, and for the first time, they're going to be in the RCA dome, seating capacity over ninety-five thousand.

"As unfortunate as the incident was, the murder in Hershey has the NFW beefing up security, which means we can infiltrate as hired security guards without raising suspicions."

The Special Agent in Charge stood up. "Harrison, Taylor, Baker, Jones, the four of you will take on security detail." He passed out folders. "Take this, study it, then contact the local authorities. We need a task force at every location."

The men took their folders and left, leaving only the female agent. Tommy hoped the SAC knew what he was doing assigning the stiff, aloof agent to the operation.

"Pierce. You're going undercover with Boden as a newspaper reporter team." SAC turned to him. "Tommy Boden, Fallon Pierce."

She looked over at Tommy, then back down at the notebook she was making notes in.

Tommy took over. "With all the hoopla surrounding Python's comeback, he and his competitors are doing constant interviews. We're set up as a reporter and photographer. We'll report and follow all their progress right up to the Brawl."

"Are the parts assigned?" was her only question, with little change in facial expression.

"Do you have a preference?" Tommy asked.

"Not really."

The SAC intervened. "From reviewing your files, Boden would make the better reporter."

"Yes, sir." The words from Pierce were harsh. Tommy wondered at their cause.

"I do have significant knowledge about the wrestling world and Python in particular," he added, hoping to ease the tension that had suddenly built in the room.

"Fine." Her words were clipped once again.

The SAC slid a file to each of them and an exasperated look at Pierce. "Here's the details. Figure out how you're going to proceed." He left the room.

"Is there a problem I need to know about, Special Agent Pierce?"

"Not unless you have one."

"Are you always this prickly?"

"Are you always so invasive?"

Rounding the table, Tommy pulled out the chair nearest to her. "Listen, we're going to have to get along in order to work together."

"Why?"

He sat down. "What?"

"Why do we have to get along?"

"It makes things easier."

She shrugged and stood. "Fine." Without another word, she stalked out.

"Whew, you are one intense piece of work." Which made Tommy wonder why the heck she got assigned to him.

As the water streamed over her, Kendal heaved a sigh of relief. Another match won, and Owen was back at the hotel safe and sound. She'd never felt so nervous or anxious. Every move and sound had her on edge, checking for bad guys around every corner.

Twisting off the water, she dried in a hurry, then unwrapped her dry hair from the towel. She hadn't wanted to use the blow dryer and be unable to hear through the connecting door she'd left open.

Groupies were no longer her worry. UCA were stationed at the front desk, and outside their doors, all prepared to intercept anyone attempting to get in. If a contract had been put out on Python, the killer would be craftier at getting in to him than any groupie would be.

She dressed in a baggy T-shirt and shorts, sick of the tight clothes her cover continued to force her to wear. When she emerged from the bathroom the top of the mirror fogged.

"Finally you're done."

Halting, she tossed her hair over her shoulder. "I didn't realize you were in here waiting on me."

"You left the door open. I thought you were expecting me."

Walking past him, she put her dirty clothes in a plastic bag. "I wanted to be able to hear if you needed me. That's all."

"Is it?"

Needing time and space, Kendal turned and could only stare. "What're you wearing?"

He grinned. "You like it?"

She pointed at his chest. "That's me!"

He looked down and nodded. "Yeah."

Amazed at the sight, she moved close to inspect the tank T-shirt. "And you."

"Right again."

"When, why–"

"It's marketing. We're a hot commodity."

"It's hot all right." Kendal traced the outline of her body, which was wrapped around a very real looking, strong Python. "I've never worn an outfit like that."

Pulling out the shirt, Owen inspected it. "It's amazing what they can do with computers, isn't it?"

"Amazing doesn't even describe it."

"This isn't why I came in here."

She suddenly realized how close she was. Too close. "No?"

"I need you."

"What?"

He put his hands on her shoulders. "I need you."

After a feeble attempt to pull out of his hold, she tilted back. "What do you need?"

"Guess." He lowered his head.

Chapter Nine

Kendal braced her hands on his chest. "This isn't smart, Owen."

Not until his mouth whispered over hers did he stop. "So?"

"I'm not the woman you want."

"Yes, you are."

She tried to step away, but he held her firm. "You want forever."

"Yeah." His lips feathered over her cheek. "I want forever."

"You don't know the real me."

Pulling back, he stared into her eyes. "I know more than you realize."

She dropped her forehead on his shoulder. "If only that was true."

Moving her hair, he kissed her neck. "What's that supposed to mean?"

"Nothing." Kendal rolled her head back and forth.

"Let's just," he rubbed his nose on her skin, "take it slow. See where it leads."

A desperate ache filled her as she lifted off his chest. "You don't–"

His mouth captured hers. Kendal knew she should want to resist, but she didn't. She wanted this man, and she wanted him now. She wouldn't be the first agent to have an inappropriate relationship, and she was sure she wouldn't be the last. Besides, Tommy already thought they were intimate.

Owen broke the kiss and nuzzled her neck. "You taste delicious."

Turning to give him better access, she closed her eyes.

"Owen."

"Say my name again."

"Owen," she breathed.

His hands traveled down her back, grasped her rear, and squeezed. "You look good. Very sexy."

"I'm in baggy clothes."

"Easy to get into, my dear." His hands slid down her sides, dipping beneath her shirt, making truth of his words. Spanning her back with his fingers, he kneaded the skin.

"You're hired," she breathed.

"You like that, do you?"

"Love wouldn't be too strong a word." She grabbed his face and kissed him hard.

"Oh, damn. You keep that up and you're gonna make me come."

"You'd better not." She jumped, wrapping her legs around his waist.

"*Oomph.*" He stumbled back, teetering at the edge of the bed. "That makes it better."

She laughed at his sarcasm. "Good."

He attacked, growling as they fell.

They rolled on the bed with Kendal ending on top. With a hand to the back of her neck, he pulled her down for a lazy, slow kiss.

Licking her tingling lips, Kendal pulled away, and he tugged once again. She put her hands on his chest. Undeterred, he rose and kissed her again. "You're beautiful."

She smiled. "Thank you, Owen." His gaze roved over her, making everything tingle inside. When he lay back, a sudden impatience overwhelmed her. "You have on too many clothes."

In haste, he lifted his shoulders and ripped off the Big K/Python shirt. Kendal attacked the buttons of his jeans. Up on her knees, she yanked the denim down. After a quick jerk and toss, his pants went flying off the bed.

Leering at her, he gripped the bottom of her overlarge shirt. "Now, it's your turn."

Dragging the fabric up, he filled his hands with her bare breasts. The shirt fell back over his fingers.

"Take it off," she demanded.

"As you wish." As he pulled the shirt over her head, she stripped off her shorts.

He stopped. "You weren't wearing any underwear?"

She looked down at the material in her hand. Donning her most wicked grin, she cocked her eyebrow. "Nope."

"Are you trying to kill me?"

"That is the last thing I'd want to accomplish at this moment."

Reaching over, he started to caress her breast, rubbing his thumb over her pebbled nipple.

"Owen," she exhaled.

"You like that?"

"Oh, yes." She straddled his hips, reached under, and grasped him.

"We need..."

She leaned close and licked his chest. "We need what?" Her fingers flexed, emphasizing her words.

"Protection," he gasped.

She stilled, releasing him.

Afraid he'd broken the mood, Python popped open his eyes. "I have some. My pants." Her immediate smile reassured his momentary panic.

Stretching, she searched the floor beside the bed. Her beautiful breast peeked out, begging him to touch it again. Unable to resist, he circled her nipple with his finger.

Her hand reappeared holding his pants in a raised fist as if they were an incredible prize. Her eyes gleamed, and he would never know if it was from his ministrations or the satisfaction of her find.

Excited, happy, and overly ready to finally have her in bed, Owen went right to the pocket with the condom.

Still straddling him, she snatched it from his hands. "Always prepared?"

"Only since you." Her smile softened as her cheeks

reddened even more, and Python knew he'd said the right thing. *Thank heavens*!

She ripped open the small packet. With infinite slowness, she rolled the thin cover over him.

"Kendal," he strangled.

"You like that?"

"Oh, man, yes."

"Then you're going to love this." Collapsing, she impaled herself.

"*Ahhh*." Grasping her thighs, he surged upward over and over again. He wanted to go slow, take things easy, but he couldn't.

As she arched backward, her hands grabbed his legs, her elbows at his knees. As if they'd been lovers forever, they moved together perfectly. The intensity of being inside her, her moist skin, the scent of her arousal, all overrode his control. "Come–here," he panted. "I–need–to–kiss–you."

She released him, falling forward, melding their lips in a hot, slick lock. Her fingers clenched his shoulders and somewhere in the back recesses of his mind, he knew she was close to climaxing. He let go of her thigh, then pressed his thumb against her.

"Owen!"

Hearing his name threw him over the edge. As he started to lose himself, his mind began to chant, *I love you. I love you. I love you.* His world exploded.

An hour later, Kendal lay in the dark, a snoring Owen at her side. Just as he'd been falling asleep, he'd mumbled three distinctive words, *I love you*.

He'd said he loved her. How could she have let this get so out of hand? He wanted a wife and kids. Not only was she not the woman he thought she was, what was he going to say when he found out she'd been lying to him all along?

Plus, she would always be married to her career. Just like her parents. They'd always put their military careers before each other. Owen would never accept that type of life. He wanted a woman who could give him everything.

Tears welled in her eyes. This was so wrong. She should be shot for not keeping this professional. She had a duty to her country, an obligation that overrode everything else in her life. A pledge she'd made and was honor bound to keep.

She should tell him. Even as the thought flew into her mind, she knew it was not an option. She could not break cover before they exposed the money laundering. And telling him the truth now could very well put his life in even more danger. Unsure of how'd he react, she couldn't take the chance.

She rolled away from the man who'd burrowed his way into her heart. Life could be so unfair. Once this operation wrapped up, he would know everything. With crystal clarity, Kendal realized one undeniable truth. Honest, openhearted, Owen would never love a woman whose entire existence in his life was a sham.

Lights flashed and Python blinked. "Hey, you got to do that so much?"

The perky photographer only shrugged and smiled an impish smile. "Does it bother you?"

He softened, hearing Fallon's sweet voice, and shook his head. "No. You just caught me off guard, that's all."

"I'm sorry. I want candid shots. They come out better this way."

Wanting to pat her little head, Python refrained, and turned back to Tommy, the supposed reporter. The guy had gone all out for the gig. He carried a tape recorder and notebook, wore glasses and a Python trademark baseball cap backwards on his head. If Python hadn't been told beforehand, he wasn't sure he would've recognized him. He glanced over at Kendal to see if there was a spark of recognition.

None.

Tommy had contacted him again, and Python had expressed his concern that she might be able to identify the agent. Tommy had assured him they'd never met except in the dark. The most she'd ever seen was the back of his head. Tommy hadn't been worried.

So, what about the photographer? Eyeing the tiny woman, Python concluded she wasn't an agent. The FBI must've figured out a way to get Tommy hired by the magazine. How they pulled that off was anybody's guess.

"I think that's enough for today. We'll be in the crowd for the match." Tommy stood. So did Fallon.

"Root for me," Python said.

"Sure thing." Tommy left, grinning, with the pixie of a woman following him.

"You're quite the celebrity."

Python turned to Kendal. She'd stayed out of range of the pictures, and had yet to come out of the corner. Right after they'd arrived at the Thompson/Boling arena she'd been called away. Ever since she'd returned, she'd been distant. "You okay?"

"Yes. These interviews aren't too taxing, are they? I mean, considering we just arrived in Knoxville."

He walked over and wrapped her in his arms. "No. They're energizing me. I feel like I can take on the world."

Kendal didn't respond with her usual enthusiasm. Instead, she broke out of his embrace and stepped away. "You've come a long way, Python. This is what all the work is for."

"We've come a long way." He started to feel anxious and wasn't sure why.

"You're going to be a star. Always enjoy it."

It suddenly hit him. She'd called him Python, not Owen. "Why are you talking like you're not going to be there?" Grabbing her arms, he shook her lightly. "We're in this together."

"Things change." She wouldn't meet his gaze. "Sometimes in midstream."

"What're you trying to say?"

"I've gotten an offer."

He let go of her. "An offer?"

"Rusen."

"What'd he offer? It doesn't matter. I'll match it."

Sad eyes stared at him. "You can't."

"How do you know?"

"I just do." She touched his arm, and this time he pulled away. "You'll be fine without me. I didn't do much. You're the one who pushed and got here in such a short time. You're a winner, Owen. Here and in life."

His hands balled at his sides, even as a tiny part of him sparked with hope when she called him Owen. "I'm not talking about wrestling. I'm talking about us."

Stepping close, she raised up on her toes. She leaned in, placing a chaste kiss on his lips. "You're a special guy, and some very lucky woman is going to figure that out one day."

She kissed him again, this time deeper. He couldn't help but respond. Breaking away, she caressed his cheek. "Be happy, Owen. Go have that life you've been dreaming of. You deserve it."

Turning, she hurried out.

"Kendal!"

The door slammed shut. She was gone. How could she leave? After everything they shared. Didn't she care at all?

Something wet hit his arm, and Python looked down. More drops. *Tears*? He wiped his cheek, and found it damp. *Men don't cry*!

Infuriated, he grabbed a chair and threw it across the room. What did he care? She'd jerked him around enough. He was done chasing after her. If she could take another job after the night they spent together, then he sure as hell could move on too. Like she said, she didn't want the same future he did anyway.

It was time he got his life back. That meant cracking this drug ring and getting the hell out of here. He shoved another chair.

The sooner, the better.

"I want him out." Kendal paced from one side of the room to the other.

Seated, Tommy shook his head. "Not possible."

She rounded on him. "Yes, it is. Rusen has hired me. We

have our in, we don't need a civilian involved anymore."

"Why'd you do it in the first place?"

Kendal cocked a brow at Special Agent Fallon Pierce. "Excuse me?"

Fallon shrugged. "Seems to me, you could've come up with a better way then having a civilian think he's uncovering some nonexistent drug ring."

A little taken aback by the candor of the younger agent, Kendal took a moment to glare. Then she dismissed the upstart without answering. "Uncover the ring. Let him think he's finished the job. He'll pack up and leave."

"What if we need him again?" Tommy asked.

"We won't. Don't forget someone wants him dead. It'll be best for all if we get him out of here."

Kendal could almost see his brain working as Tommy didn't move. He frowned. "It might work. We tell him we conducted a sting. Let him think the drug dealer spilled his guts and we have all the information we need."

"Good. That way he'll leave the tour immediately," Kendal finished.

"Yeah." Tommy's voice held all the dejection of a true fan losing his hero.

"I've set up another deal." Python pulled Tommy aside on the floor of the arena.

"What?" The agent's eyes narrowed behind his glasses.

"Tonight, the west side, staff parking lot."

"You set another one up?" Tommy grabbed his arm and yanked. Python followed him behind the temporary bleachers. "I told you, I wanted to check things out before you went and did that again."

"And I told you from the beginning, I wanted to find the drug ring and get the hell out of here."

"Why the sudden urgency?"

Python glanced over at Fallon, who sat on a bench and was busy wiping the lens of her camera. "My trainer quit."

"So?"

"So, I'm ready to move on. That means we bust this drug ring. You're not doing anything, so I did."

Tugging the bill, Tommy adjusted his cap. "From now on, you talk to me first."

"I want to get this over with."

"You were only competing for your trainer?"

"It doesn't matter. I set up the meet at midnight. In the southwest corner of the lot."

"I don't like it." Tommy tugged his cap again. "Why couldn't they make the contact somewhere more populated?"

Python crossed his arms, irritated with the agent's reluctance. "How 'bout they don't want to get caught?"

"Maybe. Deals go down out in the open all the time, though. It bothers me that they want to meet in such an out-of-the-way place again."

Tommy's unwillingness roused Python's instincts. "You think they may be out to get me?"

"It's beginning to look like it." Another wrestler and his manager passed nearby. Tommy paused until they were out of earshot. "I'll be there backing you up. After tonight, you're not to do anything without okaying it with me first."

The agent's adamant tone had him straightening. If Tommy was that concerned, maybe Python should be more wary. The last thing he wanted to do was not live to make the changes he'd been dreaming about ever since he let himself fall in love with Kendal.

The mention of her name had his hands balling into fists. He needed to forget her. Already she was working with Sloan. He'd heard the rumors about a run-in with Shockra that had caused Sloan to offer her a position in his franchise.

"See you tonight." Tommy trotted over to Fallon.

As he watched the duo leave, Python tried not to blame Kendal for moving on. He couldn't do it. She'd sold out.

After using him to get what she needed, she'd left. Just when he needed her most. The hurt went deeper than he'd ever known he could feel.

How was this any different than when his mother had

decided to overdose? Hadn't he, his younger brother and sister all been left for the authorities? After they'd been placed in foster homes, he'd taken off. He'd known then that no one would want on overgrown teenager who looked more like a man. With his past, he should be used to rejection by now.

Curbing his inclination to slam the bleachers into tiny shards of metal, he headed to the locker room. He would go through the motions of preparing for the match, but if everything went as he hoped, after tonight he would leave the circuit and never look back.

A storm had been brewing all day. This late in November, Tennessee temperatures could change in a matter of hours. It was a toss-up whether it rained, sleeted, or snowed.

Python wouldn't have known much about the weather if Stubb hadn't demanded they leave the coliseum for lunch, muttering something about a change of scenery. Then to top it all off, the guy had spent the entire time grilling him on why Kendal had quit. After such an exasperating meal, he'd used all his pent up frustration on his practice opponent in the ring.

Wind whipped around the side of the car as he flipped up the collar of his jacket. Out here, at five minutes to eleven, a light drizzle started to fall. He held out his hand to catch a few drops and rubbed the moisture between his thumb and finger.

Rain.

As he walked, he pulled a ball cap from his pocket, then stuffed it on his head. He wanted to be early, to watch the pusher arrive in order to be better prepared. In the back of the lot, several spaces away from a streetlight, a lone black SUV sat parked. The model and make he was scheduled to meet.

Were they already here? Conscious of his other close encounter, he edged nearer, staying next to a small cluster of trees. He wasn't about to make the same mistake twice.

In the dim light, he thought he saw someone sitting in the car. The rain started to pour harder, helping to protect Python from being noticed. Unfortunately, it also decreased his ability to see inside the vehicle. Crouching, he crept on, approaching from the rear. Why would the pusher show up this early?

Was there someone in there? Python was no longer sure. Maybe this wasn't the right car. Water dripped from his brim as he stood, wondering how he should proceed. He did a quick visual scan for Tommy. Surely the FBI was already here, even if he couldn't see them.

Somewhat confident he wasn't alone, Python treaded through growing puddles. A sudden deluge made seeing impossible. He lifted his hand and couldn't even make out his wiggling fingers. His knee hit something hard with a thud. Blindly searching, his fingers grazed icy metal and he realized it was the bumper of a car.

This wasn't good. He turned to run. Someone tackled him from behind. Muddy water splashed his face as he hit cement.

His arms were trapped. He shoved. Broke the hold, and twisted forward, ready to jump up. A second attacker shoved a thick cloth in his face. Fighting, he tore at the hands.

"Help me," the man yelled. The tackler came off the ground, wrapping his hands around the other man's.

Python struggled. His vision blurred as his arms became heavy. Everything went dark.

"I can't believe he set up another deal." Tommy trudged across the soggy ground in the driving rain. "You'd think having one gun pulled on you would be enough."

"We've got a problem."

"I know–" he started to answer.

Fallon sped off. He gave chase. Through a watery curtain, he saw two people throwing something into the back of a SUV. He kicked into high gear, running full out.

He and Fallon pulled their weapons simultaneously.

"Stop, FBI," she yelled.

He doubted the assailants could even hear them from this distance, as they jumped into the vehicle.

Fallon started firing. Tommy hesitated a split second before he pulled the trigger. The SUV screeched as it screamed out of the parking lot. Still firing, Fallon ran after it.

"Damn it! Damn it!" Stopping, he dropped his hands to his knees, breathing hard. "What'd he think he was doing?"

Fallon returned. "I radioed in all I could see. No license. You?"

He straightened. "No. Only black, maybe dark green, American-made SUV."

"That's what I called in."

The rain poured even harder as he motioned behind them. "Let's get going."

They both ran back, jumping into the car, soaking wet. Tommy hit the steering wheel as he started the vehicle. "Why the hell did he do it?"

"You already told me he had a hero complex. Why does this surprise you?" She pulled off her cap and shook her head.

Tearing out of the adjacent lot, he searched the road for the SUV. "You know, with that winning personality of yours, I can see why you're such a favorite with the department."

"I'm not here to be Ms. Congeniality."

"That's abundantly clear."

She adjusted the air to defrost the foggy windshield. "Why don't you stay on subject?"

"Damn it. Kendal's going to be pissed."

"Why does she have to know?"

Tommy whipped his head toward her, then back to the road. "What do you mean? She's primary."

"On the money laundering case. This isn't connected. Why disrupt the operation? We can take care of this situation, while she stays focused on hers."

"What do you propose we tell her happened to Python?"

"Exactly what she wanted to happen. He exposed a drug ring, thought he had completed his mission, and went home." She clapped her hands. "End of story."

"He wouldn't just walk away from his fans like that."

"Oh, yeah? He already did it once before, didn't he? I'm sure we can convince her he did it again."

Not sure if he liked the idea or not, Tommy stayed quiet. What if they didn't tell Kendal? It would keep her focused.

Knowing how personally involved she'd become, maybe it would be for the best.

Arriving around noon at the Von Braun civic center, Kendal went straight to the booker's office.

"I've got a job for you." As Rusen spoke, cigarette smoke licked out of his mouth like a snake's tongue. He must've decided that all those no smoking signs plastered all over the building were for someone else.

She waited in anticipation. This could be it. All he had to do was put her in position to learn how the money came in and out. All her hard work was about to pay off.

Last night had been difficult. The urge to call Owen and talk had been excruciatingly hard to squelch. All she wanted to do was assure herself that he was safe, even though she knew Tommy would never let anything happen to him. Realizing how attached she'd become to him made her profoundly glad she'd cut loose. This would make the sacrifice worth it.

"You're gonna train Shockra."

Blinking, she started to hold back her astonishment until she remembered she was Big K. "Excuse me?"

"I've been looking for a trainer who can handle the woman. Someone who won't back down." He eyed her up and down. "After what you did to her, I knew you were the one for me."

"That's why you hired me? To train Shockra?"

Another deep drag on his cigarette, and he coughed. "Yeah." He got up, hacking. He motioned for her to precede him through the door. "She's waiting. Let's go."

As they walked, Kendal reasoned that this was to be her proving ground. If this was what it took, then she'd do it. He shoved the curtain aside, and they entered the arena.

"What's that bitch doing here?" Shockra thrust her hip to the side and pointed.

Rusen grinned, his gold teeth sparkling in the bright lights. "She's your new trainer."

"You gotta be shitting me."

"Nope." Rusen lit a new cigarette from his old one. "She's it."

"That bitch hit me. You think I'm going to work with her now?"

"Not only are you going to work with her," he punched the air with his cigarette, "you're going to take her advice and practice it in the ring."

A strange look passed from Rusen to Shockra. Suddenly her face split into a too wide smile. "You decided to switch camps, Big K?" Dipping under the ropes, Shockra dropped down. "You ready to take a ride on the wild side?"

Rusen stepped in front of Kendal, halting Shockra's advance. "She ain't your plaything. She's here to make sure you get it together for the big win."

With her chest puffed, Shockra slapped it. "I'm the best."

"You used to be. Lately you've been lacking, and the fans are complaining." He shoved a finger under her nose. "Either you buck it up and get better, or your next fight will be a loss."

Shockra turned and climbed back into the ring without another word.

"She's all yours," Rusen said as he left.

Couldn't it have been anyone but Shockra? Kendal wondered. She levered herself up, then under the ropes.

"You can't teach me nothing."

Rising from her knees, Kendal stood. "We can start with proper speech."

"*Ooooh*," Shockra waggled her fingers, "you're so smart."

"In more ways than you know," Kendal added under her breath.

"What?"

"Nothing. Let's get to work."

Shockra inspected her nails. "I don't feel like it right now."

Kendal slammed into the wrestler's side. They went down in a tumble of arms and legs. Shockra snatched a hank of Kendal's hair. Feeling as if it was coming out at the roots, Kendal gritted, "I always knew you were a stiff worker."

"I am not." Shockra released her hold, rolled, and crouched.

Kendal did the same. The two circled each other. "You're soft. You're no better than a jobber."

"Your psychobabble ain't gonna work on me. I don't give a damn what you think." Shockra lunged.

Kendal dodged right, hooked Shockra's foot, and heaved up. The mat and Shockra's face met with a slap. She skidded to a stop on her cheek.

"Like I said, you're soft."

With a red streak dominating the right side of her face, Shockra bounced up. She balled her hands. "You're gonna pay for that."

"You think you can take me on?" Kendal was starting to enjoy herself.

"I don't think. I know." There was something too confident about Shockra's tone.

Or was it when Shockra glanced over Kendal's shoulder that caused Kendal's head to tingle? What was she, Spiderman? Knowing better than to look behind, Kendal tensed.

Shockra charged. Waiting, Kendal went left at the last moment. Clipped, she spun. She hit solid flesh and lashed out with her foot.

"*Umph*," a woman grunted. *Flame.*

"Grab her arms," Shockra ordered from behind.

Lashing out again, Kendal slammed her foot into a rock hard stomach. *Crap. This woman is solid.* "Can't take me on by yourself, Shockra?" Kendal rounded, working to keep both women in sight.

"I told you. You're not going to get me with all your talk." A fierce look in her eyes, Shockra pointed with her chin. "Get her."

Flame pounced from the left, while Shockra attacked from the right. Kendal gut-kicked Shockra, sending her to the mat. Then, she shoulder-slammed Flame.

Flame grasped her around the waist. Lifted, Kendal felt

like a windmill. Her stomach flipped when she was slammed to the mat. Grabbing her arm, Flame jerked it back in a perfect armbar submission move.

"I'm going easy on you 'cause you listened and got away from my man." Flame sat heavily on her back. "You want a piece of her?"

"You better believe I do." Shockra's voice shook, the anger was so intense. She stomped on Kendal's ankle.

Biting the inside of her cheek, Kendal kept herself from yelling out.

"You think you're so good. It's time you learned your lesson, bitch." Another stomp, this one to the back of the knee.

The taste of blood flooded Kendal's mouth. This was really starting to piss her off. She needed Flame to move. From her prone position, and with the two women behind her, Kendal needed to get the advantage thrown her way.

"Hey, what're you gals doing in there?" a man called from a distance.

"Just practicing," Shockra answered, as Flame adjusted her weight. Kendal shoved up. When Flame fought for balance, Kendal grabbed her calf and pulled forward. More off balance, Flame fell backwards. Kendal rolled and kicked her in the thigh.

Freed, she continued to roll until she could rise into a crouch. Hands extended, she watched as the women approached from both sides.

"What the fuck is going on here?" Rusen's rusty voice croaked.

Shockra immediately stopped. Flame followed her lead. Kendal waited, tense.

"Just practice."

"Then what's Flame doing in there? She ain't in your routine." Rusen stubbed out his cigarette.

"She was helping out."

"We don't need her. Get out."

Flame looked only at Shockra, who nodded. The big redhead climbed out of the ring.

"Looks like you need me to watch." Rusen sat in a folding chair.

"No, we're all right." Shockra leaned on the ropes, displaying her breasts over the top.

"No, you ain't. You're sloppy. You need to get back your edge. The only way it's going happen is through work. I want to see it."

Shockra huffed off the ropes, turning back to Kendal.

Unable to help it, Kendal grinned. "Looks like it's just you and me." She bobbed her eyebrows. "It's time you learned what a real workout is."

Chapter Ten

"Python's on the second floor of a condemned housing project," Fallon said, a finger pressed against her earpiece.

"How much further?" Tommy hit the gas even harder, mentally following the directions that had already been relayed to him. Finally their futile, all-night searching had paid off.

"ETA eight minutes."

"What backup do we have?" The tires hydroplaned on the slick pavement as they rounded the corner. Twisting the steering wheel, he got the car back under control.

"Three, plus locals. They're already there." She braced herself with a hand on the dash.

"Are they getting the layout?"

"Wait." She held up her left hand and scrawled in a notebook with her right. "They have the blueprints waiting for us."

"Good." He concentrated on increasing speed while still arriving safely.

"Over there." She pointed to where several federal and police vehicles were parked.

The rain, which had continued throughout the night, turned to a light drizzle as Tommy pulled in and parked. As he got out, he inserted his earpiece. "Are we ready?" he asked, walking up to the group.

"Yes, sir. We're all in place," a special agent answered.

"Where are the blueprints?"

"Here." Another special agent handed them to Fallon.

They spread the maps in the trunk of a car, sheltering them as much as they could from the rain. Over the next few minutes, they detailed out entrance locations and possible scenarios. Tommy stepped back. "Pierce and I will take the lead. We go in on three."

The agent nodded as he repeated the information to the rest of the team, already in place.

"Get the lead out, Boden. We have one minute to be in position." Fallon took off at a fast trot.

Instead of taking offense, he joined her. Together they slipped around the edge of a building. Through litter-filled, rank alleys, they ran three blocks.

Quickly, they entered a decrepit apartment building and crept up the stairs. Near the warped door, they met three policemen holding a battering ram. The only form of communication, nods.

Another team climbed the fire escape. Poised with fire axes and picks, they would infiltrate from the window.

The agent watching from across the street gave the signal through the earpiece. Tommy lifted his hand.

The men rushed. With quick efficiency, they hammered the door, busting it open.

Weapons drawn, Tommy and Fallon dashed inside.

"FBI!" Someone shouted from another room.

"Clear," an agent yelled next to him. The front room was empty.

Footsteps pounded toward them. Tommy gestured. Fallon leapt to one side of the doorway. He positioned himself on the other.

The men were closing in. He made eye contact with her and nodded. They waited, then jumped.

"Halt, FBI!" she yelled, her gun squarely on one man's chest. Tommy aimed at the second kidnapper.

The two men stopped, their gazes darting at the narrow hallway's walls, hunting for that nonexistent exit.

"Hands where we can see them." When they hesitated, he added, "Now!"

With clear reluctance, the men raised their hands halfway.

"Lay your weapons down." Fallon took a step toward the men. They bent down quickly.

"Slowly." She smacked the shoulder of one.

They complied as more agents and policemen rushed in, surrounding them.

"Where's Python?" Tommy asked.

"In the back." A cop motioned toward the far end of the hall. "He's still groggy."

Tommy left the others to take care of the arrests. Weaving his way between the boxes cluttering the cramped space, he hurried to the back. Spotlighted by the weak sunlight filtering in through the broken wood, Python sat in a chair, ropes coiled about his feet. The officer still in the room nodded as he left.

"Are you hurt?" Tommy knelt in front of him.

"I could be better." Python rubbed his head before pinching the bridge of his nose.

"Why in the name of God did you go there so early?"

Python glared up at him. "I wanted to see them arrive." With a groan, he dropped his head back into his hand. "Listen. It's over. I don't want to go over it."

Tommy stood, holstering his gun. "You're going to have to. Did they say why they kidnapped you?"

"I didn't come to until I was sitting here tied up." Python paused. "You know this is a little too reminiscent of when Mega was kidnapped. I've got a lot better understanding now of what it's like to be out of control."

"Python, focus." The pixie, Fallon, entered the room. "Did they say why they kidnapped you?"

Python frowned at her. What he had thought was a cute voice before, now grated on his every nerve. "You don't have to yell." His head hurt. "No."

"Do you know them?" Tommy asked.

"No. Can't you tone it down a bit? My head feels like a jackhammer is pounding on it."

"Okay, we'll keep it down."

With his words, Python's appreciation for Tommy increased.

"They're not from the circuit?" Fallon persisted.

"I don't know everyone. I already told you no. I hadn't ever seen them before."

Tommy looked at Fallon. "Make sure no one speaks to them before we do."

Without a word, she strode away.

Tommy held out his hand. "Let's go. We'll make a stop at the hospital."

Happy for the assistance, Python used his help to get up. "Hospital? Why?"

"You need to be checked out."

He lifted his head higher. "I'm feeling better."

Tommy shook his. "Don't even try. It's standard procedure."

"And you've made it past irritant status," Python muttered.

"What'd you say?"

"Nothing." As they exited the building, the two kidnappers were being put in the back of a patrol car in handcuffs. Fallon sprinted over to him and Tommy.

On the curb, Python watched as the men were driven away. "Is Kendal all right?"

Tommy whirled around. "Did they say something about her?"

Amazed at the agent's concern for his ex-trainer, Python shook his head. "I'm not sure."

Tommy grabbed his arm. "What do you mean, you're not sure?"

"I was groggy." He jerked away. "I could've dreamed it."

"Just tell me."

"If I wasn't dreaming, they talked about how this takes care of Big K, too." A bad feeling settled in the pit of his stomach.

"Anything else?"

Pausing, he tried to remember. "No." He poked Tommy in the chest. "You didn't answer me. Is Kendal all right?"

"As far as I know, she is."

He advanced on the young agent. "Can't you call someone? Have them check it out?"

Tommy held up his hand. "I can."

"Then do it."

"Fine, I will." He pulled out a cell phone. "Let's get out of here."

As Tommy and Fallon, who Python now knew was an agent, escorted him through dirty alleys, he wondered about Kendal. Did she worry about him last night, knowing he was missing? Or had she moved on completely?

Tommy slapped the phone closed. "She's fine."

"Who'd you talk to?"

"One of the security guards. She's in a practice session in the arena."

Once in the back of the car, Python checked his wrists. They were a little bruised from the ropes, but not much.

Fallon turned to look at him. "Do you have any idea why they didn't just kill you?"

The woman, who had seemed so delicate to him before, sure didn't mince words. "No."

She looked at Tommy. "Why would they keep him alive?" She turned back to Python. "Did they make contact with anyone else?"

"They did get a call. No names were used. I think that person told them what to do."

"Why do you say that?" Tommy met his gaze in the rearview mirror.

"Because they argued. The jerks wanted to get out of there. They didn't want to keep me overnight."

"Whoever they were talking to did," Fallon said.

Python nodded. "That's what I figured."

"Were they ever close enough to you so you could hear the voice on the phone?" she asked.

"No. They always called from another room."

"We've got to figure out who wanted you dead," Tommy said.

Python leaned forward. "You said that before. Why do you think they were going to kill me? Do they know I'm helping out the FBI?"

"Probably. That's why it'd be best if you step away."

"You mean leave the tour?" Python put his hand on the

back of Tommy's seat.

"Yes," Tommy said.

"Not possible." Even as the words left his mouth, Python couldn't believe he said them. "I'm staying."

"Not an option. You're getting off the tour now." The harsh words seemed almost funny coming out of such a tiny female.

"Sorry, no can do." Python sat back. "I'm not leaving Big K."

"Big K?" Fallon faced forward. "She doesn't even work with you anymore."

"Doesn't matter." He crossed his arms. "They mentioned her name, too. I'm going to be there in case she needs me. She's never been on the pro circuit before. I can't leave her vulnerable."

Tommy looked at him again in the mirror. "We'll protect her."

Python met his stare. "I don't think so. She doesn't even know you exist. She knows me. I'll be able to talk her into letting me stick around."

"She seems pretty tough to me," Fallon added. "I'll bet she can take care of herself."

If he didn't know better, Python would think they were tag teaming him. "She needs me. Nothing you can say will change my mind."

Fallon glanced at Tommy. The look that passed between the agents clearly said they didn't agree.

He didn't care. No one cared for Kendal like he did. Whether she liked it or not, he was going to be there for her.

"WELCOME, LADIES AND GENTLEMEN, TO TONIGHT'S EVENT," the announcer's voice thundered through the civic center. Kendal tapped her toe while she peeked through the curtain. She rolled her shoulders, giving her a sharp reminder that she was actually sore.

The workout with Shockra had been grueling. Kendal hadn't realized until then just how much Owen had held back even when she riled him. Shockra hadn't had any reservations when it came to hitting. Kendal's fighting skills had received a real honing this afternoon.

"I'm glad you're here."

She sucked in a quick breath and spun. "Owen." An incredibly handsome, delectable Owen stood very close. His delicious, pervasive scent encased her.

"You say that as if you're surprised."

"I heard you were off the schedule for tonight. I just assumed you'd decided to leave." She'd been surprised, then disappointed at learning the fact. She chastised herself for having those feelings since, after all, that had been the goal.

"It wasn't my idea to take me off."

"Really? Stubb did it?"

"No. There's something you need to know, Kendal." He took her arm. "Can you come with me for a moment?"

After glancing back out, she let the curtain drop. "Sure. For just a few minutes, though."

He escorted her to a small, empty room. There he paced away and back. "I don't know how to tell you this."

"What is it?" Knowing he was about to admit his connection to the FBI, Kendal tried to make it as easy as possible. "You're not going to tell me you're married or something?"

"Hell, no."

"Then just tell me."

"I was going to leave the circuit. I had to come back."

Somewhat confused at his tone, internally she went on alert. "Why?"

"I'm working with the FBI."

"Excuse me? You're working with the Feds? Why? What do they want?"

He rubbed his head. "I can't say?"

"You can't say?" She threw her hands in the air. "You get taken off the rotation, show up here anyway, tell me you're working with the Feds, and now you can't tell me more? Why'd you bother me at all?"

"There's something you need to know."

"You mean there's something you can say?"

"You're not making this easy."

"Am I supposed to?"

"After all we've been through together?" He crowded closer. "Yeah."

"Fine." She retreated a safe distance away. "What is it you have to tell me?"

"First off, the FBI didn't convince me to come back. They wanted me to leave."

Staying in character of her cover, she knew she needed to sound confused. "What do you mean, they wanted you to leave? You just said they wanted you to work for them."

"That was before."

"Before? Before what?" she asked.

"They're the reason I came back in the first place."

"You never even wanted to win?" Kendal made sure her voice held all the disbelief she could muster.

"Not at first. Then I did. You made me want it." Shaking his head, he approached her. "This isn't what I wanted to tell you."

"There's more?"

"Yes. The rest is about you."

"About me?" *Damn, how'd he learn?*

"I don't want you to get alarmed." He grabbed her arms. "Last night a couple guys ganged up on me."

The unexpected news made her frown real. "What do you mean 'ganged up on you?'"

"I guess you could say they sorta kidnapped me."

"Kidnapped you? Here?" Truly surprised, her brows rose. She inspected him from head to toe.

Dropping his hold on her, he stepped back. "They used chloroform."

His affronted answer told her he'd misinterpreted her concern for disbelief that someone could abduct him. "How'd they–"

"Would you shut up, and let me tell you what happened?"

Using his misinterpretation to her benefit, she said, "Fine. Tell me what happened."

"I set up a drug deal."

She opened her mouth, and he put a finger on her lips.

"I said let me finish. I was helping the FBI bust a drug ring. Somehow the dealers found out what I was up to. I think they were trying to kill me or something."

"But–"

He silenced her again. "The worst part is, now they're after you."

"After me?"

"That's right." Grasping her shoulders, he shook her. "You've got to come back and work with me. There's no other way to keep you safe."

"Come back to work with you?" Kendal couldn't believe all her hard work to get him out of here had been sabotaged. "You're not leaving the tour?"

"How can I leave with you in danger?" He shook her again. "I could never do that. I love you."

All the air in her lungs seemed to rush out, and none could force its way back in. "Wha–"

"This isn't how I wanted to tell you. You had to know, Kendal. The way we are together. Everything we've meant to each other. Don't you have something to say?"

Even having heard it before, after their lovemaking, didn't reduce the impact of hearing those three words in the light of day. "You've caught me off guard."

Letting go of her, he moved away. "That's all you can say?"

She wanted so bad to say *I love you.* She couldn't, it wouldn't be fair. Owen didn't know who she really was. When he found out how she'd misled him all this time, she didn't want to even contemplate the pain he would feel.

"I want to say more. I really do." She took a step toward him, then stopped. "I can't. Not now."

"What do you mean, not now? Then when?" He shook his head. "I don't understand."

"Big K?" The stench of cigarettes almost beat Rusen's voice into the room.

Her eyes never leaving Owen's, she answered, "In here."

Rusen popped his head in. "Python. Didn't know you came tonight." The grungy manager waddled inside. "What're you trying to do? Entice my employee back to your camp?"

"Yes."

"Of course not," Kendal said at the same time.

Rusen cackled. "I can see you're not succeeding." Pulling out a cigarette, he lit it, ignoring the no smoking sign over the door as always. "Good. Big K, you're needed. It's time."

"I'll be right there."

Rusen didn't leave. "Now."

She pierced him with her most lethal stare. "I said, I'll be right there."

Rusen shot her an answering sharp look before starting to shuffle out. "Don't be long."

After heaving a mental sigh, she focused on Python. "I have to do this. Whatever else you think, always remember, I had to do this." Going to him, she caressed his cheek, then went to the door.

"Kendal."

His soft call stopped her. Unable to take much more, she kept her back to him.

"Just tell me you love me."

The pleading and pain in his voice almost broke her. She stiffened her shoulders, even as tears started to trickle down her cheek. Without another word, she left.

"How dare you not inform me." Kendal wanted to put her fist through the pretty boy agent's face. With amazing effort, she restrained herself. Either this wrestling cover was starting to sink in or her true nature was taking over.

"Need to know, Smart." Tommy shifted, putting his back to the inside of the driver's door.

"Need to know? You're throwing need to know in my face?" This rookie was going to tell her she wasn't privy to the information? She stabbed at her chest. "I'm primary on this case. I decide who learns what."

"Calm down. Think rationally. You had a job to do. Python's capture wasn't a part of it anymore. You didn't need the distraction."

Just because he was right didn't make her any more receptive. "Just be glad you got him back in one piece."

"Is that the only reason you wanted to talk to me?" he asked with just enough superiority to raise her hackles a few more notches.

"No," she drawled, working to calm herself. "I want to know what you've learned from the abductors?"

"Nothing. Yet."

She pulled out a small notebook. "Any evidence from the apartment or the SUV?"

"I see you got briefed on the details."

The censure she heard helped to make up for some of the earlier irritation. She smiled. "Since you didn't feel it necessary to let me know what was going on, I took it upon myself to get the information."

He crossed his arms. "All you had to do was ask."

"Now you're going to get offended because I went over your head?"

Tommy didn't answer.

"Then I suggest in the future, you don't keep me in the dark."

"We thought at the time it'd be best."

"We?"

He hesitated. "Pierce and I."

Kendal slapped the notebook closed. "Is that where you got the bright notion not to inform me?"

"She suggested it would be best if you weren't distracted by the extra details."

She shouldn't bring it up, but knowing the over-ambitious Pierce had a hand in keeping her out of the loop irritated her even more. "You knew more, Tommy."

"That's why I agreed."

"Excuse me?" Had she heard him right?

"You and I both know if SAC knew how involved you've become with Python, he'd have yanked you out of the operation."

Again, his being right didn't make it easier to accept. "Let's move on. I know you brought the men here. When is the interrogation going to start?"

"As soon as we're done."

"If that's a hint, it wasn't very subtle." She punched him in the arm. "You'll let me know the minute you learn something."

"Yes."

"I'm a professional, Tommy." She grabbed the door handle. "I haven't given you any reason to doubt I'll do my job."

"No, you haven't."

"Good. Then keep me informed." She started to leave.

Tommy put his hand on her arm. "How close are you to getting evidence on the money laundering?"

"Rusen's testing me." She rolled her shoulders. "I'm whipping Shockra into shape. I think when I prove myself by working with her, I'll be in. Then it's just time."

He tightened his hold. "You'll let me know the minute you need backup."

"You'll be my first call."

He released her. "I better be."

Feeling better after letting her feelings be known, she opened the door. She climbed out, then bent down to peer in. "Do me a favor, Boden."

The hand about to turn on the motor halted. "Anything."

"Find out who's after Owen before he gets to Indianapolis." She swallowed her pride. "He can't die."

With an intense stare, he fiercely shook his head. "That's not going to happen, Smart. Not with us watching him."

"Who put you up to this?" Tommy was pretty sure the two suspects had not set up the kidnapping by themselves. Basically, they were dumber than dirt, hired muscle with little between their ears except air. Which is why they had been able to hold the men overnight without booking them.

He had picked Fritz, the one he hoped was the weaker link, to interview first. Fallon sat in a chair across the table staring at the thug, while Tommy paced the room.

Fritz stayed silent.

Tommy leaned over him from the side. "You think your pal's going down for this all by himself? You think he isn't in the other room spilling his guts?"

Fritz glanced at Fallon's steely glare. "What's wrong with you? Why you keep staring like I'm a freak or sumthin'?"

She only raised a brow.

"She doesn't like you very much, bro." Tommy leaned even closer. "And when Special Agent Pierce doesn't like someone, she just stares at them. You know, kinda like a rat in a cage."

He stepped away. "I wouldn't push her if I were you. She's got a short fuse. You don't want to get on her bad side."

The guy jerked his chin. "I ain't done nuthin' to her. Why would I care?"

She continued to stare.

"Make her stop. She's creepin' me."

"There's only one way to make her stop. Tell me who put you up to this."

The guy glanced at him, but his gaze shot back to Fallon, glaring at her as hard as she was staring at him. "What's in it for me?"

"Nothing." Tommy leaned back against the wall. It wasn't like anyone was looking at him. "We've got you dead to rights. The only thing I can do is possibly keep you out of maximum security."

"Quit staring at me." Fritz's eyes never left Fallon. "Don't you speak?"

In a well-calculated show, a slow smile edged its way across her face.

"You're weird." Perspiration beaded his forehead. "You hear me? A damn weirdo."

The antsier the man became, the better Tommy began to feel. "If you want to get out of here, you better start talking."

Finally the man's gaze darted over to him. "I don't know who it is."

Shoving off the wall, Tommy walked to the table. "How can you not know who it is?"

"He called, left us some money and instructions."

"It's a man."

Fritz rubbed the bottom of his nose with his knuckle. "Don't know. Could be a woman with a scratchy voice."

Frustrated, Tommy wanted to punch the wall. "What can you tell me?"

"The number I called."

Dumbfounded, he stared at the man for a second. "You have a phone number?"

Fritz pulled out a tattered piece of paper from his pocket. He held it out. "Right here."

Taking it, Tommy went and knocked on the door. It opened, and he handed the slip to another agent. "How'd they know to contact you for this type of work?"

"I dunno." Using his knuckle again, Fritz swiped the base of his nose, then inspected his finger. "I've never done nuthin' like this ever before."

Tommy wanted to roll his eyes at the blatant lie. "So, someone you don't know just picks you and your pal out of the crowd."

"I guess so."

Suddenly, Fallon slammed her hands on the top of the table. The big guy jolted backwards, almost falling out of his chair.

"Do I, or my partner, look stupid to you? Cut the crap. We know you've got a rap sheet thicker than Webster's dictionary. If you want a snowball's chance for special consideration when you're in front of the judge, then you'd better stop yanking us around and start talking."

Fritz threw his hands out in front. "Hey, back off. I'm telling ya everything I know."

"No, you aren't." She jumped up and looked like she was about to crawl over the top of the table.

His eyes went wide. "Get back. I'm telling ya everything."

A shared look and Fallon went out through the door, with Tommy following right on her heels. Able to watch and listen to the perp through the two-way mirror, Tommy rubbed the back of his neck. "He's not breaking."

She put her face close to the window. "Give it time. He's close."

"I'm not sure he'll crack."

A knock, and an agent thrust a piece of paper inside.

Fallon turned. "What is it?"

"They've traced the phone number." He grinned. "That crack is about to split. We've just been handed the crowbar."

Dry ice smoke billowed from hidden stacks at the sides of the black curtain.

"LADIES AND GENTLEMEN, WHAT YOU'VE ALL BEEN WAITING FOR. IT'S TIME FOR THE MAIN EVENT."

The crowd roared their approval by stomping feet, clapping hands, and shouting. Along with the pounding rock music, the noise deafened the ears. Tonight's attendance of fifty thousand was packed into one end of the Indianapolis RCA dome, concentrating the noise, while the other half of the coliseum was roped off with a black curtain backdrop. On Saturday, at the sold-out main event, all seats would be filled. The ultimate culmination, as the champions of each division wrestled.

The music blared, the beat thrumming through concrete. His body vibrating with the intensity, Python felt invincible as he waited for his cue. This was his last battle before the Brawl. Soon the title would be his again. A tremor of fear flew up his spine. Wasn't this the same way he'd felt the day Terror had died?

No. He slammed his hand into the cinderblock wall.

Kendal had told him Terror went through the ropes, not over. It hadn't been his fault. He was in control.

"BACK TO TAKE WHAT WAS NEVER TAKEN AWAY FROM HIM. THE ONE AND ONLY, PYTHON!"

The curtain spread, and a spotlight speared him. *I am in control.* Python lifted his fisted hands high. Strutting down the entry ramp through the fog, he bobbed his head. When the commentator approached with a microphone, he went through his litany of trash talk without thought. That would be the one thing he wouldn't miss for a second. A necessary evil of the wrestling world.

Ducking, he climbed into the ring. As the crowd went crazy, he in turn jumped up on the ropes on each side, heightening the fervor. Python soaked in the energy. They wanted him to win. He was their champion.

"ONCE AGAIN HE DARES TO TRY AND BEAT THE BEST. THE MAN YOU LOVE TO HATE, JAMMER!"

Jammer swaggered to the ring amidst boos and jeers, with a smattering of cheers. He spewed his brand of intimidation into the microphone. The crowd's booing rose to a crescendo. There would be no need to dub in more sound with the heat machine for this match.

Joining him in the ring, Jammer bounced from side to side leering at the crowd. When he swung by, he stomped on Python's foot. Most wrestlers played a part. Jammer lived his. There was no acting.

The referee brought the two of them to the middle of the ring. The dance began. As scripted, Python took a beating through the first few minutes. It was time to make his move.

Her hands damp, Kendal scrutinized the match and the crowd. She knew the routine. Once Owen took the offensive, he would have a spot move, the high point of the match. The finisher, his last move, was designed to drive the crowd insane, making them stream in droves to the Brawl.

None of that gave her any comfort, knowing someone was after Owen. He was scheduled to win all the way to the top. Kendal prayed he'd change his mind. If only he would throw an early fight. All she wanted was for him to be far away from danger.

That left the pressing question of who? Did they want him dead? Or was he only in danger because he'd come back to the circuit?

Owen started his comeback. A series of well-choreographed moves went as planned. Kendal's shoulders stayed tensed. It would seem impossible to hurt him in the ring, but they'd tried before. What better alibi could you have than an accidental death during a match?

"Juice," yelled a man as he pumped his hand in the air.

Blood? Kendal rushed to the side of the ring, the trickle of fear becoming a full stream. Was Owen bleeding?

The match had not been set up with blades. As far as she knew, neither Owen nor Jammer had been dressed for fake bleeding.

As Owen closed in, the left side of his face dripped red. *No*, her mind screamed. *This had better be fake*, was all she could think. She ran around the ring, keeping Owen and his damaged head in sight.

He came out of the corner. He slammed into Jammer in an avalanche move. The bodies broke apart. More blood spurted from Owen's arm. This was not planned. Jammer had a blade, and he wasn't afraid to use it.

Kendal climbed up the side of the ring. She could hear the announcer hyping her unexpected appearance. "Ref! Stop the match," she yelled over the noise.

The referee ignored her. The two wrestlers clashed again. This time Owen dropped Jammer in a front slam. Owen jerked his leg in a hanging kneebreaker. With his arm, he wiped his face, smearing blood everywhere.

"Owen," Kendal yelled, trying to get his attention. She moved around the edge of the ring.

"No," the referee shouted. "You have to tag from his corner."

Tag? Of course, that's what she could do. Quickly, she went back to Owen's corner and stripped off her heels. Stubb grabbed them from the edge. Straining, she stretched over the ropes. "Owen. Tag me!"

Chapter Eleven

Blind from the blood flooding his eyes, Python heard his name. His real name. *Kendal?*

"You hear me, you stubborn idiot? Get over here."

That was his Kendal all right. Letting go of Jammer, Python turned toward her voice. Jammer twisted, grabbed Python's legs, and slammed him back to the ground. Razor-sharp pain stabbed his thigh. "Damn! What're you doing?"

Jammer jumped up. "Taking you out."

Unable to see, Python swung blindly, hitting air.

"Owen! Get your ass over here."

What did she expect to do? They didn't ring a bell in wrestling and take a break. That was boxing.

"If you don't get over here, I swear I'll never let you live it down. Do you hear me?"

Circling, Python wiped at his eyes, trying to determine Jammer's location.

A slam to his back, and Python went flying to the ropes. Jammer hit him again with a hot shot. His head hanging over the ropes, Python's back burned from a new slice. "You're not going to get away with this, Jammer."

His body plastered on the back of Python's, the burly wrestler laughed. "I already am."

"Owen! Reach right. Extend your hand!"

What did she think she could do for him? Maybe she had a rag. Breaking Jammer's hold, Python reached out until he felt the tips of Kendal's fingers.

"I'm in," Kendal yelled. "Get him when I push."

"What's going on?" Python asked when the weight disappeared off his back. "Where's the towel?"

"You're out."

His vision still blurred, Python frowned. "Out?" Another shove. Someone grabbed at his ankles.

"Get outta there, boy." Stubb tugged on his calves.

Not knowing what else to do, Python felt his way down the ropes, then slipped out of the ring.

Kendal circled Jammer.

"This ain't in the script, bitch."

"Yeah? Well, neither was your little slice and dice routine."

"You're just gonna get the same, Big K." He swung a cupped right hand at her.

Bingo, the razor's location. "Except I know what you're doing."

"That's not gonna help you none. You're just gonna get that pretty face of yours all cut up."

"You're about to get your butt kicked like never before." She didn't care about rules or standards. They could call the match for all she cared. This wrestler was about to learn just how well she could fight.

She snap kicked his right hand. Blood spurted when Jammer flicked his wrist. She followed the silver flash. The razor landed close to Stubb.

"Get it." Kendal pointed and he snatched the tiny, lethal weapon.

"Looks like the odds just went in my favor."

Holding his bleeding palm, Jammer charged. She grabbed his arm and slung him into the ropes. When he ricocheted, she stiff-armed him in the throat. He dropped to his knees, choking.

"Kendal!"

She half-turned toward Owen, keeping Jammer in sight. Red streaks still marred Owen's face and neck, but his eyes were clear.

"Tag me."

She shook her head.

"You've got to. I need to finish the match."

Jammer staggered to his feet.

"Tag me!"

Since Jammer no longer had a weapon, she rushed over and slapped Owen's hand. She slipped out of the ring. With a huge smile, he climbed up on the top rope.

And dove.

This was his finisher. A combination four hundred fifty degree splash frankensteiner ending with his knee planted in Jammer's back.

The crowd came to their feet applauding.

After putting the spike heels back on, Kendal stalked out of the arena. Owen would have plenty of attention from the announcers interviewing him. She knew she could count on the UCAs to take care of him. She needed some answers, and she needed them now.

"Good show."

Duty called at the worst times. Even though Rusen sounded sarcastic, she decided to play dumb. "Thanks."

He puffed on a cigarette. "You want to explain why, as my employee, you went into the ring for Python?"

"It was a shoot." She'd heard about shoots, matches where one wrestler varies from the script and intentionally tries to hurt another. This was the first time she'd seen one.

"You thought it was your problem?"

Did the man have no compassion? "Jammer was slicing Python."

"Yeah." He shrugged. "It's a sure ticket off the tour. Why do you care? You got a conscience?"

Damn. The one thing a criminal doesn't want a cohort to have. "No. I wanted in on the action."

"The blood intrigued you?"

"I like not following a script."

He laughed and hacked up phlegm. "Good. That's what I want to hear. Follow me. There's something I need to do. You can help."

Nodding, she fell into step with him. She wanted to find out if Tommy was any closer to learning who was out to get Owen. With Jammer doing what he did in the ring, all hands pointed to Shockra. Why would she expose her supposed partner in wrestling like that?

They turned the corner. Rusen went in the direction of an exit.

"We're leaving?"

"Yeah." He pushed open the door. "I've got to get ready for tomorrow's final match. You're just the type of person who can help me pull it off."

Hands on the table, Tommy leaned over. "We know you've been calling a prepaid cell phone. It's only a matter of time before we track it back to the owner."

He paused to let the information sink into Fritz's rock head. Hopefully, the man wouldn't know if the perp used cash to purchase the phone, the chances of learning the identity of the buyer decreased substantially. Plus, the person who'd bought the phone from a reputable dealer might not be the same person using it now.

"When we track the person down, the time for deals will be over." He put his nose inches away from Fritz's face, and got a heavy dose of the man's vile body odor. "If you're hoping for any leniency from a judge, you'd better speak now."

The sweat stains under Fritz's arms grew. "I only know it's a woman."

Knowing the smell was only going to get worse, Tommy moved to the other side of the table. "A fact you didn't know yesterday?"

"I forgot."

Not very likely. A night in jail always seemed to help a criminal's memory. "Why is she after Python?"

"She doesn't want him to win."

Tommy sat, opening his palms, a gesture known to show openness to the subconscious. "You're telling me she's willing to kill him to keep it from happening?"

"I don't know nuthin' 'bout killing him."

Leaning forward, Tommy cocked his head. "What? You were only supposed to kidnap him?"

"That's right."

Tommy decided to continue the amicable, *I'm your friend,* routine. "I don't believe it."

"I don't care what you believe. It's the truth." He frowned, looking at the floor.

"You don't know who the woman is."

Lifting his head, Fritz nodded. "That's right."

"She leaves money, you pick it up." Tommy drummed his fingers.

"That's right."

"You have no idea who she is."

The guy shrugged. "I could guess."

"You have an idea?" Not sure the thug's opinion would matter, Tommy would listen to any theory.

"Me and Bruno, we were thinking."

"That's a scary thought," Fallon said as she entered the room.

"Fritz is about to tell us who he thinks his employer is."

"Then I got here just in time." She swiveled a chair and sat in it backward. "Go ahead."

"It's just a guess."

"It's all right. Anything you say can help." Tommy patted the table to reassure him.

"Shockra."

"Why?" he asked.

Fritz shrugged again. "It kinda sounds like her."

Without a word, Fallon got up and left.

"Okay. We'll check into it." When Tommy followed, she was waiting just on the other side of the door.

"Could be Shockra," she said.

"Why?"

"A woman bought the phone. A big-haired blonde."

Excitement started playing a vigorous round of handball in the pit of his stomach. "What are the chances it was a wig?"

"Could be." She flipped open a notebook. "Why?"

"The woman who murdered Cook was a frizzy-haired blonde."

"The one Smart smashed into the side of a building?" Fallon shook her head. "She'd have a scar. Something Shockra doesn't have."

"How can you tell under all the makeup?"

She nodded. "Good point."

He turned toward the two-way mirror. "We need to tell Smart."

"You contact her. I'll check back at the store where the phone was bought and see if he can remember if the woman was wearing a wig." She pointed her pen at Fritz. "What about him?"

"Give him over to the locals. Let them put him in the system. He can take his chances in court."

"Got a real heart, don't you?" she asked.

"For the people who deserve it? Yes. For scum that lie through their teeth to get a deal? No."

She stuffed the notebook in her pocket. "Which particular lie are we talking about?"

"The one that he wasn't going to kill Python."

A sly smile broke across her face. "You really admire him, don't you?"

"He's a hero. He deserves to realize it."

She patted him on the arm. "Go call Smart. If I'm hearing you right, we've got to get to Indianapolis and save Superman."

Python searched the teeming crowd for Kendal. Where had she gone? After coming in like an avenging angel and saving him, he wanted to say thank you.

Who was he kidding? He wanted to do a lot more than that. He wanted to hold her, kiss her, make love. There's no way she didn't love him, after what she'd just done. If it was the last thing he ever did, he was going to convince her they belonged together.

"Python, come with me." Stubb pulled on his arm.

He didn't budge. "I'm looking for Kendal."

"Who?"

Looking over the top of Stubb's head, he continued to

search. "Big K."

"I think she left."

He dropped his gaze to Stubb's face. "Left? I wanted to see her."

Stubb tugged. "Come on."

Python allowed himself to be pulled along. "Where are you taking me?"

"To the med tech. You need stitches." His hand held out, Stubb cut a path through the crowd.

"I don't need stitches."

"You at least need cleaning up." Stubb glanced back. "Stop your caterwauling."

"I'm not complaining." He frowned, but Stubb had already turned around. "Besides, what kind of word is caterwauling?"

"It don't matter." Stubb opened the door to the coliseum first aid station. "Here we are."

A pungent antiseptic smell plagued the entire room. A nurse came out. As soon as he saw Python, he hustled him into a chair and started to poke at his cuts.

Python looked at Stubb. "Go find Big K." Sudden fire scalded his head. "*Aargh.*" He jerked. "Go easy with that stuff."

The nurse glanced up, not pausing from dabbing the wounds with the drenched cotton ball.

"I don't know where she went." Stubb hopped from one foot to the other.

"Go find her."

The nurse tapped Python's thigh. "I need you to hold the edges together."

Python scowled at the nurse's bald spot. Grinding his teeth, he grabbed the edges of his skin around a cut on his thigh.

The nurse opened a sterile package. "All you're going to need are butterfly bandages."

"You gonna be able to go on tomorrow night?" Stubb asked.

"Why wouldn't I be?"

"Considering you took quite a beating tonight, I wasn't sure."

"I'm going on tomorrow night." Python poked the nurse. "Are you finished yet?"

"Just about." One last bandage was placed on his head. "Done."

Python stood. "I'm going to find Kendal." Stubb scurried alongside as he marched down the hallway.

"I told you I think she left."

Not slowing, he turned the corner. "Where'd she go?"

"Someone said with Sloan."

That stopped him. "With Sloan?"

"That's what I heard."

"Where's she staying?"

"I–"

He grabbed Stubb by the neck. "Don't even say you don't know, because you do. If there's one thing you live to do, it's put your nose in everyone's business." He released him. "Now, tell me where she is."

What a bust. Kendal had thought she was on her way. Instead, she'd spent the night counting tickets and packaging them for tomorrow's night event. She looked down at her fingers. She'd never known them to be so dry.

Tired, sore, and disappointed, she let herself into the hotel room, then flicked on the light. The bed looked so inviting, she almost collapsed for the night. Instead, she sat and freed her poor aching feet.

Feeling dirty from her bout in the ring and from being surrounded by piles of rectangular chunks of cardboard, she dragged her body to the shower. The bits of leather she wore as clothes fell to the ground.

Under the steaming spray, she relaxed as the hot water took the chill out of her bones. With renewed vigor, she washed her hair and body. One last rinse and she could climb into bed.

Turning off the water, she searched blindly for a towel wanting to keep maximum heat inside the stall. Her hand hit flesh. She jerked back.

"It's me, Kendal. It's only me."

Hearing Owen's voice, she relaxed her attack stance. "Give me a towel." Her voice came out harsh.

He tried to pull back the curtain.

She held it closed. "A towel."

"I've already seen you."

"That was before. Just hand me a damn towel over the top."

"What's the matter with you?"

After wrapping herself, she yanked back the curtain. "You scared the hell out of me. What'd you expect?"

"I thought you'd be happy to see me."

"If you had knocked on my door and not sneaked in here like a groupie, I might've been." She brushed past him out to the sink. A glance in the mirror left her grateful she hadn't had the energy to remove her contacts.

Crap. Now she was going to have to dry her hair to keep it from being wavy. Slapping straightening gel in her hand, she slathered every strand.

"What're you doing?"

"I have to dry my hair. I can't go to bed with a wet head."

Owen's eyes blazed. A look she'd come to know very well. She grabbed the hair dryer and plugged it in. As the hot air blew, she tried not to keep looking at him. She couldn't help herself.

He sat on the bed, his eyes never straying from her. Their intensity burned a path all over her towel-clad body. As fast as she could, Kendal finished. "I need to put some clothes on."

He got up, then walked over to her. "No, you don't."

"You shouldn't be here."

"Yes, I should." His warm hands grasped her naked shoulders.

"You've been hurt." Her mind frantically searched for anything to make her body stop responding.

"I'm fine."

"I don't want to hurt you."

"You could never hurt me."

How wrong he was. Maybe not physically, but emotionally, she knew in time he would be crushed at all the deception. "We can't."

"Yes," he lowered his head, "we can."

Hot. The kiss overheated as soon as their lips touched. It had been so long, and Python wanted her. Wanted her now.

Changing the angle, his tongue delved deeper. She met him thrust for thrust. "Kendal," he murmured, as he tasted his way down her throat.

"Yes." As her head fell back, she held his, with her fingertips rubbing just below his ears.

The erotic touch sizzled all the way to his toes. "I've missed you." His hand skimmed over her shoulder, ending on a towel-coated breast. She surged forward, putting more of the lush, warm orb into his palm.

"Yes, Owen."

"I want you naked." He stripped away the towel, then held her away. "You're beautiful. I–"

She put her fingers on his mouth. "Stop. You talk way too much."

Warm, soft lips teased his. Python grasped her naked rear and pulled her tightly to him. She squirmed against his jean-clad erection.

He broke the intensely sensual kiss, nuzzling her neck. "I've missed you."

"I've missed you too." She pushed him backwards. He let himself be hustled to the edge of the bed. Her hands snapped open his pants. "You need to be naked." She dragged both his jeans and shorts down, letting them pool at his feet.

"You think so?" He grinned.

"No thinking about it. I know it." She matched his grin as she pulled up his shirt. Reaching behind, he grasped the thin material and dragged it over his head. Her hands, followed immediately by her lips, explored his bare chest.

Wet, slick kisses rained over him before she centered her attention on his nipple. He clutched her hips and fell backwards. Bouncing once, they settled with Kendal straddling him. Her hair fanned over his shoulders as she went right back to her attack.

He groaned. "You're killing me."

Not lifting her head, she licked a slow path across his aching, sensitive skin. "That's the idea." Her muffled voice couldn't hide the obvious smile.

Feeling great even with his multiple bandages, he lifted her face. "Come here."

With immediate acquiescence, she crawled up his body. "You want something?"

"You."

Grabbing his ears, she fused their mouths. Her persistent tongue nudged at his lips until all he could think about was letting her in. Their tongues danced an erotic salsa and his *johnson* jerked. She grasped it, stroking him.

Breaking apart, she ripped open a foil packet. She must've gotten it out of his pants. With a slowness bordering on torture, she rolled the thin layer of latex over him.

The kiss and their bodies heated. Python rolled, ending with her underneath. He poised himself at her entrance.

He paused, even as she urged him forward by raising her hips. He held her gaze as he pushed inside. She arched to accommodate him.

He waited again, letting her softness envelop him. "You feel so good."

"So do you."

He wanted to tell her he loved her. He wanted to make her understand they could have the perfect life together. He knew she wouldn't admit it. Kendal thought her life belonged on the circuit. He would make it his mission to prove her wrong.

He started to move, and she wrapped her legs tighter around his waist. As his rhythm increased, so did the moans escaping her throat. Slipping his hands beneath her, he adjusted the angle for an even deeper penetration.

"Oh, yes." Her muscles tensed and throbbed around him.

"I want you, Kendal." Python pumped even harder. "I–love–you." He fought to hold himself back, but the pleasure was too great. Just as his body started to convulse, she milked him intimately as he poured into her.

Exhausted, he hugged her tight, not wanting to let her go. He loved everything about her. The sounds she made, their mingled smell while and after they made love, and how beautiful she looked when she climaxed.

Wiggling, she pushed against him and he slid to lie beside her. She began to play with his chest hair. He moved her hair off her forehead, then kissed her temple. "I've missed you."

She rubbed her nose over his shoulder before kissing the same spot. "You've already said that. I missed you too."

He ran his hand through her hair while she continued to nuzzle. "We can be together."

She stilled. "We are together."

"I want more." He lifted her face so he could see her eyes. "Come back. Be my trainer."

She lifted up on an elbow. "I don't want you back in the ring."

"You don't?" He squeezed her arms before lifting her to lie on him. "Okay. I'll quit right after the Brawl."

"No. Didn't tonight tell you anything? I want you out now."

"Adamant, aren't you?" Unable to help it, he smiled. "I like it. I will, on one condition."

Smiling back, she kissed him. "What condition is that?"

"You leave too."

She shook her head as she moved away. "I can't."

Not liking the distance growing between them both physically and mentally, he grasped her shoulders. "Yes, you can."

"Owen, I have a job to finish. I can't walk away from it."

"I'll take care of you. You don't need to stay."

Breaking out of his embrace, Kendal pushed to sit up.

"Why can't you just go back to Baltimore?" She pulled the sheet around her breasts.

"I think you know why. I've said it enough times."

Unable to look him in the eyes, Kendal could only stare at her hands.

"You've never said it back."

Why did he have to do this now? Damning the tears that threatened, Kendal looked up. "I care for you, Owen. I couldn't be with you if I didn't."

He sat up, then swung his legs over the side. "I'm beginning to wonder."

"What's that supposed to mean?"

"I thought we had something special. I thought you were starting to come around to loving me." Putting his back to her, he left the bed. "It looks like I'm wrong." He pulled on his shorts.

"You don't understand."

With his hands outstretched, he turned to face her. "Then make me understand. Explain it to me."

"I can't. You just have to trust me that I care–a lot."

"That's all you're willing to give me?" His hands dropped, much as she was sure his spirit had.

Kendal gripped the sheet tighter, wishing she could say more. "It's all I *can* give."

"Can or will?"

"Can." She shook her head. "If I could give you more, I would."

In two strides he was back to the side of the bed. "Quit comparing me to your past relationships. I mean what I say."

Confused, Kendal blinked. "What're you talking about?"

"Isn't that why you won't love me?" His hand lifted toward her face, but fell before touching her. "I'm not whoever you're judging me by. You need to give us a chance."

Could he make this any harder? "I've told you. You don't really know me."

The bed dipped when he sat on the edge. "I know I love you, Kendal." He fingered the edges of her black hair. "I told myself, I'd never fall for a woman who looked like you. I convinced myself, I wanted the white picket fence and minivan. I'm willing to adjust my dream. I'm willing to stay in the wrestling world for you. I'll do anything to keep you in my life."

Shaking her head to keep from losing her control, Kendal dislodged her hair. "Don't."

"Don't what?"

"Don't be so accommodating." She smoothed the sheets in her lap. "You deserve the life you crave. You shouldn't change for anyone, especially me."

"It's what you do when you love someone."

Jerking her gaze to his, she glared. "Stop saying that."

"Why? It's the truth."

"No, it isn't."

Owen leapt to his feet, then paced away. "How can you argue with what I know I feel?"

Exasperated and angry at how out of control the situation had become, Kendal yelled, "Because you don't know the real me. How many times do I have to say it?"

Striding back, he put his face inches from hers. "I just told you, you're the opposite of my dream woman. I still fell in love. What more could I possibly learn that would make me fall out of love with you?"

Gaining control, she reached out, but in a duplication of his earlier action, she didn't touch his face. "Please, just leave the circuit while you're still alive. Wasn't tonight's experience in the ring enough to convince you to get out?"

"You were there to cover my back."

"I might not be there the next time."

"I think you will."

"You can't count on me."

He stepped back and searched the floor for something. "Is that what you're trying to tell me? That you aren't long term?" He picked up his jeans.

"I can't be the woman you want me to be."

He held out the pants, shoved each leg inside, then

stopped. "I told you I can adjust."

"I don't want you to adjust. I want you to be happy."

He pulled the jeans all the way up. "And if I decide you're the one that makes that happen?"

"I'm not."

He turned his back and bent down to retrieve his shirt. "And what just happened? It meant nothing special to you?"

"It's great sex. Why do you have to make more of it?"

His head popped through the neck, and he looked over his shoulder. "You mean that, don't you?"

"What do I have to do? Hit you with a two-by-four?"

"No." He shoved on his shoes. "You've beaten me up enough. I think I finally got the picture."

Struggling to keep the sheet in place, Kendal rose up on her knees. "I never meant to hurt you, Owen."

"Yeah?" He stomped to the door. "You coulda fooled me."

"Have a safe trip back to Maryland."

Without turning to look at her again, he opened the door. "What would it matter to you?"

The door slammed. He was gone.

Kendal dropped back on the bed. She let the tears she'd been holding fall. Every time she thought she'd been through a wringer, a new, tighter squeeze wound her up in knots.

Owen didn't deserve to be hurt like this. He was a good guy with a heart of gold. All she kept doing was grinding it into smaller and smaller pieces.

If only she'd held her ground before they made love. She didn't even want to imagine what he thought about her now. In a small recess of her mind, she'd held on to the idea that maybe they'd have a chance once the case was over. That last hope was now extinguished. No matter how she groveled or explained, he would never forgive her for all this deception and pain.

She'd never forgive someone for doing the same to her. He wanted a home, wife, and kids. She was dedicated to her country. Her life was meant for service. As her parents had drilled into her day after day, duty would always be first. Family second.

Rolling over to her stomach, she buried her face in her hands. She never knew a broken heart could cause such a physical ache. Tears dripped between her fingers, spotting the sheet beneath her.

The phone rang. Wiping her eyes and nose, she twisted and reached for the receiver. "H'lo?"

"Smart?"

"Yeah. What's up, Boden?"

"You okay?"

Sitting up, Kendal threw her hair over her shoulder. "Of course I am."

"You sound like you've got a cold. Are you getting sick?"

"No. Allergies."

"In November?"

Irritated at Tommy's insightfulness, she grabbed a tissue. "Did you call for a reason?"

"Yes. There's new information."

"What?"

"We've got a lead. It seems the same woman who attacked you is the one who bought the cell phone."

"And ordered Python's abduction?" She mulled over this new information.

"That's our best guess."

"Do we have any idea who?"

"It's looking like Shockra."

Unsurprised, she nodded to the empty room. "I thought the same."

"We need to meet."

"Fine." She shifted off the bed.

"Twenty minutes."

"I'll be there."

How could he have been so stupid? In the dark room, he flopped onto the bed. Hadn't she always said she wasn't interested? Realizing he wasn't sleepy, Python turned on the

TV. With the remote in hand, he surfed the channels. He paused when Rambo filled the screen.

Watching as Stallone wiped out an entire army of bad guys, he piled his hands under his head. This is what he needed, a serious man flick. Through the machine gun fire filling the air, Python thought he heard a door close.

He hurried to the window. Inching the curtain aside, he peeked out. *This is crazy. What do I care if Kendal leaves*? Of course, having bribed the desk clerk to get the room next to hers made his own thoughts a lie.

After a quick scan, he saw no one. He dropped the fabric, then went back to the bed. The movie continued to flash on the screen. He paid it little attention.

He must've made a mistake. Kendal was next door getting ready to go to sleep. How come he couldn't keep his mouth shut? If he had, he could've held her all night. They could've made love again.

Wouldn't that have been better than him lying here alone? His jonhson bobbed in answer. "Of course, you'd agree. When it comes to Kendal, there's only one position you know. Up."

He grinned at his raging hard-on. Why couldn't that happen anyway? Why couldn't he just apologize? Then they'd make up and have one hell of a good time.

Excited with the thought, he rolled to the edge of the bed. That's exactly what he'd do. Just as he was about to stand, the connecting door opened.

Well, well, well. He was right after all. She hadn't left. It looked like he wasn't the only one who wanted to make up. He shut off the TV as he shifted back onto the bed.

The faint light filtering in from the parking lot illuminated a tall silhouette standing in the doorway.

"You looking for me?" Python grinned in the dark. This was too good to be true.

She sauntered over to him without a word.

"Are you wearing different perfume?" He hadn't heard the shower. She must've doused herself with the stuff. He wrinkled his nose as she reached the bed and placed her knee on the edge. "It's strong."

"I thought you'd like it," a too familiar voice said.

Chapter Twelve

Python jerked up, smashing Flame's face with his forehead. "What the hell are you doing here?" Rolling away, he flicked on the bedside light.

"I'm here for you." In a bikini top and skintight mini-skirt, Flame climbed onto the bed on all fours.

"Get out."

"Oh, come on, Python." She collapsed and stretched. "You and me, we're meant for each other."

"No, we're not." Pacing to the front door, Python grabbed the knob. "Leave."

"Why're you doing this? I know you and that pushy trainer ain't together." Spreading her legs, she gave him a bare beaver shot while she fingered herself. "It's time for you to learn what a real woman is like."

"No."

She lifted up on her heels and the top of her head as she inserted two more fingers. "Come help me. I know you want it."

Python could only stare at the exhibition. How many men would love to change positions with him? Flame was an Amazon of a woman with an incredibly well-built body, none of it surgically enhanced. A rarity in the wrestling world.

"Oh, oh, oh." Her hips pumped.

Did she really think this would turn him on? Then it hit him. "How'd you get into the room next door?"

"Huh?" She dropped her butt to the mattress, keeping her hand in place.

Careful to keep his distance, he edged a little closer. "You came through the connecting door. How'd you get in?"

"I'm horny here." She slung slick fingers at him. "Why

do you care how I got in?"

"Flame. Tell me."

"Fine." Sitting up, she crossed her legs. "I saw someone leaving. I thought it was your room. I picked the lock. The room was empty, then I noticed the connecting doors. I wasn't sure it was your room until you spoke."

"Ke–I mean, Big K wasn't in there?"

She glanced over at the door. "That's Big K's room? Why is it next to yours?"

"I wanted her next to me." Which begged the question, where was she?

"Why, Python? You know I'm ready for you. Why can't we get it on?"

"Nothing personal, Flame. I'm just not attracted to women like you."

"Women like me? Whadaya mean?"

"The whole wrestling scene. It's just not me."

"Is this because you and Big K split?"

He went to the window and pulled back the curtain. "No. I always felt this way."

"So, you just did it with her because she was there."

He scanned the parking lot. "Of course not. I care for Kendal."

"Kendal? Oh, Big K."

The bed creaked and he tensed, knowing Flame was moving off the mattress.

"I like you, Python. When you came back, I thought we could hook up, you know."

Not wanting to miss seeing Kendal come back, he didn't turn around. "I'm sorry."

"Yeah, so am I." He could hear her coming toward him and was ready when she put her hand on his shoulder. "If you ever change–"

"I won't." Python knew he sounded harsh. He also knew better than to show any kindness.

The one thing the wrestling world pounced on was weakness of any kind. Even though Flame sounded very convincing, he knew if she smelled even a hint of tenderness in him, she'd attack. "You'd better go."

Unmoving, he waited until he heard the door open and shut. Not until she passed by the window and waved did he take a deep breath. Staring at Flame's retreating back, he thought about his feelings for Kendal.

Was it the same way for her? Didn't she care about him? Was he asking her to feel something she wasn't capable of?

No. It couldn't be. The way she melted in his arms had to mean something. What was he thinking? How much more evidence did he need? He let go of the curtain, then turned back to look at the connecting door.

Where the hell was she?

"I don't want Python here." Kendal sat in the back of the sedan, grateful that she'd been extra careful not to be followed.

"You sound like a broken record." Fallon threw her arm over the back of the front seat. "If the man wants to wrestle, we don't have a legal reason not to let him."

As she glared at the young agent, Kendal bit back a nasty retort. After all, Fallon was right. "At least try to convince him."

"I'll do the best I can," Tommy said.

Unsatisfied, Kendal needed more assurance. "If you aren't able to succeed in discouraging him, what extra security precautions are being taken?"

"We have all that taken care of, Smart." Impatience could easily be heard in Fallon's tone. "We need to discuss the laundering."

Ignoring the other agent's irritation, Kendal sat forward. "There's new intel?"

Tommy tossed a notebook back to her. "Everything's pointing to a large payoff occurring at the Brawl."

Kendal shook her head. "Something's not right. They don't need to be so showy."

"I agree," Fallon said.

Surprised at her compliance, Kendal flipped open the

book.

"What's your take?" Fallon asked.

"I'm not sure. It's just not adding up. I don't see why they need to do this publicly."

"We don't have time to speculate." Tommy stabbed the air. "The intel says they're going to launder the money at the Brawl. We want to catch them in the act. Let's get back on target."

"Fine." Kendal wondered if Fallon was the source of Tommy's impatience. "Shockra's match will be one of the last bouts. My time should be free before and after. I can easily slip away. Even if I'm seen backstage, no one will think twice about it. I'll be in a perfect position to uncover the perpetrators. Catch them in the act."

"When you add Tommy and I being able to come and go as reporters, and the UCAs, we shouldn't miss them," Fallon said.

Kendal flipped through the pages, studying the blueprints of the dome. "Isn't it ironic that our bringing back Python is why the match is in one of the most difficult locations to cover?"

"I told you he'd be the biggest draw ever."

Looking up, she smiled at Tommy. "Okay, okay. You were right."

"Thank you." He stared over her shoulder. "There's going to be a lot of disappointed fans if we talk him into not going."

"Including you," Fallon muttered, but Kendal heard her loud and clear.

"What'd you say?" Tommy asked.

"Nothing." Fallon smiled slightly.

Closing the book, Kendal slid over toward the door. "I'll contact you only if necessary."

"Get Smart?"

Why'd he have to say it in front of Fallon? She glanced at the woman, but Fallon was somber. Kendal decided to let it go. "Yeah, Boden?"

"Be careful."

"I wouldn't be anything else." She opened the door.

A blast of cold air rushed through the already cooled interior of the car. Tommy started the engine. "There's no way we're going to be able to cover the whole dome."

"If everyone works like they should, we shouldn't have any problems." Fallon reached over the seat and grabbed the book she'd handed Kendal. Her pert little bottom wiggled in Tommy's face as she shifted back into the front seat. Their eyes met, and she frowned.

Putting his hand in front of his mouth, he coughed.

"You got something to say, Boden?"

"No."

"Then what's with the look?"

"What's with your attitude, Pierce?"

She crossed her arms. "Attitude?"

"Yeah." He gripped the steering wheel until his knuckles turned white. What was with this woman? "You put your butt in my face. I happen to notice, and you act like I've broken one of the Ten Commandments."

"Because you only noticed because I'm a woman."

Throwing her a dubious look, he held out a hand. "Well, duh."

The crease in her forehead looked like it was going to crack her face in two, she frowned so hard. "You shouldn't notice. I'm a fellow agent. Nothing else. You should see me as asexual."

"That's impossible. Men can't do that."

"Yes, they can." She jabbed her finger at him. "All I'm asking for is equality."

The hell she was. Tommy straightened in the seat. "What're you talking about? It's not equal. You get all kind of breaks."

"Are you trying to say they made me an agent because they needed women?"

Too late, he realized the deep water he was wading into. "I'm just saying you need to get over your attitude."

"Let me tell you, I was first in my class at the academy."

She thrust her finger at him again. "On an equal level, I outperformed everyone, whether male or female. Don't you even try and say I got special treatment."

Irritated that they were even having this inane conversation, he held up his hands in mock surrender. "Fine. You didn't get special treatment."

She crossed her arms again. "You've got nerve to even suggest it."

"Fine. I've got nerve." And you've got one humongous chip on your shoulder. He wasn't about to breach that subject with a ten-foot pole. Besides, once this mission was over, the chances that he'd have to work with Fallon Pierce again were highly unlikely. "How about we get back to deciding on the security."

"Fine."

"Yeah, fine." Tommy pulled out of the parking lot, thankful for the sudden silence.

Men, women, and children flooded through the doors into the RCA dome. Kendal stood holding back the curtain, searching the crowd. Could the radical group be stupid enough to make their move in such a public forum? It didn't make sense, but then again criminals rarely did.

"Hey, bitch."

Kendal didn't turn. "What is it, Flame?"

"Shockra's ready for you."

Rotating on her heel, Kendal put her hands on her hips. "And she sent her lackey to come find me?"

"Huh?" Flame frowned. "Just get in there."

Without answering, Kendal passed the red-haired female brute.

Flame hurried to her side. "You ain't so special, you know."

Kendal waved her hand. "Whatever."

"He deserves better than you."

Not caring about Flame's opinion, Kendal picked up her pace.

Flame grabbed her arm. "Hey. I said Python doesn't deserve you."

Just hearing his name made her skin tingle. Jerking out of Flame's hold, Kendal slapped her hand. "Why don't you go play with yourself."

"It's all your fault that he wouldn't hook up with me."

Rounding on Flame, Kendal slammed her fist into the other woman's chest. "His not liking you had nothing to do with me. Get over it."

"Wh–"

Kendal pushed open the doors to the locker room. "I'm tired of this conversation and you." The metal door clanged in Flame's face.

Shockra stood in front of a locker adjusting the strap of her spandex outfit. Kendal strode over to her when she heard the door reopen from behind.

"It's about time you got here," Shockra said.

"You're ready. I didn't think you'd need a pep talk."

Shockra cocked her hip. "I don't need a pep talk. Rumor is Bomber's gonna swerve."

"She can't change the outcome of the match. Someone's trying to mess with your head that she'd even attempt to. Rusen has put on the push. He has you scheduled to win through the rest of this year." Conscious of the weapon tucked in the small of her back, Kendal flipped her long leather coat out before sitting down on the bench. "Don't listen to the hype."

Shockra stepped close, towering over her. "I'm telling you it's not hype. You've got to watch my back."

"Fine. I'm there."

The wrestler stepped away. "Good. That's all I wanted to hear."

With a frown, Kendal stood. Shockra had never been concerned before. It was out of character.

One-handed, Flame shoved the door open. "You better keep my girl safe."

Kendal threw what she knew was a lethal glare. "Why

don't you concentrate on your own career? Quit being second to Shockra."

As Kendal strode out, Flame followed. "Hey! What do you know?"

Kendal rounded on her. "I know you're just as good as Shockra. What I can't understand is why all of you let her be the one on top. You could easily take her. Your moves are crisper, better defined. With the right trainer, and a great push, you could be the one at the top."

Flame's face scrunched. "Wha–"

"Flame! Get your ass in here." Shockra stood in the locker room doorway.

"I think your master is calling. You'd better be a good little girl and do what she says."

Flame gave Kendal a confused look before rushing back to Shockra. That wouldn't be happening for much longer if Kendal had anything to say about it. As soon as they disbanded the homeland terrorist group, it was going to be her personal mission to put Shockra behind bars for Owen's kidnapping, at the very least. She'd prefer to put her away for murder. The best part about being the woman's trainer was it gave her the chance to gather evidence.

A blur of color had her turning her head. Was that Owen going into the men's locker room? She hesitated. A man in gray overalls carrying a large metal case strode by. All her instincts went on alert. As she turned to watch, the man disappeared into a stairwell.

Something wasn't right. One of the main FBI training sessions was to teach recruits to always rely on intuition. Kendal knew now was not the time to change years of belief. After a quick look around, she followed.

Listening, she was just able to hear a door close above. She sped up three flights, dismissing the first two levels. As she started to open the door, a murmur of voices and footsteps could be heard. She stepped out onto the hall of deluxe suites.

The floor was full of people mingling as they made their way to their assigned VIP suite box. Straining to see over the crowd, Kendal scanned for the man in overalls.

Gone.

Determined to find him, she hustled through the groups. The man was nowhere to be found. He'd disappeared. Returning to the stairwell door, she found it red with bright white letters reading *Emergency Only*.

The alarm was disconnected. Her head tingled from the discovery. "I am definitely becoming Spiderman?"

"Nah, you look more like a colorful Zena to me," a nearby man commented.

Turning, Kendal forced herself to smile. "Yes, I suppose I do, don't I?"

He sidled up close. "Could I interest you in watching the matches from my private suite?"

"Nope. 'Preciate the offer, though." She plowed through the remaining groups as she used the public ramp to get back down to the main floor. Once past the box seat ticket takers, the throngs of people grew until she felt like a salmon swimming upstream.

With a constant eye out for gray clothing, she couldn't have been happier when she spotted another door leading backstage. She strode straight to the security guard on the left.

"Gray overalls, five eleven, medium build. Suspicious."

Not even by the flutter of an eyelid did the Special Agent confirm she had spoken. As soon as she went through the door, she heard him relaying the information. Wrestlers, crew, and more security filled the back area, almost as crowded as out in the front. Amazing how the bookers got all of the matches scheduled once the RCA dome had been set up.

Keeping a rapid pace, Kendal passed another hallway. A gray blur stopped her. She retraced her steps. Overalls was moving away at a fast clip. Again her instincts went on alert.

With a quick scan, she confirmed there were no other agents available. She was on her own. The man darted into another stairwell.

Aw, shit. Why couldn't he stay on the same level? She ran. As quietly as possible, she opened the door seconds behind him. His footfalls echoed on the metal stairs as he climbed. She waited until his steps faded slightly before she ventured inside. Again another door shut. She headed up.

What the hell was Kendal up to? Python wondered as he followed her. He knew Shockra's match was still a few bouts away, since she was the female headliner. He'd thought Kendal would be sticking close to make sure everything was going as planned. He'd tried to get her out of his head. Tried to forget her. It wasn't going to happen.

Today he'd fight and win. Then he'd convince Kendal this was his destiny. He'd finally accepted what he hadn't wanted to. This was going to be his life. Staying behind, he slipped up the stairs.

Seeing her in that bright green, midriff-showing leather outfit had him thirsting to see her back in black. Although, he had to admit the knee-length leather coat was a nice touch. When they were working together again, he'd have one made with a python embroidered on the back. He smiled with the thought.

Just as he slipped around the edge of the first stairway, a door closed. He rushed up the last flight. Whipping out into the hall, he slammed into her back.

She crouched as her hand flew inside her coat. "Wha–Owen?"

"Sorry. I didn't mean to hit you."

She pushed him back toward the door. "What're you doing?" she hissed.

"Stop pushing me." He grabbed her shoulders. "What're you doing up here?"

"None of your business." She glanced over her shoulder.

"Why are you so test–*umph*" She crushed his mouth with hers. Stunned, his hands flexed once, then his arms wrapped around, forcing her against his chest.

She tasted so good. He nudged at the seam of her lips with his tongue and she resisted. He continued to try and she pushed him. He stepped back against the door.

Suddenly, he stumbled when the support behind him

disappeared. "Huh?"

Shoving again, she followed him into the stairwell, slamming the door behind her. "What're you doing?"

"You seem to be stuck on that question." Python leaned back on the railing.

"Listen, I need you to go back downstairs." Turning, she cracked open the door. "Right now," she hissed over her shoulder.

"Why?" He pushed off. "Are you meeting someone?"

"Yes."

Python couldn't believe she came right out and said it. Was *sucker* written across his forehead? "Then by all means, don't let me stop you."

He started down the stairs.

"Owen, that's not what I meant."

He halted, each foot on a different step, and peered at her over the rail. "Yeah? Well, it's how it sounded."

"Fine." She shook her head. "Think what you want."

Shrugging, he stomped down the stairs.

Kendal didn't have time to worry about him. Overalls had been at the other end of the deserted hallway. To keep him from being suspicious, she'd kissed Owen. If only things were different and they really were just a couple of wrestlers searching for a place to have a good time.

She peeked out. The hall was empty. Rushing out, she checked every door. No sign of the man. Disgusted, she rechecked all the doors before lifting her wrist, where a thick leather bracelet hid the transmitter.

She pressed the small hidden button. "Boden? Over."

No response. Kendal assumed he needed to find a secure place to talk. She licked her lips and tasted Owen. This was not what she needed right now. Distractions killed agents.

"Boden here. Over."

"Suspect in gray overalls. Over."

"Affirmative. Over."

"Over and out." As Kendal switched the transmitter off, she strode to the stairs. Unable to track the elusive Overalls, she needed to make her way back to Shockra. Contemplating the excitement she felt at seeing Owen and her trepidation at the danger he could be in, she exited the stairwell into chaos.

The hall swarmed with people. A popular hard rock band would be performing after the main event, making the crowds larger than ever. With a hand extended, she plowed through the masses to the women's locker room.

"What?" Shockra's voice pierced the solid door as Kendal entered. Flame stood at the edge of a row of lockers. Shockra must be around the corner, out of sight.

"I just saw Python." Flame bounced on her toes. "He's the bomb."

Kendal edged inside, not wanting to interrupt.

"Why are you so stuck on him?" Shockra's harsh voice echoed throughout the room.

Flame stopped bouncing. "Cause he's cute and the best."

A locker slammed. "No, he ain't."

"What's eating at you?"

Rounding the corner, Shockra pushed Flame. "Nothing."

"Hey!" Off balance, the redhead crashed into the lockers.

"Just stay outta my face." Shockra stormed toward Kendal. "Where the hell have you been?"

Ignoring her tirade, Kendal shrugged. "It's time to get warmed up."

"Not now. I've got to take care of something."

Kendal grabbed her arm as she tried to pass. "It's time to warm up. There's nothing more important right now. If you don't believe me, maybe we should ask Rusen."

"You wouldn't," Shockra snarled, pulled out of Kendal's grasp, but stayed put.

"You willing to chance it?" Kendal held her breath with the bluff. She'd pushed the envelope.

Shockra stepped close, nose-to-nose with her. "You need to back off, bitch. You don't know who the fuck you're messing with."

"I know a lot more than you realize. If you know what's good for you, you'll step back." Kendal stared until the larger woman moved away. "Get ready for the match."

"Bitch. Flame, get over here."

Sitting down on the hard bench as the women left, Kendal placed her head in her hands. She had a bad feeling about tonight. A real bad feeling.

A loud blast shook the room.

Chapter Thirteen

Kendal was up and running before fully registering the intent to do so. Outside the locker room, the place was pandemonium with people rushing in all directions. The explosion had to have come from the dome.

Shoving through, she forced her way past the curtain. Thick smoke filled the air. Kendal coughed as she waved her hand through the stench.

"LADIES AND GENTLEMEN, PLEASE REMAIN IN YOUR SEATS! THERE IS NO CAUSE FOR ALARM. EVERYTHING IS UNDER CONTROL. PLEASE REMAIN SEATED!"

Aware that she'd be unable to hear the transmitter on her arm, Kendal searched for a UCA. Through the lifting haze, she spotted a guard. "What happened?"

"Fireworks accident. It's part of the rock band's gig," he said.

"Everything else going as planned?"

"Yes, ma'am."

Kendal did a quick visual check around them. "Anything new on Overalls?"

He shook his head. "No, ma'am. Nobody matching the description."

She nodded. No one else had seen him, and she couldn't give any reason to suspect he was anything more than an ordinary repair guy working for the RCA dome.

"LADIES AND GENTLEMEN. PLEASE TAKE YOUR SEATS. THE BRAWL WILL BEGIN IN EXACTLY FIVE MINUTES."

Remarkably, the air continued to clear as most of the fans began to heed the announcer's instructions. With a quick nod to the undercover agent, Kendal returned backstage, her heart finally starting to calm.

"Are you okay?"

Hearing Owen's voice so close sent chills over her body. She turned to find him standing off to the side. "I'm fine. I didn't see you there."

"I know. I was looking for you. You ran right by without seeing me."

Before she thought about it, she reached out and touched his arm. "Are you all right?"

"I was changing. Nowhere near the excitement."

"Good."

"Were you worried about me?"

How did he always bring it back to such dangerous ground? "Of course, I was worried. No matter what else, you have to know I care. I only want what's best for you."

Taking her elbow, he steered her behind extra privacy walls being stored on the side of the hall. "That's what I want for you too." He traced her chin with his finger.

"Oh, Owen. You make this so hard."

"It doesn't have to be."

Kendal gazed at the man who had stolen her heart. She sighed inwardly. Could he really forgive her when he learned the truth? Could they figure out a way to make things work? Right now, she didn't care.

She grabbed his face. "This is wrong, but I don't care." She crushed her lips to his.

His arms wrapped around her waist, and he pulled her firm against him. Unable to help herself, when his mouth opened she delved inside, tasting him deeply. Wanting more, she slid her leg up the side of his until her knee hooked over his hip.

His hands adjusted to the back of her thighs. He lifted her up as he spun. Knowing what would happen, she threw her arm behind just as they slammed against the concrete block wall.

Confident that her gun was wedged tight and unharmed,

she pulled her hand free, flattening her breasts against his chest even more. She wiggled, searching for the perfect fit.

He responded with a deep groan and spread his legs. She fell into him, placing the aching apex between her legs in direct contact with the bulge in his pants. She squirmed, wanting the friction and much, much more.

Python broke the kiss. "Why do you put us through this misery? You know we want each other."

"Stop talking." Grasping his ears, she pulled his lips to hers once again. She gyrated more, grinding herself on him.

She was killing him. Python wanted to be inside her. Deep, deep inside, filling her, her softness surrounding him. His hand massaged her thigh before traveling under her skirt hem and up. Pushing under the leather and past the strip of material she called underwear, he found her slick. His fingers slid over the full lips, then he teased the tip until it became a hardened nub. He thrust a finger inside.

"Owen," Kendal screeched in his ear.

"I want inside, instead of my finger." He inserted a second finger and pushed up.

She tried to pump. He held her tighter against the wall, making her immobile. "You're killing me."

"No." Python sucked on her neck. "I want to see you come."

With glazed eyes, she laid her head back on the wall. "Not here." Her eyes closed as she began to pant.

"Yes, here." His fingers thrusting in and out, Python's hips began to match the rhythm. Oh, he wanted to be inside her.

"Owen–Owen." Her head popped off the wall, and she kissed him hard. The intensity almost had him coming in his pants even as he continued to stimulate her. Leaving his mouth, she brushed aside his shirt, attacking the top of his shoulder. A sudden bite had him thrusting even harder.

The bite intensified almost to the point of pain as the muscles around his fingers began to contract. He continued to massage her until the last contraction ceased. Closing his eyes,

Owen tried to calm his over-stimulated system.

"Oh, no, you don't." Kendal's legs loosened around his hips. She dropped her feet to the floor.

"What?"

Before he knew what was happening, she'd unsnapped his pants and filled her hands with his aching flesh.

"You don't ha–"

Her mouth took his in another searing kiss. Within seconds, a powerful release overcame him. He shuddered with its force.

Their foreheads resting together, Kendal rocked her head back and forth. "I can't believe we just did that."

Owen kissed her nose. "It just shows we belong together."

"It shows we can't keep our hands off each other." She shook her head. "What are we? A couple of high school kids?"

He pulled her into his arms. "You did this in high school?"

She cocked her eyebrow. "You didn't?"

"Okay. Let's not go there."

Laying her head in the crook of his neck, Kendal snuggled. "I knew you were a smart man."

"I don't know about smart, I just know what I want."

She pulled back to look up at him. "Me."

"Now, you're getting the picture."

Disentangling, she said, "We'll talk."

"That's all you can say?"

"It's the most I can give right now." Using only the tips of her fingers, she held his face and kissed his lips gently. "I promise you, no matter what happens, we'll take the time to sort this thing out."

With his hands on her shoulders, he massaged her already loose muscles. "You giving me a guarantee?"

"You betcha."

"Then you've got a deal."

"We'd better get back." Wanting to lean into him even more, Kendal made herself pull away. "You've got a match to win." She made a face. "And I have a witch to coach."

"Are you saying I'm the best wrestler you've ever coached?"

Grinning and feeling good about the future, Kendal punched his shoulder. "Yes."

"I love you, Kendal."

Even through the uncomfortable pregnant pause, she held his stare. She couldn't say the words now, when everything was a lie. Once he learned the truth, he would never believe she had meant them. No matter how much it hurt, she had to wait until he knew the real Kendal.

"Can't you say it back?"

"Not now."

"What do you mean, not now?"

Tracing his face with her finger like he'd done to her, Kendal sucked in a breath. "I want to. I really do. I can't. Not now."

"That makes no sense."

She understood his frustration and wished she could explain. She couldn't, no, wouldn't, endanger everyone on the case just to appease her own guilt due to her weaknesses and mistakes. Her military upbringing had instilled in her the true meaning of duty. "One day it will, Owen. I promise. One day it will."

They broke apart, and she immediately felt the loss. Which was crazy, since she'd told him more about how she felt than ever before. If anything, things were looking better and brighter between them.

As he fixed his pants, Owen looked up. "I'm going to keep you to that promise."

"I wouldn't want it any other way."

With a hand on her back, he led her out of their impromptu love nest. "Come find me after my match. We can watch the band together or something."

Her mouth twitched. "Or something?"

They reached the women's lockers.

"Yeah."

"I'll see you later?" The minute the words came out, Kendal heard the pleading tone in her voice.

"Didn't we just plan that?"

She laughed, and the sound was shaky. "Yes, we did."

"Are you okay?"

Berating herself for even the momentary weakness, Kendal straightened her shoulders. "Of course. I was just a little distracted." She kissed his cheek. "I'll find you later." Pushing open the door, she let it slam behind her.

"LADIES AND GENTLEMEN! IT'S TIME FOR THE ULTIMATE MATCH OF THE NEW MILLENNIUM. THE MAN WHO CAN'T BE BEAT. THE MAN WITH THE LETHAL STRIKE IS READY TO DOMINATE AND TAKE THE TITLE OF BEST WRESTLER IN THE WORLD. LADIES AND GENTLEMEN, WELCOME TO THE RCA DOME, PYTHON!!!

Feeling strong, vibrant, and proud, Python strutted out to the deafening roar of the crowd. This was his moment. He was about to take the NFW's highest title.

He'd come up with a new plan for the future. He was getting back with Kendal, and he was going to propose. Tonight, he would convince her to become his wife.

He felt the grin on his face grow and thought it would surely split his face in two. Of course, this was not the appropriate facial expression for the match. With a great deal of fortitude, he schooled his features.

Halfway to the ring, he stopped. Scowling, he fisted his hands. He bowed his arms, making the muscles in his back tense and flex. He turned a complete circle, growling and snarling to the crowd.

This was another part of the performance he was not going to miss. He couldn't wait until he told Kendal about his new idea. Yes, he would be leaving the ring. Together they would sponsor and train new, upcoming wrestlers.

As he continued, eager fans stretched over the barriers and security personnel to try and touch him. Python extended both hands, briefly slapping fingertips as he passed.

They'd make a great team. Once they were established, they could retire from the road. Young men and women would come from all around to be trained in the latest and greatest techniques from the best. And that's what they would be–the best.

Reaching the edge of the ring, he climbed in, lifting his hands high over his head. The crowd roared their approval. Python wished Kendal was in his corner. Man, what a show he would've given them tonight.

"LADIES AND GENTLEMEN. THE ONLY MAN WILLING TO TAKE ON THE KILLER. A LEGEND IN HIS OWN MIND. HOLD ON TO YOUR SEATS BECAUSE WE ARE IN FOR A WILD RIDE. HERE COMES SLAUGHTER!"

As booing permeated the dome, Python wondered if the marks ever knew how well they played into the drama of the event. The hard-core fans had to know how much of the match was predetermined. Yet, they still came in massive numbers, always providing the right sounds at the right time.

Slaughter stomped his way to the ring. He plowed through the ropes. His huge arms looked like tree trunks as he lifted them above his head and took his turn around the ropes.

Damn, the man was big. You always went through the motions in practice. The hard hits weren't put in until the wrestlers were in front of the crowd. Slaughter topped the scales at three fifty. It was all muscle.

Python loosened up his neck muscles and shook out his arms. This was it. His very last match. It was time to go out with a bang.

"LET THE MATCH BEGIN!"

Kendal stood at the curtain at the edge of the wrestlers' entrance and exit ramp. Python and Slaughter continued to charge and attack. Every time they hit, the dome shook from the intense reaction of the fans.

She'd spent the better part of all the matches going through various parts of the dome searching for anything out of the ordinary. Nothing. Much to her disgruntlement, Rusen had not asked her to help with the money side of his operation yet. If the homeland radical group planned to move money here tonight, she wasn't going to have a front row seat to watch.

Connecting with Tommy had only confirmed that no one had seen anything. It appeared that the radical group had gotten spooked. Most likely they had decided to wait. A decision she would've made if she were heading the operation. Why take such a chance with so many people around, including extra security?

The back of a piece of cardboard blocked her view of the ring for a moment. When she scanned the arena, homemade signs dotted the crowd, including a few propositions. She shook her head. You couldn't beat a wrestling fan. They loved and hated with a vengeance and were proud of it. A pride Kendal found herself becoming increasingly familiar with. Who would've figured?

Her palms dampened when Slaughter gave Owen a solid punch. After witnessing the number of stiff workers in the sport, she'd become increasingly nervous watching Owen's bouts. The good news was, Slaughter was a straight shooter. Even as a tremendous heel, he had a strong following. Kendal wouldn't be surprised if he turned. She easily could see him becoming a huge face.

Owen pinned Slaughter with a grandstand finisher, bringing the crowd to its feet. "God, Python is one fine piece of meat." Flame's voice grated on Kendal's last nerve as lips smacked near her ear.

The woman needed to keep her pushy eyes and hands to herself. Ignoring her, Kendal tried to see past the fans as the referee paraded Owen around the ring. Once he made his way to the ramp, she'd convince him that staying for the concert was not top on her list.

"Too bad you couldn't keep him satisfied." Flame patted her back. "Don't you worry about it. I'm going to give him the ride of his life tonight."

Rounding, Kendal felt like decking her. "You need to back off."

"You gonna make me?"

"Yeah."

Her eyes narrowed. "When?"

"When you least exp–"

Overalls!

Kendal pushed Flame to the side and rushed toward the unidentified suspect. He still had the large case. If he was a workman, she'd apologize. But something inside kept screaming there was more to it.

He disappeared behind temporary bleachers. Rushing, Kendal caught a glimpse just as he slid behind a black curtain. She followed, finding a hidden door. After a slight hesitation to give him time to move away, she opened the door and found herself in the underbelly of the stage. Above, the rock band warmed up for their performance.

What would a repairman be doing under here at this point? Slipping her hand under the leather coat, she wrapped her fingers around her weapon. The metal felt good–right.

She stayed in the shadows, stepping over steel bars as she edged up to where a wall made a sharp L. With her back to it, she peeked around the edge. The intricate support system had created a dead end. The man knelt on his hands and knees with the large case open in the corner. *Trapped like a rat.*

With a smile, Kendal lifted her wrist and whispered, "Code red. Code red." A sharp glint caught her eye. A thin piece of wire stuck out of the side of her bracelet. Upon closer examination, she realized her transmitter was smashed.

She'd successfully saved her gun when she and Owen had acted like a couple of teenagers, but she'd ruined her only method to call for backup. She was on her own.

Pulling the weapon free of her waistband, she held it nose level, preparing to sneak up on the man.

"Get the hell away from me! I saw her go in here."

Owen?

"She's not good enough. Why're you so stupid?"

Kendal rolled her eyes. Flame, too? She did not need this right now. Hiding the weapon, she turned, heading back the way she came. "What're you guys doing here?" she hissed as Flame tried her best to grab and hold a very irate looking Owen.

"I thought–"

Waving her hands, Kendal hushed Owen as she approached.

"–we were meeting," he finished in a hoarse whisper.

"We are. I just need a moment. Then I'll be right there." She pushed his shoulder. "Why don't you go get a shower? I'll meet you at the locker room."

"Yeah, come on, Python. I'll take care of ya."

Jerking out of Flame's grip, Owen punched the air. "Will you leave me alone?"

"Would you both please be quiet?

Owen turned to her with a puzzled look. "What's wrong with you? Why are you worried about noise? You can barely hear down here with all that racket going on above."

That much was true. Thank God. There was a good chance her hand hadn't been tipped. "Fine. Listen, Rusen needs me to check out a couple of things down here. You go, get cleaned up. I'll meet you, just like we planned."

His puzzled expression grew and he frowned.

"Just get her out of here, will you?"

He looked like he was going to argue, then turned and grabbed Flame's arm. "Fine. You'll come meet me."

"Yes, yes." Kendal wanted them out, now.

Flame looked more than happy to leave as she latched onto Owen in return. Over her shoulder, she threw Kendal a wide smirk.

Don't get too comfortable, little girl. That man is mine. Happy Owen had agreed, she turned back. It was time to find out what Overalls was doing. Pulling out her gun again, she made her way back to the edge of the wall. The guy was still hunched over the case, working with his back to her.

She stepped out, weapon extended. With deliberate steps,

she approached. The band started to play above. Inside fireworks blasted. Her gun sight centered between his shoulder blades, Kendal inched closer.

With the barrel mere inches away from him, she reached out and tapped his back. His head rapped the gun when he whipped around. She held the weapon firm.

Wide, startled eyes stared at her.

"FBI! Hands up," she shouted. His hands shot in the air as he turned and faced her. It was debatable whether he actually heard the words or fear had him reacting instinctively.

Keeping him in her sights, she inspected the open case.

A bomb!

Shoving the gun into Overall's nose, Kendal bent down near his head. "What the hell are you doing?"

Movement! Kendal spun. Ready to attack, she hesitated for a split second when a colorful head bobbed in front of her.

"*Umph.*" Knocked to the floor from behind, her weapon went skidding out of reach. Overalls was running. Scampering to her feet, she debated a split second about finding her weapon. She took off after him.

She felt, more than heard, Owen join her, running a few steps behind. Rounding the corner, they came face to face with the blunt barrel of a Smith and Wesson.

Chapter Fourteen

"Dina!" Kendal knew her voice was lost beneath the blaring music, but the shock of a blonde, frizzy haired Dina holding a gun stunned her. The last time she'd been up close and personal with the woman had been when she was prying her off Owen in his motel room. Thinking back to her in that cheerleading outfit seemed like an eternity ago.

Unable to hear, Kendal heeded the direction of Dina's waving hand and stepped back. Simultaneously, Owen joined her. Aware of the ticking bomb, Kendal wondered if this comedy of errors would ever end. If and when it did, would she be dead? This was not the way she intended to die. Shaking off the morbid feeling, she visually searched the ground for her weapon.

Owen bumped her shoulder with his. She looked over sharply to see his head nod ever so slightly. Following his line of sight, she saw the butt of her semi-automatic sticking out from under the edge of a stage support bar.

The Smith and Wesson flashed under her nose, and Kendal looked into Dina's wild eyes and moving lips.

"QUIT LOOK–" the music's sudden stop halted Dina's rant, "–ing around," she finished more softly.

Above them a member of the rock group announced the band's excitement at being in Indianapolis. The crowd went wild.

Dina cleared her throat. "As soon as the band starts playing again, the two of you are dead."

And no one hears a thing. Kendal needed to stall. "Why?"

"Why?" Dina laughed. "Why the shit should it matter now?"

The rock star introduced the lead guitarist. Wild cheers ensued. The band would start playing again as soon as the introductions were over. With time slipping away, Kendal forced herself to block out everything but her training. "Call me curious. Why'd you kidnap Python?"

"I needed to."

Nothing about this case was making sense. "Why do you want to kill us?" Kendal asked.

"Python is the one who has to die. You're just in the way."

Going out on a limb, Kendal made a huge assumption. "This isn't the first time you tried, is it?"

"No."

The superior look that came over Dina's face was all the evidence Kendal needed. "You almost succeeded before. That must've taken some planning."

So many people thought it cliché that criminals confessed when they thought they were in the clear. What they didn't realize is that the typical bad guy had a huge ego. The one thing they loved to do was show how clever they were.

"Yes, it did." She pointed the gun at Owen. "You don't deserve to live."

Kendal felt Owen tense. She gave him a sharp look, hoping he got the message to stay quiet. "Why?"

"I don't have to tell you." Dina waggled the gun between them. "Listen, I'm sorry you gotta die, Big K. I really don't have a beef with you. But you two dying in a lover's spat is too good to pass up. It's going to be a sad day in the wrestling world, just like it should've been before."

"Before?" Kendal asked.

"Nothing." Dina scowled as she pointed the gun at Owen's chest.

So much for the big-ego-and-I-want-to-tell-everything theory. The instant the band started again, Kendal knew she had to act. The drummer was introduced. Tensing her muscles, knowing the music would be starting up at any moment, she calculated the distance between her and Dina.

The first note blared.

"*Aaaaah*!" Owen charged before Kendal could move. His shoulder connected with Dina's stomach. Her first shot went wild.

Kendal dove for her weapon. Grabbing the steel, she rolled. There was no clear shot. Owen and Dina were a mass of legs and arms. Jumping up, she ran to them.

Owen flipped Dina, pinning the arm holding the gun to the floor. With a well-paced stab, Kendal pierced Dina's wrist with her spike heel.

Dina screamed, immediately releasing the gun as blood gushed from the gaping hole. Kendal leaned down, grabbing the Smith and Wesson. She spoke directly into Dina's ear. "Too bad. You know how it is, the best laid plans and all."

As Kendal put the extra gun in the small of her back, Dina rolled to her side, cradling her injury.

The music slowed and a ballad began. Standing, Kendal visually checked Owen for injury. "You weren't hit?" She still had to yell to be heard.

Owen stared at her for a moment. "No."

Satisfied with his short, loud answer, Kendal reached down to pull Dina to her feet. The woman resisted. "If you don't get your butt off the floor, you're going to bleed to death."

Her hand still dripping, Dina rose, leaving the frizzy wig on the ground.

"Use the edge of your shirt and wrap it around the wound." Kendal nodded at Owen. "I need you to get her to security. They'll book her, make sure she gets medical attention."

"What're you going to do?"

Ready to march past him, Kendal shouted, "I've got something to take care of."

His hand landed on her shoulder. "I want to know what's going on. Why does Rusen have you down here?"

"I don't have time to explain, Owen. Take Dina to security. Tell them to call in code red to this location."

"Who are you?"

Kendal shook her head. "Yeah, I knew you'd say that one day."

He frowned, and she knew he couldn't have heard her.

Raising her voice, she held out Dina's arm. "I'll explain later." When he grabbed her, Kendal pushed his shoulder. "Just go."

Finally, he headed away. Kendal wedged her weapon into her front waistband. The band changed tempo once again, and the volume increased. The fast, thundering beat made her teeth rattle.

Her bomb experience was limited to the few weeks at the bureau dedicated to distinguishing the types. Only those who went on to be trained on how to unarm the nasty buggers learned more.

Right now, she wished she'd been so inclined. Keeping her back to the closed corner, she squatted and studied the many colorful wires. She shifted to the opposite edge and found a timer. It wasn't set.

They'd interrupted Overalls before he could set it. Looking closer, Kendal searched for the wire allowing remote detonation. She took her time, found the correct wire, and followed its path.

Not connected. Thank God for small favors. Sitting back on her heels, she took a deep breath.

A blur of movement brought her head up. Tommy came rushing in. He pointed to her wrist transmitter, a question looming in his eyes.

She mouthed, "Broken," and held up her arm.

He nodded. Moving close, he yelled into her ear. "The bomb squad is on its way."

Bobbing their heads, they switched positions. She yelled back, "It's unarmed. How'd you know it was a bomb?"

Pulling away, Tommy gave her a puzzled look before leaning close again. "We caught the guy in overalls."

"That's good." That was the best news she'd heard. The slimy guy hadn't gotten away after all. "The timer isn't set. To the best of my knowledge, the remote detonator isn't connected. We interrupted him before he could activate it."

Tommy grabbed at his waist. He yanked off the beeper, reading the text message. Kendal stood to lean over his shoulder.

Two bad guys secured. More active bombs.

Kendal felt her blood run cold.

Damn, she hadn't stopped anything. How had they missed that the radical group wasn't laundering money? It seemed obvious now that all the group wanted was to make a statement. The one thing everyone had learned over the past few years was that blowing up innocent people definitely got you noticed.

Well, they weren't going to get away with it now! As if Tommy had read her thoughts, they both started to run.

"Come on, Python. Let's make a deal. You let me go, and I'll make you rich," Dina yelled over the pounding music.

He leaned in. "You've got to be kidding. Seconds ago you were going to kill me."

"I was only getting even," she shouted. "You understand that. If you save my ass now, we'll be even."

Not sure what the heck she was talking about, he was curious enough to ask, "Even for what?"

"You killed my brother!"

Python halted, his grip never loosening on her arm. "Terror was your brother?"

A smug smile filled her round face. "Yeah. We didn't tell no one." The smile faded. "Then you killed him."

Amazed at the news, he shook his head. "You're willing to forgive me if I let you go?"

"I would've forgiven you a long time ago if we'd hooked up." She lifted her nose in the air. "You're no better than me, you know."

Keeping her in his grasp, Python pulled her forward without answering. He did think he was better than most on the circuit. If not having sex with every groupie and wrestler had given him a reputation of being a sex snob, then so be it.

"You weren't my type."

"I could be." She rubbed up against his side.

He threw her a disgusted look as the security guard grabbed her good arm. With her bleeding hand wadded inside the bottom of her shirt, Dina glared as she was pulled away. Her mouth contorted, and Python knew she was cursing. Strobe lights from the stage gave her harsh features an even uglier glint, exposing the underlying evil.

She was willing to kill him, because she thought he'd killed her brother. Of course, he'd thought the same thing until Kendal had entered his life.

Kendal!

Python headed back under the stage. It was time to learn exactly what was going on. He stopped, the throbbing music beating around him.

What the heck was her last name? He hadn't even thought about it until just now. They'd never even told each other their full names. What else didn't he know?

More determined than ever, Python took a step just as Kendal and Tommy came rushing out. "He–"

They ran past, never breaking their speed. Python gave chase. He followed them into the backstage area toward the locker rooms. They rushed through groups of people, then slammed into a stairwell. He stayed right on their heels.

As Kendal turned the corner, she peered over the rail. "Owen, get out of here."

Her announcement made Tommy glance back, even as he continued rushing up the stairs. "Python, leave."

He wasn't going anywhere but wherever Kendal was going. Of that, Python was perfectly sure. He shook his head, even though the two of them never looked back. Guess they thought he'd just follow their orders. *What a stupid assumption.*

They all charged out into the hall.

"Which way?" Kendal's head swiveled, her hand down at her side holding the gun.

That was the hardest part of what he was witnessing,

Kendal knew guns and how to use them.

"Owen! Leave!"

"This way," Tommy said, pointing, at the same time as Kendal yelled.

They both started running to the other end. Python ignored her demand and chased after them. Rounding the corner, he skidded to a stop to keep from hitting Tommy.

Kendal glared back at him, putting her finger to her lips. Python looked past her. A man sat hunched over something on the floor. What the devil was going on?

Unbelievably, with her gun grasped between both hands, Kendal stepped to the left while Tommy went right, approaching the man.

Python's brain whirled. Kendal? FBI? In the span of a few seconds, so many things about this entire incident began to fall into place. So he hadn't been the only one recruited to help bring in the drug dealers.

Suddenly, the music stopped. The man's head popped up. The announcer's indiscernible voice boomed in the distance.

"Freeze! FBI," Tommy shouted. "Put your hands where I can see them."

Aware she had a small opportunity of surprise, Kendal inched closer when the man, in matching overalls like the other perp, jerked his head toward Tommy. They must've gotten to the band. The dome evacuation procedures had most likely commenced.

With the possibility of more bombs, and the radical's group ability to detonate them remotely, she knew it had to have been a difficult call. The brass would've been hard-pressed to know which would be safer, clear the arena which would tip off the radicals and force them to start activating the bombs or try to find and defuse them without any evacuation.

"Hands on your head, NOW!" Tommy took another step.

"Stop." The man stood, holding a small remote, his thumb hovering over the button. "Don't come any closer or we all die."

"You don't want to do that." Tommy took a step back. He

held up his hands, pointing his weapon to the ceiling.

"Oh, yeah, I do. It's important to our cause. People must die."

As Kendal got closer, she noticed the pimples across his forehead and chin. He had to be all of sixteen years old. Probably a runaway or mixed up kid, the perfect target for radical sickos.

"No, they don't," Tommy continued. "People don't have to die. There are other ways to get your message out there."

"No!" The young man waved the remote laden hand. "This is the way. We have to let the government know we're serious." Sweat beaded on the boy's upper lip.

"Calm down." Tommy lowered his voice. "Just calm down. Let's talk."

Taking small steps, Kendal inched nearer. She had to get the remote out of the boy's hand without setting off the bomb.

He stayed focused on Tommy. "This is the only way."

"No, it's not." Tommy lowered his hands to shoulder height.

Kendal took another small step. The young man whirled. "Stop!" His head jerked between her and Tommy, before rebounding to the middle.

He spotted Owen, Kendal concluded, when his eyes widened at most likely the sight of the colorful bald head.

"All of you get back." He pointed at each of them. "Or I'm gonna push the button."

"Okay, okay. Calm down," Tommy said.

"Stop telling me to calm down." The young man wiped his mouth with the back of his hand. "Stop talking." He shook the remote at Tommy. "Just stop talking. I need to think."

"Snowman? Snowman, are you there?" A radio cackled.

With his free hand, the young man pulled a walkie-talkie out of his back pocket. "I'm here. Ready to burn."

"Abort. Abort mission."

The radio flew through the air, crashing into the wall.

Wrong words, Kendal's mind screamed.

"No," Tommy shouted.

Snowman hesitated. "I've got to, man." Tears rolled down his cheeks. He shook his head. "If I gotta die, I gotta die. It's for a good cause."

"No, you don't." Tommy stepped closer. "This isn't right. There's something inside of you saying this isn't right."

Snowman shook his head, the tears streaming now, his hand shaking.

"Listen to me." Tommy moved almost within touching distance. "You don't want to die. It doesn't have to be this way." He reached out with one hand. "Give me the remote. Just hand me the remote, and this whole thing will be over."

Using his other arm, Snowman wiped his face on his sleeve. "I don't know."

"Come on. Hand it over." Tommy's fingertips were at the edge of the remote. "Jus–"

An explosion.

As if in slow motion, Kendal flew, then hit the wall. Struggling up, she blinked. Had Snowman hit the button? Her mind registered the answer *no* as quickly as she asked it.

She ran over to where Snowman lay. No remote in his hand. Tommy groaned. She turned to look for the detonator and a hand grabbed her shoulder.

"This what you're looking for?" Owen held up the remote.

"Yes." Glancing back at Tommy, she knew she had to act fast. "You've got to stay here until I can send the bomb squad. If this isn't the bomb that went off, then another one did. I have to find out what's going on."

"I'm going with you."

"Owen, you can't. I need you to keep Snowman from getting away and–"

"Good. You got the remote." Tommy rubbed his head as he held out his hand.

Glad to see Tommy up and ready, Kendal turned toward him. "Your radio working?"

Tommy put his earpiece in, keeping his finger pressed over it. "Command? Boden, over," he said into his wristband. He straightened. "Code red, sir."

Snowman rose to his knees. Kendal sidestepped Tommy. She put herself between the young man and the bomb, her weapon aimed at his back. "On the floor and spread 'em."

The boy slumped back to the floor.

Tommy dropped his finger from his ear. "The explosion was on the west side of the dome."

"Dead?" Kendal asked.

"A lot of damage. It was the roped off part. There are some casualties. No dead reported, yet."

Kendal squatted, putting her gun at Snowman's temple. "How many bombs?"

"I don't have to tell you nothing."

"Well, that's where you're wrong, little man." She poked his head with the barrel. "If you choose to keep your mouth shut, you're going away for a long, long time. Or if you actually use that itty bitty brain of yours and tell me what I want to know, you may get out of jail before you're eighty."

"You can't scare me. I'm a martyr for the cause. It's who I am."

"Fine." She rubbed the gun over his cheek. "Why don't I make you a martyr right now?"

"You–you won't kill me. You're a cop."

"No, I'm FBI. I'm not bound by the rules that cops have to follow. Besides, who's going to know? I can always say you had to be shot to keep you from blowing up the place." Kendal paused, praying the boy was dumb enough to buy her bluff.

"Five."

Hot damn, he was. "Tommy, find out how many they found."

Putting his finger to his ear, he raised his arm. "Command. Number of bombs secured. Over."

It seemed like an eternity as Kendal stared at Tommy waiting.

He smiled. "Four, including ours."

"With one exploded." Kendal smiled back before returning her attention back to Snowman. "Okay, Snowman. One last question and I'll tell the DA you cooperated. How many of you are here?"

"I don't know."

"Wrong answer."

"I don't know," he squeaked. "None of the people in my group came tonight. I was the only one. The rest of the bombs were brought by other parts of the organization."

Unfortunately, this was often the case in radical groups. One cell wasn't aware of the other members. That way none of them could rat the others out. "Then how'd you know how many?"

"I don't know. They told me."

She looked over at Tommy, and he nodded.

"What? What am I missing?" When Owen spoke, Kendal blinked.

She'd almost forgotten he was in the room. "Snowman might think he knows how many bombs. There's a good chance he doesn't."

Owen looked up at the ceiling, then back. "Meaning there could be more out there."

She tapped her weapon on Snowman's head. "Yes, meaning there could be more out there."

"Hey!" Snowman complained.

Realizing she was still thumping him, Kendal halted the movement. "It's got to be chaos out there." She stood. "Has the place been evacuated?"

"Mostly." Tommy pulled out cuffs. He slapped them on Snowman.

Kendal heard what he wasn't saying.

"So one of them could still be in here." Owen said it aloud.

"That's right," Kendal agreed. "Boden, did you get the locations of the ones they found?"

"Except for the one under the stage, the rest including this one were set along the perimeter. The west is where the one blew, this one on the east side, the other two on the north and south."

Shoving the weapon into her waistband, Kendal thought

about the details. "Okay, I need you to wait for the bomb squad."

"Yes, ma'am."

Great, now Tommy finds respect. "I want the entire premises searched for more bombs."

Tommy nodded. "It'll take awhile to get enough suited people here."

Kendal paced over to Owen, dragging her hand through her hair. "We can't wait."

"It's too risky." Tommy lifted Snowman to his feet. "We can't ask the locals to take that kind of risk."

Making her decision, Kendal nodded. "Then I'm going through the area."

"I'm going with you," Owen said.

"I don't–"

Since he was close, he put his finger to her lips. "I'm going."

No time to argue, Kendal threw up her hands. "Fine."

"I don't know, Smart."

"Boden, you just read Snowman his rights. Then make sure that bomb gets permanently deactivated."

"Yes, ma'am."

She gave him a smirk. "Now, you *yes ma'am* me?"

He smiled at her. "It seemed appropriate."

Kendal shook her head before starting down the hall.

"Get Smart!" Tommy yelled.

Exasperated with him, she still had to bite back a smile before looking over her shoulder.

Tommy's face was somber. "Be careful, okay?"

"You got it, Boden." She ran to the stairwell with Owen breathing down her back. Taking the steps two at a time, within seconds they were back on the bottom floor. "Stay behind me. Whatever you do, stay behind me."

He matched her stride for stride. "Where're you going?"

"Did you hear me say, 'stay behind me?'"

"Yeah. Where are you going?"

"You're one thickheaded guy, you know that?" she tossed

at him.

"I've heard it before."

"I'm sure you have."

Owen pushed aside the curtain, and they entered the dome.

"Oh, my God." She waved a hand in front of her face, but the thick smoke barely shifted. Lifting the edge of her coat, she covered her mouth and nose. "You need something." She gestured at her face, telling Owen to follow her lead.

Out of his back pocket, he pulled a blue and white bandana.

As they started further into the room, the smoke lessened, allowing Kendal to see more of the damage. Uniformed men and women scurried around to aid the wounded. Having gone through the training, she'd seen the pictures, even experienced controlled explosions, but now witnessing the casualties amidst the destruction. . .

Her thoughts trailed off as a woman with half of her face covered in blood was helped to her feet.

"Where are you headed?" The handkerchief muffled Owen's voice.

Knowing she had to project through leather, Kendal raised hers. "Where there's no damage."

"Why?"

"Because that's the most likely place we'll find any unexploded bombs." Stopping, Kendal put her free hand on his arm. "You don't have to do this."

"You're not going alone."

She tried to read his expression, but with only his eyes exposed, she found it hard to figure out his true feelings. "Why didn't you listen to me when I told you to leave the circuit?"

When he didn't answer, Kendal turned and carefully stepped through twisted chairs and debris.

"I wanted to be here to protect you."

She stopped again. "Protect me? I can take care of myself."

"Yeah, stupid me. I thought you might need me."

Kendal hesitated, then started walking again. *What do I say to that? Yes, I need you more than you could ever imagine? Or no. I don't need anyone or anything but my career?*

She stumbled over a blown up chair. *What am I thinking? This is not the time to let my mind wander.*

Putting her personal feelings aside, she scanned the dome, trying to not be affected by the sounds of pain echoing through the room. "Over there." She pointed to the north end.

"Why?"

"It's where the people were. If I was going to blow this place to smithereens, I'd have double rigged the populated areas."

"Makes sense."

"Thank you."

Python stared at her, trying to come to grips with everything. "You're welcome."

She gave him an odd look before striding away, her leather clad rear exposed since she was still covering her mouth with the front corner of her coat.

He wiped his brow. Damn, the tension between them had gotten as thick as the smoke. It was probably his fault, but his brain was having a hard time taking everything in.

He hurried to catch up. Kendal was an FBI agent. That fact was the hardest of all. Had she been truthful about anything?

She disappeared behind a curtain shielding the northern entrance. Python swiped it aside, bumping into her back. "Uh, sorry."

She glanced back, stared for a moment, then shrugged.

He wished he knew what she was thinking. *Hell, he did know.* Her only thoughts were on finding more bombs. Nothing else mattered to her.

Hadn't she made that clear time and time again? Sure, in the beginning he'd thought it was because she was a trainer. Either way, her dedication was the same. The goal was the only thing that had changed.

She nudged his arm.

"Wha–"

"*Shh.*" Her voice was low. "You stay here. I'll be back."

He grabbed her. "Uh-uh. I told you I was sticking, and I am."

"Only if you stay behind me."

"Fine."

"I mean it, Owen."

"I said fine." When she turned away, Python made a face. She sure was bossy. Maybe he needed to think about that.

This part of the dome showed little to no damage. She darted into a restroom. Python followed. Just inside the door, she motioned for him to stop. She squatted, craned her neck, and he guessed she was looking for feet inside the stalls. Her motions reminded him just how flexible she was.

Kendal rose. She walked over, throwing open the door of the first stall. She quickly went across the aisle and checked each one. Within seconds she had checked the entire bathroom. Without a word, she stalked by him.

He could definitely see her FBI-ness. How come he couldn't see it before? He trailed behind her into the women's side of the restroom.

Leaning on the wall, he watched as she repeated the same actions as before. This time when she started to stalk out, he grabbed her arm. "If I helped, it would go faster."

"You shouldn't even be here. You're a civilian."

"That's what I've always been to you, huh?" He let her go and headed out of the restroom, not wanting to hear her answer. Halfway down the hallway, he spotted an *Authorized Personnel Only* door. "How 'bout in there?"

"Yes." She passed him, her nose in the air.

So, he'd finally gotten under her skin. His mouth quirked. *Good*! She'd been under his since the beginning. Feeling better, he stepped up his pace, reaching the door first. Smiling, he opened it, tilting his head slightly.

"Cute, Owen. Real, cute."

He wasn't positive, but he could've sworn her lips almost

smiled. *Good, again.*

Inside, they were under the stadium seating. They'd moved a couple of steps when Kendal put out her arm and stopped. She put her finger to her lips. Owen listened for whatever she heard. A slight rustling came from straight ahead.

She pulled a gun from beneath her coat. "Stay behind me," she hissed.

At least she didn't even try to tell him to stay where he was. On her toes, she crept, staying close to the side of the curved concrete wall. Inch by inch they moved. She stopped and craned her neck. Python leaned around her to look. A man in overalls was hunched over a toolbox.

Suddenly, his head jerked up and toward them.

"FBI! Freeze!" Kendal rushed toward him with her gun extended. "Put your hands up. Now!"

The man rose and turned slowly, his hands, palms out, at shoulder level. "I–I don't have a gun. D-d-don't shoot. Please, don't shoot."

The voice cracked and Python knew he was only a boy, too young to be helping to blow up an arena full of people. He should be out playing basketball, worrying about how to ask that first girl out on a date. Not here, becoming a murderer.

Kendal approached the boy. "It's too late. It's over."

"I wasn't gonna do anything."

"You're standing over a bomb, in overalls that match the men we've already arrested. I would say that constitutes as something."

"But–"

"Do yourself a favor. Don't say another word. It'll be better for you in the long run. Owen?" She shifted. With her gun aimed at the boy, she looked over at him.

"Yeah?"

"I need you to go find any cop. Have them call this in and send the bomb squad. I'll stay here and wait."

Python didn't want to leave her, but knew he had to. "Okay." Not liking it, he turned to head back the way they'd come.

The boy's eyes darted past Kendal twice.

Uh-oh. She glanced over her shoulder. Another man!

The boy plowed into her side. Off balance, they fell to the floor with the boy ending on top. He tried to rip her weapon from her hand. The man rushed out of the shadows. Kendal wrestled with the boy, trying to gain the upper hand, but the sucker was squirrelly.

"Get the gun. Get the gun," the man called out as he neared.

"I can't," the boy grunted as she fought him. "She won't let go."

"Grab her arm. I'll get it."

"The hell you will," Kendal gritted, determined not to relinquish her weapon. The boy got her arm, and the man crouched.

"*Aaargh.*"

The man's head snapped up just as Owen tackled him. Kendal had never been so glad to see someone in her entire life.

Thrusting upward with her body, she flipped the boy off. He rushed back. Flat on her back, she shoved her gun in his nose. "Don't move or I'll blow your brains out."

His eyes blazed, and Kendal knew the stuttering, unsure teenager was gone. Replaced by a hardened radical group member prepared to die.

"Go ahead. I don't care." He lunged.

She rolled and slammed into someone's back. The gun flew out of her hand.

"The gun! She lost it!" The kid scrambled over her legs, effectively pinning her. She grabbed his legs, holding him in place.

Grunts and thuds of fists hitting flesh sounded behind her as Owen and the other man continued to fight. She had to get this situation back under control.

The boy reached back, clawing at her hands, drawing blood. He started to kick. Kendal felt her grip loosening.

"No!"

He kicked and clawed harder, breaking her hold. Shoving, she pushed his legs to the side. Her freedom won, she scrambled up, rushing for her semi-automatic even as she pulled the Smith and Wesson from the small of her back.

The boy beat her by two seconds. Throwing himself on the gun, he rolled and came up holding it in both hands. He pointed it directly at her chest as she pointed hers at him.

"Did you know you were gonna die today?" The sick smile spreading across his terribly young face left Kendal with no doubt that he had every intention of killing her.

"Not today, boy." Hearing Owen's voice made Kendal's entire body go cold. This teenager was prepared to die, no matter what. Owen shouldn't be here.

A quick glimpse of the prone body of the unconscious man proved he was secured. Owen crouched, ready to attack.

This is not going to happen. She looked back to the armed boy. "You don't want to do this. Killing an FBI Special Agent is only going to get you a death sentence."

"So? I'd be dying for the cause."

"Don't make me do this," Kendal pleaded as she moved her finger to the trigger. She didn't want to kill the young man. "There's so much for you to live for."

"Not with this government."

"NO!" Owen yelled.

Kendal jerked to see him diving. She snapped back just as the boy shifted the barrel at Owen. "NO!" she screamed, lunged, and pulled the trigger.

The earsplitting blast deafened her as she fell to the ground. She ignored everything except securing the boy. He was lying on his side, clutching his shoulder. Trying to go to him, she found she couldn't move. Owen rushed over, her gun in his hand.

Kendal tried to smile, but frowned instead. Owen grabbed her, lifting her off the floor, surrounding her with his heat. Why couldn't she move? That's when she realized she was cold. So very cold.

"Kendal? Kendal? Can you hear me?" Owen sounded as if he was in a tunnel.

"Ye–" Unable to speak, she tried to cough, then swallow. Her mouth was dry.

"Don't talk." Owen's face was white as a sheet. "We've got to put pressure on it. There's too much blood."

Too much blood? The kid? They needed to get help. Kendal tried to lift her hand and couldn't. A sudden burning engulfed her. She gasped. "I–I'm–"

"*Shh.*" Owen laid her flat on the ground. He pressed his hands near her left shoulder. "Don't try to talk. You need to save your energy."

She was hit? "How bad?" Her own voice sounded small and weak.

"You're going to be all right." He pressed harder. "Save your energy."

She closed her eyes and tried to breathe. The pain she hadn't noticed before now overwhelmed her. Needing to clear the air, needing to let Owen know, she opened her eyes.

Tears dripped off his cheeks. It was then that she knew this was her last chance.

"Owen," she whispered.

"Why won't you listen, and not talk?"

Unable to speak any louder, she tried to implore him with her eyes to come closer. When he lowered his head, she realized he must've understood. "I need–I want–to say. . ."

"What? What is it, sweetheart?"

Seeing the tears, hearing his voice so choked with pain, Kendal felt her heart break. Her eyes closed. She'd been so stupid. Why had her career been so important?

With every last ounce of energy she had, she reopened her eyes. "I love you, Owen."

His eyes widened and she forced herself to smile. Finally, the man she loved knew who she was.

Her eyes closed one last time.

Chapter Fifteen

Spotlighted, the ring sat in the middle of the dome.

The mist-shrouded crowd screamed as he strutted to the blue glowing mat like a moth attracted to a bright fluorescent light. He was the king. No other wrestler could beat him.

He climbed through the ropes, then extended his arms high over his head. The crowd went wild, clapping, stomping, chanting his name. As if the cheering were a physical being, his body enlarged, filling with the intensity and excitement of the mob. Bringing his fists to the front he made an O, scowling, in a perfect pose to show off his arm muscles.

He sensed a presence behind him, even before the booing began. Turning, he prepared to defeat this newest adversary.

"Kendal?"

Out of the shadows, dark hair whipping around her shoulders, she appeared, dressed in a glistening white, flowing dress. She pierced him with an icy glare, her anger palpable. Her mouth moved, but he could hear no sound. The crowd noise increased almost to the point of pain.

"What? What are you saying?"

Not moving from the corner, she pointed at him. Her words lost.

"I can't hear you." Python tried to go to her. He couldn't move. His feet felt cemented to the floor.

Suddenly, a man in overalls rushed from the mist–an ugly, black gun in his hand. Python tried to run, tried to move, his arms flailing, as he tried desperately to reach her.

A flash, then the shot.

Kendal's eyes widened, her mouth gaping. Slowly her head dropped as she lifted her hands to her stomach.

Red soaked the white material. She looked up, her eyes

rimmed in pain. Reaching out her hand dripping with blood, she begged for his help.

He tried to move again. His legs felt like tree trunks anchored to the land. Why couldn't he go to her?

Her beautiful, green, tear-filled eyes pleaded, telling him without words that she needed him.

"No!" he yelled.

She slumped to the floor, landing in a pool of blood.

Falling to his knees, he shouted, cursing the heavens. He lifted his head and stared at her unmoving, red-stained body.

He was unable to do anything–again.

"Why does it take so long?" Python paced over, then back. When he glanced up, he caught Mega giving Joe a peculiar look. "What? What aren't you telling me?"

She came over to him, touching his arm. "Why don't you sit? Have something to eat."

She seemed so small to him now, so fragile. Not like Kendal, a woman made just for him. Or so he had thought.

"Megan's right, Python. Sit." Joe went into the condo's kitchen, then opened the fridge. "How about some cheese and wine?"

Python didn't budge. "I didn't come here for food or drink. I came here for answers."

Mega bopped him on the arm as she passed. "Cheese and wine sound good." She seemed so at home here. Python had been a little surprised to learn that they had decided to live in the condo overlooking the Inner Harbor instead of moving into Little Italy behind the bakery.

"I might not have any answers for you." Joe placed a cutting board on the counter.

"Don't give me that." Python came to stand on the other side of the counter. "You're a Fed. You can find out anything."

Mega took the hunk of cheese from Joe, handing him a bottle of red wine. Probably some fancy Italian brand, not like the eight-ninety-nine bottle Python was used to buying and drinking.

"You know that's not true." Joe pulled out a high-tech looking contraption and popped the cork in seconds. "Every case is a need to know. I don't have any need to know."

"You'd know if an agent was okay or not. All I want to know is how Kendal is? It's been two months. Hell, I don't even know if she made it." He threw his hands in the air. "She could be dead for all I know?"

Again they shared a look.

"All right, that's it." Python pointed at them both. "Stop looking at each other like that. Tell me what's going on."

Joe poured the wine. "The only thing going on is that you have to testify tomorrow. You don't need to worry about anything else."

"What if I don't?"

Joe put down the bottle and stared at him hard. "Don't even kid about something like that. You of all people should want to put those men away."

"Me of all people?" He raised his brow. "Why me, of all people? Why should I be angrier than others? Is that what you're not telling me? Did they kill Kendal?"

Joe filled a second glass. "None of that matters. Just know that your testimony is important to put these guys away for a long, long time."

"How come you never told me you used to be a wrestler?" Mega came into the living room with a tray of cheese.

"It wasn't important."

"It was a big part of your life, yet in all the years I knew you, you never said a word."

He followed her toward the sofa, shrugging as he sat in an overstuffed chair. "Like I said, not important."

"But–" she started.

"It wasn't something I was proud of. I wanted to have a regular life."

She frowned at him while Joe brought the glasses. He set them down on the coffee table.

"Why weren't you proud of it? From what I've learned

you were very successful. I mean, compared to what I thought. . ."

"Compared to what you thought?" He straightened his back. "What'd you think?"

She blushed. "Well, it's not important now."

"To me it is. What did you think?"

She looked at Joe, who'd sat next to her on the couch. He shrugged as he chose a piece of cheese. Python didn't need an interpreter for that look. Joe wasn't getting involved.

"Mega?"

She looked at her hands, then back at him. "You were always just sitting around at Tiny's tattoo parlor. I just assumed you didn't have a job or any skills."

"You thought I was a bum?"

"Not exactly a bum. Just someone who hadn't found their niche in life yet." She spread her hands. "Who was I to say anything? I hadn't found mine either."

Joe lifted her hand and kissed it. "Look at you now." He smiled at Python. "The bakery's never been so successful. Between her memory and marketing skills, we have people from all over Baltimore driving in for our pastries."

Python sat back and looked at them. She'd thought he was an aimless bum. In more ways then one, she'd been right. But in one very important way, she'd been wrong. Very wrong.

She shook her finger at him. "You know, Python, we never got around to writing you up."

Joe pushed her hand into her lap. "You don't sell insurance anymore."

"I know." She stayed focused on Python. "You should always be prepared, and term life insurance is so important. He–"

"I've got to go." Python stood. He really didn't need to hear her sales pitch tonight.

"Now? You just got here." She rose too.

"Yeah." He started edging out of the room. "I've got some errands to run, and I've got an early flight out tomorrow. I'm on the stand in the afternoon."

Joe joined his wife, and together they escorted him to the front door.

"You'll call us if you need to talk?" Mega placed her hand on his arm.

Joe grinned over her head, when Python's face must've showed how befuddled he felt.

"Don't worry about it, Python," Joe said.

"Okay." He hugged Mega.

She smiled. "Take care of yourself."

"I will." He shook Joe's hand.

"Relax. Just tell the truth tomorrow," said Joe.

"That's the plan."

"By the way," Mega started, "what's with the hat and bandana?"

"Just thought I'd try out a new look." He grinned. "What'd you think?"

She tilted her head. "Different."

"Yeah, that's kind of been my mantra." He waved. "See you later."

It wasn't until the door closed behind him that he realized how effectively they'd diverted him from asking more questions about Kendal. Pushing the button for the elevator, he thought back over the past two months.

The dream had come almost every night, depriving him of much needed sleep. Was she dead or alive? Why wouldn't they tell him?

She'd been so white. She'd lost so much blood. It would've been a miracle if she lived. Right now, he didn't believe in miracles or love.

Kendal washed her hands while staring at her reflection in the restroom mirror. Her shoulder was still sore. Thankfully, she'd regained ninety percent mobility. Even though the rehabilitation had been torturous, it had also been the best way to keep her mind off Owen. Following the orders not to have any contact with him had been the hardest part of her recovery.

How Wilson had learned about her personal relationship

with Owen was still unknown. She did have a sinking suspicion it was Fallon, but didn't have any evidence to back it up.

The door opened.

"Well, speak of the devil," she muttered to herself.

"I heard that." Fallon walked over to a stall.

Kendal shrugged. She didn't care what people thought anymore. She smiled at her reflection. She'd grown as a person during her undercover work. A growth she felt good about.

"I didn't rat on you."

She met Fallon's eyes in the mirror. "Did I say you did?"

"No. But if I were you, I would've assumed it was me."

Kendal didn't even try to disagree. She turned to look at the diminutive woman. "Why are you telling me this?"

Fallon kicked the bottom of the stall wall. "No reason."

"My opinion matters?"

"Let's just say, I've got enough natural enemies in the department. I don't need any extras."

Kendal started to walk out, then stopped and turned back. "Let me give you a piece of advice from what I've just recently learned myself." She paused, giving Fallon a chance to decline.

The young agent nodded. "What?"

"Be true to yourself. Stop trying to be what you think the bureau wants or needs."

Shaking her head, Fallon started into the stall. "Easy for you. You're not five-foot-nothing, constantly having to prove yourself."

As the door closed Fallon in, Kendal sighed. *If you'd stop trying to prove yourself, you might find out you've already gained the respect you don't think you have.*

Fortunately, it wasn't Kendal's problem. Right now, she had a courtroom appearance to tackle. On the way to the room, she went over the instructions given to her by her superiors. She was not to talk to the press. Nor was she to make eye contact with anyone in the courtroom except the attorneys questioning her.

She could understand all the precautions. The entire episode had become a media circus with reporters clamoring for an exclusive. Due to her injury, up to this point, she had been an unknown. Today, all that would change. They would whisk her away as soon as she testified. Hopefully, she could disappear inside the bureau until the fervor died down.

The court officer she was supposed to meet escorted her to a side entrance where she would wait. Minutes passed before the door opened. With her head held high, Kendal entered the courtroom.

Python had chosen the last seat in the far corner of the courtroom. He wasn't sure why he stayed. The initial questioning had been straightforward. The cross-examination grueling. Thank God it was over.

"The prosecution calls Special Agent Kendal Smart to the stand."

Every hair on his body stood on end. *Kendal? His Kendal? Alive and well?* His head snapped around, scanning the room for her. How could he have missed her?

A gray-suited woman walked stiffly into the room from a side door. He visually searched around her, looking for Kendal.

"Do you swear to tell the truth, the whole truth, and nothing but the truth?"

He did a double take as the rigid lady sat down. *Kendal?* That couldn't be her in a tailored suit with a conservative shirt buttoned up to her neck. He straightened in the chair and craned his neck to get a better view. Then the power of what he'd just learned hit him.

She was alive! His body vibrated with the news as his hands began to sweat. He wiped them on his pants.

Her brown hair was pulled back in a strict bun. Brown hair? This couldn't be his Kendal. She was the complete opposite of the woman he'd fallen in love with.

Her clipped voice answered the attorney's questions

precisely. He stared at her, wanting to make a connection. She never looked anywhere. Only at the person asking the questions.

Something about her face was different. He couldn't tell exactly what from this distance. He rubbed his eyes. How could he not have seen any evidence of the woman sitting in front of him now? Was she that good an actress?

The defense attorney stopped questioning Kendal, probably because she couldn't break through the icy façade. Kendal rose as stiffly as she'd sat. Although he bobbed his head, desperately trying to get her attention, she left the courtroom without ever glancing his way.

Immediately, he got up. Stepping over the feet of the people filling his row, he stumbled out to the aisle. Maybe he could catch her in the hall. He opened the door, and a flood of flashbulbs flared in his face.

Damn, forgot about the press. Using his hands, he shielded his eyes.

"Python! Can you tell us your version of the events?"

"What'd you say on the stand?"

"When are you returning to the NFW?"

Microphones and questions hurled over each other all aimed at him. Without a word, using maneuvers typically reserved for the ring, he extended his arm, barreling a path through the reporters.

"Python, are you returning to the ring anytime soon?"

"Don't you have any comment for your fans?"

They chased him through the hall, then out the front of the courthouse. Even as he ran, he searched the area for Kendal. Stumbling to the curb, he knew he had to get away.

He headed down the street, now searching for a taxi. A few persistent reporters followed him, while the rest went back inside. Hailing the cab, Python happily slammed the door in their faces.

He sat back. It was time to get back to Baltimore and make some changes.

* * *

At her desk, Kendal tried one more time to concentrate on the case file in front of her. She shut the folder. *This is stupid. I'm a professional. I will not allow a man to overtake my every waking minute.*

Jerking open a drawer, her hand stopped in mid-reach. On top of the pens and sticky notes sat the Python doll–uh–action figure. Unable to prevent herself, she lifted the toy, then moved its arms. Tracing the little flesh-colored bald head, she turned it over and smiled at the tiny tattoo of a python on the back.

"That's where it went."

Hearing Tommy, her immediate response was to throw the doll back in the drawer and shut it. She squelched the reaction and calmly looked up. "Yes. Do you need it?" As strange as it felt, she didn't want to give up the action figure. She'd given up so much already. Losing this small piece of Owen would be the last straw.

"Uh, no." He came into the cubicle, then sat down on the edge of her desk. "As long as I know where it is, that's cool. It's a collector's item, though."

She turned the muscle-bound wrestler in her hand. "It really doesn't look like him."

"It does."

Kendal heard the defensive tone and her spirits lifted. She knew how he felt. Maybe not for the same reasons, but she was definitely protective when it came to Owen. Reluctantly, she handed the toy over. "Here, you take it. I wouldn't want anything to happen to it."

"Are you sure?" He clearly didn't mean what he said, as he reverently took the action figure.

Smiling more in the past few minutes then she had in the past six months, Kendal felt like grinning. "Yes, I'm sure."

He put the action figure in his pocket, his expression sobering. "How're your cases going?"

She fiddled with the file. "Fine. How about yours?"

"Good." He touched one of the files on her desk. "You did a good job in Indianapolis."

Swallowing her pride, she confessed what she hadn't admitted even to herself. "I made a rookie mistake."

"Getting involved–"

She waved him off. "No. Not that."

"Then what?"

"I didn't search the shadows for a second perp."

"Everyone we arrested was working alone. Besides, the idea that they would come back in to get the bomb instead of leaving it was absurd. No one could've guessed that."

"My mistake could've killed Owen."

"It didn't. That's all that matters."

Picking up a pen, she bounced it on the desk. "You'd think, huh?"

"Why don't you go to him?"

She fumbled the pen. "I don't know what you–"

"Do we have to go back to the beginning, Smart?" He moved her desk stapler. "I thought we'd at least become friends."

Not sure she could trust herself to even talk about it, she made a sudden decision to take the chance. "Yes, we did."

"Then, why don't you go see him?"

"I'm not sure he'd want to see me."

"Is that the fearless, nothing-ever-scares-me agent I've always known talking?"

"Just forget it."

"Smart, I was kidding." He knocked her in the shoulder. "Loosen up. Go see him."

"He doesn't know me."

He frowned, then nodded as if it took a minute for him to get her meaning. "So, let him learn."

"It's not that easy, Boden."

"Yes, it is."

"You don't understand."

"Yeah? I'm a man, aren't I?"

She scanned his body. "Well–"

"Funny. You're a real laugh riot." He shifted his feet. "The point I'm making is, if he fell in love with you, he fell in love. Your appearance doesn't change that."

"What are you? A lovelorn advice column?"

"I'm just telling you the way it is for a man. We fall in love and that's it."

She leaned back in her chair. "You know this from personal experience?"

"You could say that."

"Anyone I know?" Did he and Fallon have something going on?

"No." He moved the stapler again. "It happened a long time ago."

Curiosity getting the better of her, Kendal asked, "Where is she now?"

"It didn't work out."

She raised her eyebrows. "You're giving me advice?"

"Trust me. He wants to see you."

Since he answered her jest so seriously, Kendal sobered as well. "Do you still want to see the woman you're in love with?"

"My ex-wife?" Tommy shook his head. "No. I'm not in love with her anymore."

"Sure doesn't sound that way to me."

Tommy straightened. "We're not talking about me."

"Oh?" Seemed Tommy's personal life was a taboo subject.

"Go see him."

"I don't know where he lives." It was a weak excuse, but she was willing to grasp at anything.

"Good thing for you, I went there once." He motioned at the drawer. "I need pen and paper."

She gave him what he wanted and waited while he jotted down the address.

"Here. Go now." He handed her the slip of paper.

"It's the middle of the day." She studied the address. "This isn't the best part of town."

"That changes your feelings?"

The harsh words took Kendal aback. Did money have

something to do with Tommy's bad marriage? "No." She stood, grabbing her coat off the back of the chair. "It does make a lot more sense to go now and not later."

He slid off the desk. "You'll let me know."

"You know, Boden, you keep this up and I might think you care."

"Don't kid yourself," he said with a wide smile.

"I wouldn't dare." After putting on her coat, she pulled out a knit hat from the pocket, took a step, then stopped. "Thanks."

"Anytime, Smart. Anytime."

Leaving the bureau, she realized he meant it. Tommy was one of the good guys. Too bad some woman had burned him so badly.

Out in the parking lot, she brushed off the dusting of snow on her bureau issued car, wishing she'd parked in the garage. The drive from the west side of Baltimore to the east gave her plenty of time to think about what she was doing.

Tommy might be right about her appearance, but how could any man get past being lied to? Owen had been by her side when she got shot. Wasn't that proof positive that he cared even after he knew she was FBI? Or was it his knight-in-shining-armor personality coming through? Hadn't that been why they'd chosen him in the first place? Feeling like she should just bang her head against a brick wall and stop thinking, Kendal gripped the steering wheel tighter instead.

Before she knew it, she was parked outside a decrepit apartment building's door. *What is wrong with me? I've stared down hardened criminals, taken on tough, dangerous assignments, yet here I sit with my palms moist.* Thinking she must be going crazy, Kendal forced herself to leave the car.

With her head down, she crossed the street, hurrying inside. The smell hit her first. If she had to guess, she'd have thought one of the apartments had a rotting body in it. She put her hand over her nose.

Owen's apartment was located on the second floor. Picking her way through the trash left on the stairs, she realized many of the residents didn't quite get the idea of taking out the garbage. They seemed to think the hallway was far enough.

When she reached his door, she paused to take a deep breath. He was only a man. What was the big deal? She knew the answer, but wasn't wiling to let herself dwell on it.

She knocked. Waiting for him to answer, she kept watch on the hall. It might be midday, but in this neighborhood, she wasn't about to let her guard down.

No answer. Putting her ear to the door, she listened. No noise.

Pulling off her gloves, she knocked again, this time louder.

No answer.

Maybe, he's asleep. She banged on the door.

"Hey! What'a tr'in to do? Wake t' dead?"

With her hand at the small of her back, Kendal swiveled to find a stooped elderly woman standing in the opposite doorway. "No, ma'am. I thought maybe Owen was asleep."

"You lookin' fer Python?"

"Yes, ma'am, I am."

"You too late."

"Excuse me?"

"He left."

"Left?" Shaking her head, Kendal knew she needed to stop repeating what the woman was saying.

"Yessiree. Them reporters kept comin' 'round. I thought you were 'nother one."

"No, ma'am. I'm not with the press."

"Yep, I see that."

Not sure what she meant, Kendal continued, "You wouldn't happen to know where he went, would you?"

The old lady eyed her up and down before lifting a cup and spitting into it. "Nope. He di'nt say."

Not believing the woman for a minute, Kendal reached into her suit pocket. She pulled out a nondescript business card. "If you happen to see him, would you mind giving him this?"

A bony, gnarled hand took the card. "I s'pose I can."

"I'd very much appreciate it." Kendal turned to leave, then turned back. "Have you complained to the landlord about the smell and condition of this place?"

"Don' do no good. He don' fix nuthin'."

Kendal pulled out another card and gave it to her. "Give me a week. If he doesn't start making improvements by then, call me."

"You betcha, girly." The woman's bright eyes overshadowed her brown-toothed grin.

Kendal waved as she descended the stairs. Her happy mood stayed with her all the way to her car. Once inside, she slumped.

Owen was gone. Sure, she could use the bureau's resources to find him, but that was strictly against policy. That wouldn't stop her as much as his moving did. He knew this was the address Tommy had. He'd probably moved wanting to make sure he never saw her again.

Dropping her head on the steering wheel, she rolled it back and forth. She shouldn't have given that woman her card for Owen. If he ever came back and she gave it to him, he'd think Kendal was desperate.

She lifted her head, wondering where all her self-confidence had gone. *Why is it when you fall in love every insecurity possible finds its way to the surface*?

With a twist, she started the ignition. A neon sign caught her attention. *Tiny's Tattoos*. Owen had said his friend owned a tattoo shop. Maybe this was it.

She paused, her hand on the keys. Hadn't she just told herself that if he'd wanted to see her again, he wouldn't have moved?

Oh, what the hell.

After turning off the car, she got out. She'd never forgive herself if she didn't at least give it a try. Entering, the store, it appeared cleaner than she expected, especially after Owen's apartment building.

The small room had one other doorway covered with a

curtain depicting a wizard. With no one around, she unbuttoned her coat, then took off her gloves and hat while she studied the walls covered with drawings.

Why would anyone want to etch ink into their skin? She thought of Owen's head and shook her own.

"May I help you?"

Kendal pulled her attention from the wall, turning to find a man as large, no larger, than Owen standing in the curtained doorway. His entire body, what she could see of it, was covered in colorful ink.

"Are you here for a tattoo?" His voice and body language told her he knew she wasn't.

"No. I was hoping you might help me locate someone."

He rubbed his chin. "You a cop?"

"No." She held out her hand. "I'm Kendal Smart. I'm a business consultant."

Shaking her hand tentatively, he suddenly frowned. "Did you say Kendal?"

"Yes."

"There can't be that many women with that name," he muttered as he started to circle her. "You don't fit the description at all."

Her heart skipped a beat as she swiveled to keep him in sight. This was Owen's friend. "You know Owen?"

"Owen?" He smiled for the first time. "Yeah, he's a good friend."

"Do you know where he is?"

He cocked his head. "Right to the point, aren't you?"

"I'm sorry." She wasn't about to back down now. "It's imperative that I see him."

"I don't think I can help you."

Somewhat taken aback, Kendal moved closer. "It's important."

Staring into her eyes, he leaned in as well. "I don't help liars."

She jerked back. "Excuse me?"

"You aren't a business consultant."

She debated for a millisecond. "You're right. I'm FBI. Special Agent Kendal Smart."

He smiled even as he crossed his arms. "That's more like it."

"And you are?"

"I'm Tiny."

After a quick scan of his enormous body, she lifted a brow. "Tiny?"

"You got something to say?"

Raising her hand, she smirked, "Not me."

He laughed. "You know, your personality doesn't fit the look."

"Excuse me?"

He waved up and down. "The suit, the bun. The whole third-grade-teacher-from-hell thing."

She lifted her nose. "It's appropriate attire for my profession."

"Now, that attitude fits the package."

She stared at the huge man. "You're direct."

"When the woman who screwed with my friend comes walking in? Yeah, I get that way."

Kendal went immediately on the defensive. "There were extenuating circumstances."

"So I heard." He shrugged. "Doesn't excuse what you did."

Already hurt, she wasn't about to take his accusations lying down. "I couldn't tell him I was with the FBI. The mission would have been in jeopardy." She threw up her hands. "I don't know why I'm even telling you this."

"You don't get it."

Ready to stop dancing around the truth, she blew out a breath. "Then why don't you explain it to me."

"You could've called and told him you were still alive."

His words stunned her. She started to reach out to touch him. At the last moment, she caught herself and snatched her hand back. "What do you mean? I was told they notified him that night."

"You were told wrong."

She paced away. "I can't believe they lied to me. Why would they do that?" Even as the words left her mouth, she knew the answer. Since she thought he knew she was fine, she'd followed orders not to contact Owen without a fight. How wrong she'd been.

"So you're not the only one who lies in the FBI."

Pacing back to him, she put her hands on her hips. "I may not agree with the method, but the goal needed was achieved by the deception."

"Does your mouth hurt when it talks like that?"

Unable to help it, she laughed. "Okay. I'll slack on the vocabulary, if you tell me where Owen is."

"Uh-uh, no can do."

"But–"

"How do I know you're just not going to lie to him some more?"

"How do you–" Kendal stopped, then smiled. "I think I have a way to show you I mean business."

Chapter Sixteen

"Three days ago? She came by here too?"

Tiny sat on a short stool, making a delicate incision into a man's back. "Yep."

Antsy, Python shifted on his feet. "That's all you have to say?"

As his forehead furrowed, Tiny nodded. "Yep."

Even knowing Tiny didn't like to talk, always concentrating fully when he was working, didn't keep Python from being persistent. "What'd she want?"

"You."

His heart started to pound. "She said that?"

"Yep." Tiny's attention never wavered from the tattoo he was creating.

"I should go see her."

"Yep."

Tiny would take at least thirty to forty-five minutes to complete this latest piece of artistry. Python couldn't wait that long to learn more. It was time to find Kendal.

Practically running out of the parlor, he hurried to his vehicle. Settling into the plush seats, he inhaled deeply enjoying the new car smell. When the engine purred to life, he patted the dash like a well-trained puppy. A quick check over his shoulder and he merged into traffic, heading for the west side of Baltimore.

What was he going to say?

"Hi, Kendal. Long time no see." *Could I sound more desperate*? His fingers drummed the steering wheel.

"Hi, Kendal. Didn't you want to see me?" *Yeah, that sounds brilliant.*

Maybe he should just stand there and let her make the first

comment. He pulled into the FBI front parking lot. The nondescript building could house any number of businesses. Instead, this one held his future.

As he crept by the parking garage, he noticed the need for a pass. Moving on, he parked in the open lot. Before getting out, he checked his reflection in the rearview mirror.

Feeling like he was walking up to a suburban house to pick up a girl on his first date, Python wiped his hands on his pants. What if she didn't want to see him? What if she'd been coming around only to give him the brush off? How come he hadn't waited and asked Tiny more questions?

He shook his head. This wasn't helping. He'd find out soon enough what her intentions had been.

He was ten feet away when the darkened glass door opened. Kendal came out, waving goodbye to someone as she and another man turned toward him.

Quickening his pace before he lost his nerve, Python got within a couple of feet. "Kendal."

She stopped, cocked her head, and stared. Taking two steps back, she put her hand into the purse hanging on her shoulder.

He put his hands up. "Kendal, it's me."

"Do you know this person, Smart?" the man on her left asked.

"Uh..."

Extending his hand, Python said, "I'm Owen. Kendal and I worked together on a case."

"Owen?" Kendal repeated as her hand left the purse. With a slight frown, she stepped closer.

The man glanced between the two of them, then took Owen's hand and shook. "I'm Gibson." He turned to Kendal. "I'll see you Monday, Smart."

Kendal nodded without taking her eyes off Owen.

Wondering if she was involved with Gibson and not liking her speechlessness, Owen shuffled his feet. "You didn't know it was me?"

Of all the reactions he'd played in his head, her not

recognizing him hadn't been one of them. Stupid, now that he thought about it.

She pointed. "You–you have hair."

He rubbed his head, still not used to feeling the soft mass up there. "I let it grow."

"You were bald on purpose?" She moved closer, and his heart raced faster.

How he wanted to grab and hold her. Nothing would make him happier right now then to have her in his arms. "It seemed like the thing to do at the time."

She circled him. "None of your tattoos show." Back in front, she reached out as if wanting to touch him. She pulled back before making contact.

Not dwelling on her withdrawal, he concentrated on the pleased look on her face. A hand on his head, he ruffled his hair. "You like?"

Her gloved hand pulled the coat around her neck tighter. "You've given yourself a pardon."

"What?"

A slight smile formed on her lips. "Nothing."

A gust of wind blew hard against his side. "Can we go somewhere and talk?"

"Now?"

Doubt cloaked his newfound confidence. "You don't want to?"

Her eyes met his. "I would like to very much."

Her hesitation had scared him more than he cared to admit.

She stepped off the curb, heading to the parking lot. "There's an IHOP in the Security Mall parking lot. Why don't we meet there?"

"You could ride with me."

Again her hesitation tore at him.

"Okay."

With a hand at her elbow, he guided her to his vehicle.

"A black minivan." She trailed her hand along the hood and smiled. Staring at her lips made him ache to hold her.

He dragged his gaze away, confident her smile told him more than words that she liked his choice. "I had to have it special ordered. Black isn't a very popular color for minivans." He opened the passenger door. "It was one of my goals."

"Yes. I remember."

Her words replayed in his head as he hurried around the front of the car. She remembered. That was a good sign. Getting in, he started up the van, and heat poured from the vents.

She stripped off her gloves. "Oh, that feels good."

Her voice brought back memories of them wrapped around each other. He felt himself twitch in the most inappropriate place. "Would you mind if we just drove around?"

"Drove around?"

"I'd like us to be alone."

"Alone?" *This repeating thing has got to stop*, Kendal chided herself. *So, I'm a little nervous. It's to be expected.*

"Do you mind?"

"No. I don't mind." She sank back into the rich leather seat and thought how she'd hoped this day would come. Tiny had said he would let Owen know that she'd been to his tattoo parlor, and had assured her Owen would contact her. She'd thought it would happen by phone.

His surprise appearance had thrown her for a loop, not to mention his having hair. Beautiful, golden brown, wavy hair. Who knew he could grow it? She turned to stare and felt a stab of disappointment.

He glanced her way. "What?"

"I kinda miss the tattoos."

He chuckled and shook his head. "You miss the tattoos?"

Pulling on the seatbelt, Kendal shifted in the seat toward him. "They were such a part of you."

"They're still there."

She sat back and smiled. "I guess they are."

Outside the parking lot he turned right, heading away from the beltway. The minivan provided such a smooth, comfortable ride, she found herself relaxing.

"I miss..."

She turned back toward him. "You miss?"

"It's nothing." He didn't take his eyes off the road.

Emboldened merely by his showing up, she reached over and touched his arm. "I want to know."

"The way you used to look."

She snatched her hand away, instantly regretting her brusque reaction. "I'm sorry." She reached back over. "You caught me off guard."

"Because I liked you before?"

"This is why I wouldn't tell you how I felt." This time she brought her hand away gradually. "I wasn't the person you got to know. That was a part I was playing."

"Are you saying none of Big K exists in you?"

Hesitating, Kendal pondered the question for a moment. "Part of my cover allowed me to be more expressive than I am on a natural basis."

"Tiny said you did that sometime."

"I did what sometime?"

"Talked like you were reciting from some kind of textbook."

"I don't think-" she cut herself off. "Yes, he said something very similar to me."

"You came by to see me."

Even though he said it as a statement, she heard the doubt. "Yes, I did."

"Why?"

Surprised, she raised a brow. "Didn't Tiny tell you?"

"No." He shook his head. "He was working on someone. All I got out of him was that you came by and the way you talked."

"It was three days ago." Hearing the censure in her voice, she cringed. She sounded like a pouty teenager.

"I've been, uh, without phone service."

She felt immediate remorse. Who knew how much debt he'd had prior to his going undercover for the FBI. "I'm sorry.

I didn't–"

"It's okay." He waved a hand. "You wanted to see me about something?"

She looked down at her hands in her lap. "I didn't like how it ended."

"I saw you at the trial."

Her gaze popped to his. "You were there? I didn't know."

He turned back to the road. "I know. When I went searching for you, the press hounded me."

Watching his strong hands turn the steering wheel flooded her mind with images of the two of them together. How he held her tight, took her to new heights of pleasure...

She decided it was time to clear the air. "The Bureau told me they'd called, let you know I was fine."

"That's why you didn't call?"

He sounded relieved, making her feel moderately better. "They didn't want anything interfering with my rehabilitation."

"I thought you were dead. I mean, all that blood."

She didn't have to hear the heartache in his voice to know the hell he must've gone through. She placed her hand on his arm again. "I'm sorry you didn't know. I'm afraid the FBI works on a need to know basis. My survival wasn't leaked, in order to increase the anxiety of the arrested radical members. The intention was to get them to divulge more information, roll over on other members including their leader."

Without looking at her, he nodded. "Did it work?"

"Yes."

"I guess that's all that matters, huh?"

Her fingers tightened on him. "No."

When he didn't answer, she let go. Facing forward, Kendal felt tense. Their reunion was not going the way she'd imagined.

He pulled over to the side of the road. For the first time, she realized they were in a residential neighborhood. "Owen, I wa–"

"Do you mind if I stop for awhile?"

"What? No, no. Of course not."

He unsnapped his seatbelt. "Good. I think it'll be easier to talk this way."

She undid her belt as well.

Shifting toward her, he hung one arm over the steering wheel, the other on the seat. "Just tell me why you came to see me."

She shook her head. "Just tell you." The request sounded simple. But she knew a great deal rode on the words she chose.

"I'd like to know."

"I wanted to explain. Let you know how I feel."

"Okay."

"This isn't easy, you know. You're asking me to spill my guts without my knowing what you think."

"Yeah, I am."

"All right." *In for a penny, in for a pound.* Why her grandmother's words came back to her now, Kendal didn't know. "I didn't mean for us to get so involved during the operation. It wasn't proper. I could've lost my job because of it."

"That's what you came to tell me?"

"Not exactly. I came to apologize–"

"Let's go inside." He opened the car door and got out, not letting her agree or disagree. She hurried from the car, scurrying to catch him as he marched toward the front door.

"Owen? What're you doing?"

Not answering, he shoved a key into the knob. With a sharp twist, the door opened.

"Owen? I asked what. . ." her words trailed away as she entered the gorgeous home.

Rushing after him, she'd taken little notice of the outside. Now inside, she took in the lovely surroundings. She was standing in an open foyer of glowing oak hardwood floors. The walls were a warm, welcoming cream color with matching oak molding.

He continued, and she followed him into an expansive living room. "Who lives here?"

"I do."

"You do?" She turned in a complete circle. "I don't understand."

He started to rub his head, then stopped and stared at his hand. "That seems to be the one thing that is constant between us."

When she only frowned, he shrugged.

"Misunderstandings. Isn't that about the only thing we do well?"

"No, Owen. It isn't." Prepared to clear up everything, Kendal walked over. "I thought we made a pretty good pair."

For the first time, he reached out, touching the side of her face. "I thought so, too."

"What I don't know is if you can forgive me for all the lying." She searched his eyes for any clue.

He smiled. "I already have."

"Owen." His name came out on a breath as her hands surrounded his face. Keeping his gaze locked with hers, she rose on her toes. Lightly, she rubbed their lips together. "I missed you."

"Stop talking," he ordered as his mouth settled on hers. His arms circled her waist, pulling her tight against him.

Kendal couldn't remember ever feeling this warm, good, or safe. As the kiss deepened, her whole life seemed to right itself. All the doubts, anxiousness, and concern she'd had since the operation ended, disappeared with his kiss.

Her fingers found their way into his new head of hair. The honey dipped ends twirled around her fingers. She flexed them, loving the feeling while massaging his hidden colorful skin.

He broke away, nuzzling her cheek. "I've been wanting to do that for a long time."

"So have I."

A smile lit his face, making her smile back.

Snuggling closer, she hugged him hard. "I've missed you. I thought about you every day. It killed me not to be able to call."

"I'm sorry you had to go through the therapy alone. I

know how hard it is."

With one hand, she traced down the front of his shirt to where she knew his scar lay beneath. "You do, don't you?"

Lifting her hand, he kissed the fingertips. "I love you, Kendal. I always will."

Having waited for this moment, she suddenly felt uneasy. What if her saying it didn't give him the pleasure she'd hoped it would? What if the build-up and delay would make the whole thing anti-climactic? "I love you, Owen. I have for a long time."

He swooped her in the air, swinging around. "Yes! I've waited a long time to hear those words again."

She braced her hands on his shoulders and laughed. "I was a little worried they wouldn't be that great after the lengthy wait."

Settling her back on her feet. He cradled her face with his hand. "I would've waited a lifetime to hear you say them over and over again."

"You're too forgiving."

"Am I?"

"I'm so sorry for all the lies."

He led her to a large sofa in the middle of the room. As he sat, he grabbed her hips, guiding her into his lap. "Stop apologizing. You had a job. Now that I know most everything, I understand."

"Most everything?" Her back straightened. "There's something about me that still concerns you?"

"No, not about you."

Shifting, she settled more comfortably, putting an arm behind his back. "Then what'd you mean?"

"I guess I never understood how it all came out."

She debated a half second about confidentiality and telling him it didn't matter. "The radical group wanted to get the government's attention by killing innocents. We were wrong to think it had anything to do with money laundering. Rusen was accepting their money for information about the matches. With his help, they were able to infiltrate the dome before we even got there."

He toyed with the bun at the base of her neck. "There was never a drug ring, was there?"

"No. We didn't want you in more danger than necessary." She kissed his cheek. "Of course, we miscalculated how active you'd be in wanting to solve the case yourself."

"I just wanted to get you out of harm's way. Funny, now when I think back, you must've thought I was a real dope."

She felt her hair unbinding from his ministrations. "That's not what I thought at all. Your constant concern only made me feel guiltier about lying to you. Then when you were shot at. . . It almost had me telling you everything."

"I still can't wrap my mind around the idea that Dina did it all because she thought I killed Terror."

"Her attacks were linked to her brother's death, but not the way you think. She and Terror tampered with the ropes, and you were supposed to fall through them. I don't think they were trying to kill you, only get you off the circuit. Terror wanted to be the top wrestler. Dina wanted you, period. You weren't cooperating on either front."

Her hair fell over her shoulders. "Then you came back. You continued to reject her and pushed Jammer, the wrestler she was now secretly backing, out of the limelight. That's why she killed Bernard Cook. He was supposed to convince Rusen to keep Jammer on top. He reneged. She shot him. The psychiatrist who examined her said she's borderline psychotic. Not enough for an insanity plea, but close."

"The drug dealer?"

"We found no link between him and Dina. I don't know why he had a gun. He was definitely going to use it. Boden had to take the shot."

Tommy was having a hard time justifying the action. She'd assured him the shoot was legit, but every agent dealt with his or her conscience differently. She hoped he could eventually put it behind him.

"I'm glad it's over." He hugged her even tighter.

With the arm behind him, she hugged him back. "You

know, if we hadn't gotten you to go back in the ring, you'd never have been in danger. I'm really sorry, Owen. I never meant to intentionally put you in harm's way."

"*Shh*." He put his finger on her mouth. "You didn't do it. I chose to work with the FBI. I had my own demons to overcome."

"Yes." She ruffled his hair. "You've finally forgiven yourself."

"You said something like that earlier. What're you talking about?" Gently, he traced the side of her face.

"You gave yourself a life sentence by tattooing your head. A place I thought you'd never be able to cover up without a hat. I didn't know you were choosing to shave it."

"You think since I let my hair grow, I've forgiven myself for Terror's death." His eyes and tone were somber.

She matched his seriousness. "Add to it the fact that you introduced yourself as Owen today, then yes, I do."

"You may be right." He shrugged.

Feeling the best she had in months, she grinned. "I love you."

"I don't think I'll ever get tired of hearing that."

"You don't think so, huh?"

"Will you marry me?"

Kendal blinked, her heart racing as the words registered. "You're sure you want me?"

"I was thinking you might not want me." His grin betrayed his real thoughts.

Willing to play along, she intentionally peered over his shoulder. "Does the house come too?"

"You like it?" The teasing lightness had left his voice.

She focused back on him. "It's beautiful." Then it dawned on her how she'd misperceived something again. "You didn't have a phone because you were waiting for a hook up. Not because you couldn't afford one."

His hand squeezed her side. "You think I'm broke?"

"It doesn't matter. I make a pretty good salary. I think we'll be fine." She held his face. "Yes, I'll marry you."

With a smile, he kissed her. "Kendal, I'm not broke. I bought this home for us."

"Your dream." She kissed him again. "It's wonderful. I'm more than willing to do whatever it takes to make everything you've ever wanted come true."

His mouth twitched, as if he held the most incredible secret. "The only thing you have to do is be there."

Eyeing him carefully, she patted his shoulder. "Plus contribute funds to the budget."

He shook his head. "You're not getting what I'm saying."

"Then what are you saying?"

"Money is not going to be a problem for us."

"Owen." Understanding men and their egos, Kendal knew she had to pacify him. Let him know it was okay. She started massaging his back. "I went to your old apartment. I realize you squandered away whatever you had earned as a wrestler and have no income. I love you. We'll make it work."

"I have plenty of money."

Her hand stilled. "Excuse me?"

"Now that I think about it, you're probably right."

Totally confused, she frowned. "Right? What're you talking about now?"

His stare seemed to be directed at some point over her shoulder. "I made a lot of money the first time around on the circuit and never spent much. I guess I was punishing myself."

Finally catching up, she flexed her hand. "Now, you're allowing yourself to spend it."

He looked at her. "Exactly."

"Wow. This is pretty amazing."

"That I have money?"

"No." She giggled. Would they ever be on the same page? "That you were really thinking about me all this time. I thought you'd never forgive me. You can't know how happy you're making me."

"I think I can imagine it."

"I can't offer you houses or cars–"

He kissed her. The heat exploded between them as their

bodies melded. She wanted to be closer. She rubbed her chest against him, needing more.

He broke away. "All I want is you."

"All I want is you, too." Her hands roamed over his body. "I can even prove I wanted you even when I thought you had nothing."

"Yeah?"

She started to unbutton her shirt. His eyes dilated, and she felt his unmistakable interest from underneath.

"I have a big bed that's dying to be initiated."

"Not yet." A subtle wiggle and her shirt dropped off her shoulder. "This is for you."

"Wha–" Owen's eyes widened as his attention fell to the top of her left breast.

"I wanted you near my heart for the rest of my life."

"You did this for me?" He poked his finger around the edges of the tiny intricate tattoo of a python.

"Ouch." She grasped his fingers. "It's still a little sore."

"Then I should kiss it." His sly grin made her laugh as he touched his lips lightly to the colored skin. "I can't believe–" His head popped up. "Wait a minute. Did Tiny do this?"

"Of course. Who else would I use?"

"He saw your breast?"

Kendal grinned and hugged him. "You're too cute. He saw less than I showed in the outfits I wore as Big K."

"Are you sure?"

Feeling like she'd smiled more today than she had in her whole life, Kendal started to unbutton his shirt. "I was there. I'm sure."

"Then the last thing I need to do is change my name."

She halted. "Change your name? Why?"

"I was thinking in order to be your partner, it would be more appropriate to be known as Agent Ninety-Nine."

She punched his arm. "You're so funny. When'd you learn my last name?"

"At the trial." He lifted her off the couch, carrying her down the hall. "That's where I learned it was time to become an agent in order to *Get Smart*."

As Owen turned to take her into the bedroom, she pulled his mouth to hers. Deliriously happy, Kendal decided that for the first time in her life she didn't mind the joke.

Meet the Author:

The best part about success is celebrating the journey. Well aware of life's ups and downs, T.A. Ridgell knows it takes more than a bright attitude to keep motivated. Having survived teaching earth science to middle school students, obtained a masters degree in environmental biology, and successfully motivated numerous agents as a finance company vice president, Ridgell more than appreciates the quiet times at the computer while pounding out new stories.

Visit T.A. Ridgell at

www.taridgell.com

Chapter One

"Whoa, where'd she come from?"

Joe Franconi glanced up from his palm pilot to see who Tommy thought was so special. A skirted woman rounded the corner near the van. "I don't think the FBI is paying you to ogle women."

The new recruit sat up straighter. "Yes, sir. Sorry, sir."

"Relax, I was jok–" Joe jerked back as the woman drew close to the window, spread her lips and rubbed her teeth with her finger. Placing his finger over his mouth, he motioned to Tommy for quiet.

Her green eyes sparkled as she lifted a small cylinder, pursed her lips, and smoothed on lipstick. Joe crushed his instant, and unusual, physical response to this surprise vision.

Tommy clutched at his heart as soon as she stepped away. "That scared the hell out of me. Walking right up to the van like that."

Joe dragged his hand through his hair. Having a woman come up and practically kiss the window was not a common occurrence. "Yeah, even I forgot about the mirrored windows."

Propping his elbows on his knees, Tommy swung his ever-present headphones on the tip of his finger. "After that shock, I'd vote for bugging the place."

"A bug wouldn't last. You know, they sweep on a daily basis. Plus, they move too often."

Turning to the side window, Joe studied the blue-suited woman crossing the street. She definitely didn't fit in the neighborhood. Women down here were more likely to wear mini-skirts or skintight pants with cropped tops.

Taking his time, he surveyed her from the top of her blonde head to the tip of her sensible, low-heeled shoes. Her wavy, shining hair was pulled back and a thick braid swayed around her shoulders. Even the boxy suit couldn't disguise her incredible figure.

A low wolf whistle echoed through the van. "Look at those legs."

Frowning at Tommy's reaction, Joe stayed focused on the woman. Silently he agreed–her legs could make a man's mouth water. Like his was starting to do.

Up close, she'd been pretty, but now that he could see the whole package even 'beautiful' or 'attractive' was too tame to describe the woman standing on the other side of the street. A walking fantasy for his underused libido was better. He rolled his shoulders as if he could physically shake off the uncomfortable emotion.

"Her briefcase," he stated almost to himself, as she balanced it precariously in her hand. "Could she be the new runner?" He slapped Tommy on the shoulder, ignoring an odd flash of regret that she was one of the bad guys. "Your ogling may be right on the money, buddy. This could be the new contact."

"You think so?" Tommy craned his neck to look out the side window. "She sure doesn't fit the profile."

Joe leaned closer to the window. "Look at her case. Who else would be in this neighborhood with one?"

"The runner usually doesn't go to the house with the briefcase. They pick it up there."

"Maybe they changed their routine again. She's definitely headed for Scalfone's front door." Pointing across the street, Joe nodded. "It would appear we've just found the mob's newest runner." With conflicting emotions, Joe felt certain about his conclusion.

* * *

"The next one is it," Megan O'Riley said to herself, talking under her breath. "Every sixty-four doors and you'll get a yes."

At least that's what she'd been told during a training seminar. With raw knuckles from the first sixty-three, she sincerely hoped her instructor was right. Who'd have figured so many homes in downtown Baltimore wouldn't have doorbells. Rubbing her nose, she humored herself by wondering if it was flatter from the speed with which those doors had been closed in her face.

Staring at the solid one looming in front of her, Megan glanced to the side. The corner store caught her eye. "Is your breath fresh?" read the poster advertisement. She faltered.

Having just checked her teeth and refreshed her lipstick, thanks to the handyman's van, she now had a new worry. Cupping her hand in front of her mouth, she puffed. *Who knows?*

Better safe than sorry, she thought as she opened her briefcase. Holding it in one hand, she rummaged up to her elbow searching for a mint. Her fingers shoved aside discarded wrappers and lint. *Shoot, no mints.*

Megan looked again at the ad with the smiling woman and her bright, white teeth. She scrounged once more, catching her briefcase before it spilled over. This time her nimble fingers searched for coins. Jackpot! She fisted her money.

Hurrying to the store, she pushed open the door and a bell jangled. The musty smell of the cramped, dimly lit store engulfed her as she entered. She smiled at the girl behind the counter and received a blank stare in return.

Swiping at her wispy bangs, she headed straight to the wire display holding the candy selections. She chose a small plastic box of oblong mints, then smiled again at the young woman behind the stained Formica counter.

"That it?"

Megan widened her smile as her purchase was rung up. "Yes. Are you from around here?"

The girl stopped and stared. "What's it to ya if I am?"

With force, Megan kept her smile in place. "Nothing. I was just wondering."

The girl shook her head as she held out her hand for the money.

Megan counted out the coins and grinned when she still had a few left over. Dropping them back into her briefcase, she glanced out the barred, dirty front window. "Nice spring day, isn't it."

The girl shrugged. "You need a bag?"

"No thanks." Megan reminded herself not to waste time with

someone who didn't fit her sales profile.

The bell over the door jingled as she exited back to the sidewalk. Shoving her case awkwardly under her arm, she struggled with the top of the little box before finally snapping it open. Popping a few of the oblong pellets in her mouth, she nodded at the model in the ad.

After dropping the small pack in her briefcase, she took two steps before tripping over the cracked, raised sidewalk. Self-conscious of the people sitting out on their stoops, she tipped her head and adjusted her gait to give the false appearance that she'd meant to do that. In a continued attempt to look casual, she smoothed the side of her hair. Her fingers tangled, pulling a few strands free from her braid. Rolling her eyes, she looped the loose hair behind her ear.

"This is it," Megan told herself again. "I won't take no for an answer. I'm getting into this house and making a sale." Her words took her up the four steps to the front door. She checked the doorframe and sighed. No doorbell. Rapping loudly three times, she shook off the minor pain.

As the door opened her gaze rose and then rose some more taking in one of the biggest men she'd ever seen. Mustering her courage, she extended her hand. "Hi, I'm Megan O'Riley," she said just as a large truck rumbled past.

When he habitually responded by stretching out his hand, she stepped forward and he retreated into the house. *It worked!* Just the thought of it made her giddy. It had happened just like she'd been taught. Now if she could get to his kitchen table, she'd be on her way.

Continuing forward, she made her way over the threshold. There she hesitated letting her eyes adjust to the dark interior. The smell of stale cigar smoke wrinkled her nose.

"I'd appreciate a few moments of your time." She advanced further into the foyer. "To explain a couple of great programs I have to offer."

The large hulk stared at her without speaking, then his big head drew back and he sneezed.

Megan jumped from the force of his blow. "God bless you." Immediately she searched her briefcase and pulled out a crumpled tissue. Bending down, she placed her case next to the wall, before handing it to him.

The hulk took the tissue and she used the opportunity to close the door. With her sight adapted to the darkened room, she waved her hand and a thick haze moved in the breeze.

Another blast, this one worthy of a volcano, exploded out of the massive man. The thin tissue disintegrated. Undaunted, the hulk rubbed the cotton remnants from his fingers on his pants, then wiped his nose on his sleeve.

Ignoring his personal habits, Megan proceeded on inside and looked around. An old manual TV played in a corner of the living room surrounded by orange and green furniture reminiscent of the fifties. Thick curtains covered all the windows blocking out any available sunlight.

A bare bulb hung from the center of the ceiling, producing an eerie glow through the smoke layering the air. His rates would be higher since he's a smoker, she thought bleakly, another difficulty to overcome, if she wanted to make this sale–and boy did she need to make this sale.

She turned back to the large man and discreetly put the mint in her cheek. "Have you ever thought about how your family would survive if anything were to happen to you?"

The hulk frowned at her. "What're you talkin' about?"

Crap! She'd forgotten to get his name and compliment his house. "I'm afraid I didn't get your name, Mr.?"

"Squid."

She smiled her most trusting smile, the one she'd practiced in the mirror. Something else she'd been taught. "Mr. Squid? Now that's an unusual name."

"No, not *Mr*. Squid. Just Squid." He scratched his head. "Why're you here?"

She tapped her finger on her chin. "Squid? Is that what your wife calls you?"

"I'm not married."

Megan felt her lips tip downward. With effort, she forced them back up. "Do you have children?" *Oh please, please, please have children*, she silently begged.

He frowned. "Not that I know of." He sneezed again.

She wanted to stomp her foot. She'd gotten in the door and the man didn't even need what she was selling. "Doesn't anyone depend on you?"

"Depend on me?" Squid asked, clearly confused as he wiped his blunt nose on the sleeve on his shirt.

"Don't you support anyone besides yourself?"

The big guy grinned as he nodded. "My Mamma. I send her money every week."

Every nerve in her body went on alert. "And if something was to happen to you, would she have difficulty financially?"

"What?" Squid shook his head. "Wait a minute. Who are you? Did Uncle Sal send you?"

Not sure who Sal was, Megan adlibbed. "I did receive a call. I was told you needed to make sure your mother was taken care of if anything happened to you."

Another sneeze. Visible beads of sweat popped out on Squid's forehead. "If somethin' happened to me? Uncle Sal said that?"